PHTHOR

PHTHOR

Piers Anthony

To order additional copies of this book, contact:
Xlibris Corporation
1-888-7-XLIBRIS
www.Xlibris.com
Orders@Xlibris.com

CONTENTS

Prologue			9
Chapter 1	*Chthon*	§426	11
Chapter II	*Death*	§460	71
Chapter III	*War*	§426	89
Chapter IV	*Tree*		107
	Interlog	∞	126
Chapter IV	*Tree*		126
Chapter V	*Thor*	§426	133
Chapter VI	*Life*	§460	179
Chapter VII	*Phthor*	§426	185
Epilogue			203
Author's Note			205

PHTHOR(thor), form of English noun *phthore,-ine,* old name for element fluorine; derived from Greek *phtheiro*, destruction.
1. Armageddon Gotterdammerung, Ragnarok. 2. A chthonic god.

Sector Cyclopedia, §426

'Fluorine is the only element known which forms no compound with oxygen.'

Eliot and Storer, *Inorganic Chemistry*

Prologue

Destruction
The only answer

F
Fluorine
Compounded with oxygen
Phthorine
Our essence
Inimical to the chemistry of life

Paradox:
Life is a horror
It must be expunged
Yet life must be cultured
A tool
To destroy life

Aton:
Half-minion
History of his coming to Chthon
A six-sided hexagon
Past – Present – Future
Represented as halves of each face
No escape from that parallel circuit

Arlo:
Quarter-minion

History of his manifestation as Phthor
Bifurcate, a figure Y
Past – Present – Future
Represented as segment of the limbs
Four escapes, and none

The only answer
Destruction

CHAPTER 1

Chthon

Arlo paused as the glowmole scurried toward him. The little creature's feet terminated in sharp spikes that drove into the stone by drillhammer action, so that it ran on the walls with a sharp clicking.

'What's with you, pokefoot?' Arlo inquired verbally. He did not need words to communicate with these animals of the caverns, for he could speak through Chthon. But Coquina insisted on frequent verbalization. Otherwise, she claimed, he would forget the speech of his heritage.

His heritage? All he knew of that was what she had told him of the tremendous universe beyond the caverns of Chthon – whole planets filled with men, not animals. That was hard to believe, especially since he wasn't allowed to see for himself. Or maybe his mother meant LOE, the big *Literature of Old Earth* book she had used to teach him reading. All the stories of times past, yet not one about the caverns . . .

The glowmole turned about and clicked back the way it had come, its fine body hair shining blue. It was one of the glow feeders, foraging on the nutrient wall fungus and picking up some of its illumination. Almost the whole of Chthon was lighted this way: never bright, but never so dim as to make traveling hazardous. Except for those temporary shadows where the larger feeders had recently foraged.

'What's it want, Chthon?' Arlo asked, turning his attention inward to that place inside his skull where his friend normally manifested. But this time he received no answer.

Well, Chthon's ways were individual, and the matter was not important. Arlo followed the mole.

It clicked upward to intersect one of the narrow cavern rivers, then sped along the upper reaches while Arlo splashed through the water. This section of this river was safe; he had been here often and knew its idiosyncrasies. The small pot-whales could not get at him, and he could hear the caterpillars from far off.

They went upstream until the walls narrowed and the stalactite-drips that were the river's source became numerous. 'This is a dead end,' the boy complained. 'Are you teasing me?'

He was wrong. It was no longer a dead end, for something had broken a hole in the wall to open a new passage. A mansize rockeater, he judged, by the height of it. Harmless creature, and solitary – but powerful! The wall here was only the thickness of Arlo's thumb; the stupid rockeater must have bashed it in the usual fashion, thinking it solid, and fled when the whole section blasted apart.

'So that's what you brought me here for!' Arlo exclaimed, pleased. 'Thanks, little friend. I would have found it myself soon anyway, but this makes it quicker. A whole new section to explore!'

But the glowmole didn't stop. It clicked through the hole and went on.

'Something more?' Now Arlo was excited. He had a keen sense of adventure – 'You get that from your father!' Coquina liked to say, tousling his red hair – and excellent hiking ability. 'From your mother,' Aton would say, winking his eye. This was confusing because Coquina never hiked. She stayed only in the oppressively warm caverns near the boiling stream.

Actually, his parents seemed always sad, and not merely because the one had lost his eye and the other her mobility. Perhaps it was because they still remembered their first son, whose name he had never heard. That boy had died as a child before Arlo was born; he knew of it only because old Doc Bedside had told him. Thus the A of the Firstborn had come to Arlo – a nomenclature he would not otherwise have had. He knew that he was second born and second-best in the eyes of his parents, though they never suggested this to him. They did not need to.

Now Arlo was careful, for new passages could be deadly until their points were known. This section seemed routine – but he was not fool enough to rely on appearances. He sniffed the air, questing for telltale scents. Sometimes the chimera lurked in dry territory like this . . .

His nose caught something else. A new smell, familiar yet strange. Animal, certainly – but not any cavern species he knew.

Silently he proceeded, deviating from the direct path of the mole, alert for ambush. The glowmole would not betray him into danger, but it could easily be fooled. If something had sent it to him to lure him within range . . .

Arlo bared his teeth in an expression he had seen Aton use on occasion. He had a long, sharp stalactite strapped to his thigh, and two flakes of metal stone cached in his cheeks. He could slice the eye out of an attacking animal at a distance of ten times his own body length. Twenty yards, in the Old Earth measurement. This talent was useless against the stronger predators, but he could avoid or outmaneuver most of those. All he needed was a little warning.

The odd odor became stronger. There was always a little wind in the caverns, even most of the dead ends, and he was downwind from the quarry. His bare feet touched the warm rock with no noise, and his tongue stroked one of the cheekstones. This was the sort of experience for which he lived! Danger, adventure, suspense, action!

Then he heard something. It was a kind of ululation audible above the distant tinkle of the moving water: the cry of a wounded animal, perhaps. He zeroed in the sound and poked his head cautiously around the curve of the wall. It was there, huddled in the center of a bowl-shaped cave, disappointingly small.

It was a naked human being.

It took him a moment to grasp this, for he had seldom seen others of his species, apart from his parents and Doc Bedside. Others were pictured in LOE, so he knew they existed – but all of those wore clothing.

Maybe it was a zombie. Zombies looked human, but they weren't really – and not merely because they were naked. Arlo himself doffed his confining garments the moment he was away from home. Zombies had no minds. They move only at Chthon's direction and avoided real people. He had never seen a young zombie – but the caverns were full of surprises.

At any rate, he had little to fear. This one was small and evidently incapacitated. The sounds he had heard were crying. No wonder they had seemed so strange!

Even a zombie deserved some consideration. Sometimes Chthon forgot them, leaving individuals to fend for themselves beyond their normal habitat, and then they were helpless indeed. He could guide this one to its companions.

'Hello,' he said, stepping close – but not too close. One could never tell about a zombie.

The head came up. Tears streaked the dirty face, and large eyes shone from behind tangled yellow tresses. 'Hello.'

Arlo started. It had spoken! Zombies spoke only when under direct Chthon-control. He had thought the god was absent. 'Chthon?' he inquired, glancing inward.

'What?' the child asked.

Arlo looked into the lifted eyes. They were pale – and Chthon was not there, either. Which meant – 'You're human!'

'I'm lost.'

'You speak yourself! You have mind!'

'Don't hurt me!'

'How did you get here?'

'The old prison – I wandered too far, couldn't find my way back -'

'The prison! That's day's travel from here, for me. Much longer for you.' Arlo knew himself to be a swift traveler. He could outdistance his father because he was stronger and knew the caverns better– and could call to Chthon to hold the predators back.

'It's been several days – I think,' the child said. 'I can't tell time here.'

That was interesting. Arlo could tell time by certain rhythms in the great caverns, the pulse of Chthon, that he automatically translated to the hours and days that registered on his parents' watches. 'I will guide you there.'

The human child stood up. 'Thank you.'

Now he saw that it was female. Or at least not male. The chest was manlike, but no appendage hung from the crotch of the legs. 'Are you a girl? He inquired curiously.

'Pretty much.'

He shrugged and turned toward the river. 'This way.'

'Please –' she said. She had stopped crying, but there was still misery in her voice. 'I'm hungry and tired. Have you anything to eat?'

'There's plenty of glow,' he said, gesturing to the walls.

She looked dubiously. 'That green color? You eat that?'

'Sometimes. Or I kill an animal. Or a plant.'

'Plants don't grow down here! There's no sunlight.'

Neither statement made sense, so he didn't answer.

She considered. 'An animal, then.'

'There are some in the river.' He led the way to it.

She followed unsteadily. He wondered how she could have made it this far without food if she had not eaten the glow. And without becoming food for a predator. Most animals stayed away from the prison tunnels, because they were too hot and dry, but she had to have passed through several other habitats. Still, she showed no sign of understanding the caverns.

She must therefore know how to fight. If so, she was dangerous. Aton could fight, and Arlo knew better than to engage his father in serious combat – ever. In fact, even gentle, weak Coquina had somehow hurled him into a wall a year ago when he had, as she put it, become too big for his britches. Britches were legging of LOE vintage, unused in Chthon – but he had gotten her meaning. One day he meant to learn that fighting art . . .

So that seemingly helpless girl-child bore watching – until he was sure of her capabilities. Perhaps it would be possible to test them, covertly.

He swooped a jellywog out of the cold river water. The thing struggled and tried to get its stinger into his hand, but be broke its pseudo-spine with a practiced motion and let it subside. There was a kind of fascination in killing, but also a kind of guilt, so he never did it randomly. '**Here.**'

She recoiled. 'That?'

'Animal. To eat.'

'Raw?'

He looked at her in perplexity. 'It's dead. I killed it. Did you want it live?'

'You didn't cook it!'

Irritated, he set it down. 'You mean, burn it?' Coquina did that to meat, ruining it.

'Yes.'

'Why should I?'

'To make it edible!'

'It *is* edible!'

She sat down and leaned against the wall, her legs extended toward the water. They were different from his legs: less muscular, more rounded. Nice, in their way. 'Please – can we cook it?'

'When we get to a firespout,' he said. His gaze followed her smooth legs up to their joining point, where instead to a genital there was a crease. For some reason, this intrigued him.

'All right,' she agreed with a little sigh. 'A firespout.' Her tone suggested that he was being irrational.

Irritation warred with curiosity. 'Let me see that,' he said.

'What?'

'That.' He poked his forefinger into her crease. He knew al-most instinctively that he was acting improperly, but this only spurred him on. He was ready to block and jump if she attacked him; she was in an awkward position for combat, which was an-other factor he had considered. How fast and effective was she? 'How are you made?'

She did not protest. Her body was completely relaxed. 'The same as any other girl.'

He probed until his finger touched the rock under her buttocks, but found nothing. 'How do you urinate?'

'Do you want me to do it on your hand?'

'Yes.'

'I can't. Let's go find that firespout.'

Frustrated on several scores, he got up and headed for the nearest jet of flame. The feel of her strange, soft, inadequate anatomy had aroused an intense emotion in him, but he could find no clear expression of it.

'You never asked my name,' she said, following.

It hadn't occurred to him to be curious about that aspect of her. 'You never asked mine,' he said gruffly.

'What's yours?'

'Arlo Five.'

'Hvee!' she exclaimed.

He stopped, surprised. 'What do you know about Hvee?'

'Those number-names. They're from Planet Hvee. Everyone knows that, because it's the only place the hvee-plant grows. And your name's an A, so you're the firstborn line. You're lucky?'

He was pleased. 'My mother is Coquina Four, third line of a higher Family.'

'I guess that's the nobility of Hvee. She must have been sad when you got convicted.'

'Convicted of what?'

'Of whatever it was that sent you to Chthon, silly! What was it?'

'I was never sent here! I was born here.'

'You don't have to lie about it!'

'My whole family lives here. We're not prisoners – we're natives.'

She shook her head. 'I haven't been here long. But I know that nobody ever gets born here. There's something contraceptive about the caverns. Too hot, maybe.'

'It's not hot here by the river!'

She considered, 'That's right! The wind's down, and there're living things here. Breeding must be possible after all.' She looked up at him, her light hair flung back. 'I'd like to meet your mother.'

'You can't. You're going back to the prison section where you got lost from.' But that made him think again. 'What did a child like you do to get sent there? You're unmarked.'

'We never speak of our pasts,' She said diffidently.

'You were just asking *me* about -'

'Still,' she said.

Disgruntled, he made as if to strike her. He was quickly becoming furious.

She neither flinched nor fought. Suddenly she smiled – such an impish, carefree grin that he realized she had been teasing him. He smiled back, appreciating the humor of it - and she turned abruptly sullen.

She came from the prison; that was his only hint. So she was a criminal, cast out from her own kind. But surely not merely because her moods were mercurial!

The prison caverns were not completely familiar to Arlo for several reasons. They were hot and windy, so that a person without a supply of water soon dehydrated; they were far removed from his normal haunts; they were partially closed off from the main caverns so that it was hard to reach them and Aton had forbidden him to visit them. Thus he had seen little of the prisoners, and regarded them much as he did the zombies: creatures of a different environment, not his kind. All of them were adult, some old; the men were stringy and muscular, the women with full or pendulous breasts and furry hair on their underbellies. They were ugly compared to Coquina despite their nudity; but sometimes, considering them, he had discovered his genital swelling up hard.

'Your penis is getting long,' the girl said.

Embarrassed for no discernible reason, Arlo moved on downriver, forcing her to scamper to keep up. 'Why *don't* you speak of your pasts?' he fired over his shoulder.

'I don't know. It's just convention, I guess. I don't-'

'Don't step in that!' he cried suddenly.

She halted, one foot poised above the water. 'I can't jump across all the time the way you do! It's not deep here.'

'This is a sucker section.'

'What's a sucker?'

'I'll show you.' He dipped the jellywog into the clear river and wiggled it, keeping his fingers out of the water. In a moment there was a shimmer of motion.

When he pulled the wog out, two thin, transparent tails hung from it. Already a ribbon of red was forming within each one as blood from the meat siphoned into the parasite's digestive tract. 'Suckers hurt,' Arlo explained.

'Ugh!' she agreed, shrinking back.

Arlo bashed the jellywog against the wall, dislodging the suckers. They dropped back into the water and disappeared with quick swirls.

'Why didn't you kill them?' the girl asked.

'They don't taste very good unless they've just gorged.'

'I don't mean to *eat*! I Mean to make them dead.'

'Why?'

'They're dangerous!'

'Not to me.'

'You just showed me how they-'

'Anyone stupid enough to put his foot in their waters-'

'You still haven't asked me my name.'

'I forgot.' He went on downstream. She followed, not able to jump over nimbly enough.

The firespout jetted from a cleft in hot stone. Arlo held the jellywog over it, letting the fatty flesh singe.

'How does that work?' the girl asked.

'Aton says it's a leak from the gas-cavern system. Most of the gas goes to the big tunnels above the prison, but some squeezes a long way through rifts and leaks out in places like this. Aton lit this one so it wouldn't foul our air.'

'You sure know a lot!' she said admiringly.

'I'm fourteen, almost. I know how to read.'

'I'm eleven. I read, too.'

'What did you do? Kill someone?'

'You never asked my name.'

'If I asked your name, will you tell me what you did?'

'No. I'm not supposed to tell.'

Arlo shrugged, though he was furious at being balked again. This child did not seem like a criminal – but according to Aton, only the worst offenders were sentenced to Chthon-prison. What *could* she have done, to deserve this?

'I could tell you a lie,' she offered. 'I'm good at that. You wouldn't know the difference, would you?'

'I would if you told me it was a lie!'

'But I could pretend it was the truth.'

Arlo found her reasoning too devious. 'Coquina says people should always tell the truth.'

'Do you believe that?'

He thought of the necessary lies he had told his mother. 'No.'

'Well?'

'All right. What's your name?'

'Vesta. That's a lie, too.'

'Why?'

'Because my real name might give away what I did.'

'Then why were you so eager to give me your name?'

'So you'll know me.'

'I don't need a name for that!'

'Yes you do. A girl's name is excruciatingly important.'

'Not to me.'

'Call me Ex for short.'

'I don't need to call you anything!'

'You're lovely when you're mad.'

'Here's your food,' he said, shoving the scorched and bubbling meat under her nose.

'It should be Esta, or maybe Es, but I like Ex better.'

'So why are you in prison?'

'I'm not. I'm out in the caverns, here. I'm an Ex-prisoner.'

'That isn't what I meant!'

'Ugh!' she said, snuffing the jellywog. 'Maybe we should have left it raw.'

'You told me you'd tell me if I asked your name!'

'I told you I'd tell you a lie,' she said. 'I did.'

'The name-lie doesn't count!'

'The lie,' she said carefully, 'was that I would tell you why I was sent to prison.'

For a moment he was baffled. 'I don't understand you!'

'Do you need to?'

'Yes!'

'Why?'

'I don't know,' he admitted, dismayed.

'You could take back your burned fish.'

'Why?'

'To get even for the lie. Punishment. Revenge.'

'That would waste the food.'

'Then you could hurt me some other way. Hit me, maybe.'

He thought about it. The notion was peculiarly attractive, but she was probably teasing him again. The blow would never land – or would be accepted as the gambit for a deadly counter. That was the way Aton fought, and even in play it was dangerous. Still, this could test what she really knew about combat. If he struck hard and fast, blocked the counter shot and jumped away simultaneously, it might be worth the risk. 'Yes.'

'Hit me!' she said, putting her hands behind her back and lifting her small chin. She was very pretty that way.

Arlo hit her.

Swift and hard, his fist caught her on the chin and knocked her back. He was pleased – he had actually foiled the counter and gotten out of range unharmed!

Ex fell like a broken stalagmite. The back of her head cracked into the stone wall. She collapsed into a huddle similar to the one he had found her in, but this time she was not crying.

Immediately Arlo was sorry. He had not realized how much

larger he was than she, or how little resistance she would have. It
was obvious now that Ex was not a trained fighter. She had aggravated him and invited retaliation, not expecting more than a token
strike. He had been angry but had never meant to destroy her.

He squatted, looking at her head. There was blood on it, seeping
through her yellow hair, turning it red. He scooped some water from
the river – this was beyond the sucker section – and splashed it on,
trying to clean the wound. She was not dead, but he knew that head
injury could kill her slowly or make her like a zombie. Loss of blood
was not good either, and its smell would attract predators.

Arlo realized that he was much better at killing than at healing. 'Chthon!' he cried in anguish, appealing to his friend the god
for help. But still Chthon was absent.

Quickly he considered his alternatives. He could put her in the
river, letting her body float down to the nearest pot-whale. It happened to be a medium-sized one, capable of consuming the carcass in
a few hours. But she wasn't dead yet, and despite all the annoyance
she had caused him, he still didn't *want* her dead. Never before had
he had company, other than adult; now he knew he needed it.

He could tell his parents. But Aton would be suspicious of
human intrusion into the caverns, and Coquina would be upset.
They might make Ex go away, back to the prison-tunnels—and
Arlo wasn't ready for that either. This little girl had made an im-
pression on him – of what nature he wasn't sure. But he could not
let her go until he knew.

He could take her to his hvee garden, a secret place even his
parents did not know of. Ex had said hvee grew only on Planet
Hvee, but this was not true. In his garden it would be easy to take
care of her and feed her until she recovered – if she did recover. If
not—there were plenty of pot whales.

So his mind reasoned, but his emotion was already committed.
He had hurt her; he must make her well. He hardly knew her, yet she
promised to fill a void that was no less intense for its recent discovery.

He picked her up, amazed again at how little she weighed,
and carried her downstream. Her bare legs dangled across his left

arm, and her blood-damp hair across his right. He felt again the unaccustomed agony of remorse.

Never again would he strike a person thoughtlessly.

In due course he passed a glow chipper – a gray, man-sized creature with close-fitting scales, standing on its hind legs and bracing against its tail to reach the edible height of glow with its buck teeth. It was strong but harmless; in fact, it was possible to ride on its back even without Chthon's intercession. Few cavern creatures were that docile!

'Good!' Arlo exclaimed. 'Chipper can carry the burden!'

But he soon realized that this would not do after all. Riding was one thing; making the stupid creature carry was another. Only Chthon could tune it to that degree. By themselves, the chippers followed their natural bent. They knew that Arlo was not a threat to them, so they ignored him. No help there.

The burden was not great, but travel was cumbersome with his arms engaged. He might have slung her over his shoulder, but he was afraid her dangling head would bleed worse. He was unable to take advantage of the most direct route to the garden because he could not swim or climb this way. Few of the linked caverns were conveniently level; their reaches twisted like monstrous wormholes—lava tubes, Aton called them—cut through by streams and fractures. The most dangerous animals tended to frequent the lower reaches of any given cave—the very region Arlo now had to walk. And he could neither throw his cheek stones nor wield his stalactite-spear while carrying Ex.

It was amazing what a difference one girl made.

He was in no trouble yet. The animals of the caverns were not as smart as he and would not realize his limitations immediately. But this was increasingly nervous business, for news of his strange behavior would already be spreading through Chthon. Free, strong, and agile, he had few mortal enemies; handicapped, he would have many. The chimera . . .

Arlo shuddered momentarily. He could not risk that!

There was only one dry, level-route shortcut to the garden: through the labyrinth of the dragon.

Arlo did not fear the dragon, but that was because it was unable to leave its own tunnels. It was huge body was so constructed that it could operate effectively only in its own territory; in a larger cavern it would become clumsy, easily escaped. But within its ten-foot diameter tubes it was a juggernaut, ferocious and irresistible. It was carnivorous, feeding on those creatures large and small who foolishly wandered or dropped into its premises and were unable to find their way out in time.

Now Arlo was about to enter that region. For the sake of a bothersome girl who would probably die anyway. He knew he was acting irrationally –being a fool, as Aton put it—and a part of him raged against that. Still he went.

These passages were not natural. They were round, scraped out of the solid rock by the mighty claws of the dragon. True, the rock was soft here; Arlo could chip it himself with his stalactite. But it would have taken him months of tedious labor to make even a small tunnel – and these were not small!

He entered through a reduced-diameter tube, left over from that time, perhaps centuries ago, when the dragon had been young. It had widened most of the passages, but there were a lot of them to cover and it had neglected some at the fringe. Perhaps it had merely changed the design, so that they were not needed anymore – or even left them deliberately for the entry of prey. Obviously more were caught than escaped, or the dragon would have starved.

Arlo had been all around the burrow, extensive as it was, and knew that it was largely two- dimensional. The dragon's bulk was such that it would be crushed by its own weight in any fall, so it didn't like to climb. Old Doc Bedside had explained that; he knew a lot about the way animals functioned.

Also, the dragon normally slept at this time and it was not readily roused. So the gamble was not intolerable.

The small tube debouched into a great one. Claw-scrape marks showed the dragon's handiwork, constantly scraping the passage walls to accommodate its increasing girth. The overall pattern of the complex was not complicated; the tubes radiated out from the hub-chamber like the spokes of one of the wheels depicted in LOE. A spiral tube intersected them, making several complete rounds before it terminated in a dead end. All the spokes carried beyond the spiral, dead-ending also. Most creatures that wandered into the labyrinth got lost because their minds could not fathom the nature of the pattern. When pursued by the dragon, they instinctively fled out ward and landed in a dead end—where they were sure prey.

Arlo carried his burden swiftly toward the center. It was escape-noise to which the monster was primarily attuned. Approach-noise it tolerated because it wanted the prey to get as far inside the system as possible and get lost. So long as Arlo walked firmly and without fear, the dragon was unlikely to be alerted.

Still, Arlo wished this stage of his journey were over.

The spokes were short compared to the spiral, but it would have taken Arlo ten minutes to traverse the pattern empty-handed. Now it would take double that.

He came to the hub. The dragon was there, asleep within the mighty folds of its skin. Even in repose, it was almost twice Arlo's height. Of course it stood no higher when active; its legs were short and its torso stretched out for a leaner running posture. The smell of it was stifling, for its dung lined the chamber and flavored the entire burrow. It was snoring: a whooshing like that of a distant wind-tunnel.

He skirted it, forcing himself to walk boldly so as to maintain the 'approach' pattern. The outer trek would be more ticklish. He could have used the spiral tube, but that would have taken much longer and would have been more likely to alert the slumberer. It was not the nearness or loudness of the sound that counted so much as their nature and direction.

Ex stirred in his arms. That was good because it suggested she was recovering, but also bad because he would not caution her to silence. The sound of his voice would bring the dragon to troubled life!

The girl sneezed.

The dragon started. Its massive tail twitched.

Arlo continued walking. Any change in his motion-pattern

would be fatal – if his situation were not already hopeless. A sneeze was not fear-noise; it just might pass . . .

The great beast rolled over, its metal-hard rock-hewing claws coming into view. Each foot was the size of Arlo's chest, and each nail was backed by the peculiar musculature and bone leverage that gave it phenomenal driving force. The dragon, Arlo realized, could be a distant cousin of the glowmole because of that special foot structure.

Now he entered the far tube he had selected, and the dragon did not stir again. They had gotten past. Arlo shuddered with relief.

'Where are you taking me?' Ex inquired loudly.

There was a snort. Arlo did not need to look back to know the dragon was alert now! They were in for it.

'Fool!' he cried angrily dumping the girl down on her feet. 'Run–if you can. Straight down this tunnel. There's a hole near the end—I'll go another way.'

Already the dragon was moving, ponderously because it was still sleepy, shaking the rock with pounding of its feet. Arlo screamed as if in terror – no difficult task! – and charged down the spiral tube.

The dragon reached the intersection and hesitated, confused by the presence of two items of prey. Which one to follow? But in a moment it decided: the frightened one. Sinuously it turned the corner, coming after Arlo. Ex stayed frozen as the lengthening torso slid by her. Arlo could tell without seeing her directly; there was no sound except that of the dragon.

He had intended to lure the monster, but now he was in trouble. He might avoid it for a while by dodging at right angles into other cross-tubes, for its mass and velocity would make it less agile than he. But that could not last forever – and it would not save Ex, wounded and lost as she was. The moment the dragon gave up on him, she would become its prey – and standing still would not fool it this time! Why wasn't she running while she had the chance?

The rock shook as the dragon's awful claws landed, propelling its torso forward. Its breath blasted out like burning gas, smelling of carrion. Now Arlo understood some of the reason so many trapped animals acted foolishly or collapsed early. The shuddering stone made the footing seem uncertain, leading to misjudgment and diminished mobility. The very wind from the monster's lungs tended to blow the prey over. And the heat and odor of that breath might paralyze the prey.

A cross-tube loomed, and Arlo dodged into it. The dragon skidded around the corner, losing velocity. Good he needed that leeway! Perhaps he could confuse it while it was still sleepy, and double back to find Ex and direct her to the escape. A slim chance, but—

A wiggle in the tube, then a blank wall loomed before him. He stared, dumbfounded. He had blundered into a dead end! He should have veered the opposite way, toward the center, where there were many options. Instead he had been headed outward, like any dumb animal – and fallen into the dragon's trap.

The sides of the tunnel were smooth here, with no claw marks. Evidently the dragon had plastered the wall with its thick spittle, making it resistive to the ubiquitous green glow that grew on the stone everywhere else. Why?

It was hopeless now, but he had to fight. The bulk of the monster blocked the entire passage; no way to slide past! Its two tiny eyes focused on him as it bore down, jaws gaping.

Arlo spat one stone into his hand, took aim, and skated it at the dragon's right eye. But the creature blinked, letting the sharp flake slice its leathery eyelid instead. Arlo threw the second stone at the other eye – and again the dragon blinked. This ploy had not worked – and even had the monster been blinded, it could have dispatched the prey readily.

The stalactite-spear was Arlo's last weapon, apart from his cunning. He drew it forth, waiting for the huge jaws to snap at him so that he could leap aside, bestride the snout, and plunge it into an eye. The eyelid would not stop *this*!

For good measure, he made several feints with his arm, forcing the dragon to blink unnecessarily. It did not know he was out of stones.

The head lunged, eyes closed. Arlo bounded high, landing across the hot black nostrils. He scrambled up toward the eyes – but his feet skidded in the slime of the nose and he landed instead directly before the closing jaws. He could not reach the eyes!

He thrust the spear into the soft, runny membrane of the nostril. The dragon bellowed and hunched away. For a moment its thickening body met the slick walls of the tube, creating a vacuum as it scraped back. Had he found a way to balk it?

Then the jaws opened wide, showing what were surprisingly small teeth. Air hissed out, and saliva, forming an opaque cloud.

'Venom!' Arlo exclaimed as its stinging mist encompassed him. Now he was done! 'Chthon! Chthon!' he cried.

Here, friend, the voice in his brain said. Chthon had returned!

The dragon's body thinned. Fresh air sucked in around the edges. Arlo gulped it avidly, clearing the pain from his lungs, letting the tears wash it out of his eyes. He was safe now; no creature in the caverns could prevail against the god's control.

Arlo let go a burst of gratitude and query: Chthon had saved him – but where had Chthon been until now? 'Come see what I found!' he said aloud, remembering Ex.

Then Chthon left him. Dismayed, Arlo stood looking about, as though his mere eyes could locate that presence. Was this a rebuke? What had he done?

Yet Chthon's absence was not complete, for the dragon remained quiescent. What did this refusal to communicate mean?

Arlo shrugged. He ran back to recover his fallen weapons, then loped down the tunnel toward the spot where he had last seen Ex. First he must get her and himself out of the warren; then he could ponder Chthon's meaning at leisure.

She was there, sitting crosslegged in the passage. Apparently she never had recovered the wit to run! Her head lolled forward, and sweat glistened on her body.

No—not sweat. Slime. Foul-smelling, glistening white, forming all over her skin. Had her head wound done this—or the
dragon's poison?

No, there had not been time for the monster to exhale its
venom on her. This was myxo, the mucus of Chthon. Once before
he had seen it, on his father Aton, when the man had attempted to
go where Chthon had forbidden. And Doc Bedside had discussed
it. It was the god's way of punishing a creature with brain and
willpower to resist the mandates of the caverns.

'No!' Arlo cried, putting his hands on the girl. She was burning hot: another sign. 'She is not an enemy! I hurt her, I brought
her here – I must save her!'

Chthon paid no attention. More thickly now the awful white
sludge formed, encrusting Ex so that she looked like forming stone.

Never before had Arlo sought to oppose his will to that of
Chthon. Now it had to be done.

He drew his stalactite and placed the point to his own breast.
He clasped both hands about the base and tensed his muscles.
'Stop – or I die!' he cried.

Suddenly the will of Chthon was on him, forcing his muscles to
go limp. Arlo fought, pressing the point in to cut his skin – but the
force against him was incomparably greater than that of the dragon.

Before him the girl stirred. Flakes of white fell off her as she
tried to stand. Arlo could not assist her. All his being was locked in
the struggle with the god – a struggle he knew now he could not
win. Chthon was too powerful; Chthon ruled all the caverns! To
fight against Chthon was to become – a zombie.

Yet Arlo fought. White began to form on his own skin, the
first glistening of the myxo slime. Heat raged within him – not
the heat of passion, but of decimation. Slowly, inevitably, he was
being crushed, but he would not quit.

Abruptly it stopped. He held his sword a moment longer, to
be sure the siege had not merely been shifted back to the girl, then
relaxed. Chthon had gone again.

The dragon hissed, the noise reverberating through the passages. Chthon had let it go, too!

Arlo took Ex out of the labyrinth in a hurry, before the dragon could reorient. Then on to another stream, a safe one, where he washed the repulsive myxo off her body and the blood from her hair. Then he brought her to his private garden.

The garden was in a tremendous cavern, so tall that the ceiling could not be seen from the sculptured flood. It was bright and warm, for not only did the walls and floor give off an especially fine glow, so did the delicate green and blue plants nestled in alcoves. But more than this, it was illuminated by steady, yellowish flame across the upper reaches: burning jets of gas, monstrous fire spouts that cast light and heat all the way to the bottom, except when clouds formed. The garden was also noisy – not with the rush of wind, but with the merging roar of falling water and jetting fire.

Arlo carried Ex to his favorite bower and laid her down beside the spuming base of the great waterfall. He fetched moss to pillow her head, but as he placed it, she sat up so alertly that he knew she had been awake for some time. 'Hi,' she said.

He stared at her blankly. 'What?'

She had spoken in a language of Old Earth, rather than Galactic. He was familiar with it, thanks to LOE, but had hardly expected this dead tongue to emerge from a living mouth.

'Oh, it hurts!' Ex cried, clutching her head and falling back.

Distracted, Arlo forgot the question he had been about to ask. He packed the moss under her head while she grimaced with evident pain. If only he had not hit her! He felt helpless, not knowing what he could do that would really help. She writhed for some time, groaning, while his apprehension and guilt mounted. Her head was bleeding again, staining the moss black.

Just about the time he became convinced she would die, she relaxed. Her eyes closed and she appeared to sleep. He watched her for some time, but she did not move, and gradually his alarm subsided.

It was replaced by another siege of irritation. Why hadn't Ex told him she knew how to speak Old Earth? And if she had recovered while he was carrying her from the dragon's maze, why hadn't she let him, know? She had been able to move well enough for a while in the tunnel, before the myxo siege, then relapsed. Or so it had seemed.

It also occurred to him now that her latest seizure had arrived very conveniently for a girl who did not like to answer questions. Yet she *had* been injured, so he could not be sure she was pretending. What was he to believe?

Torn by doubt, Arlo left her and walked through his garden. The vegetation was tall and luxuriant, with that faint, pleasant odor associated with hvee, the love plant. Old Doc Bedside had brought him a sprig of immature hvee several years ago, a personal gift. Arlo had never liked or trusted Bedside, but the madman had a disquieting knack for doing genuine favors at opportune moments. The hvee had been a major example.

Perhaps Bedside had merely intended that Arlo wear it in his hair, as the men of Planet Hvee did. But the same immaturity that allowed the hvee plant to pass from man to man without becoming attached, enabled it to grow again in the ground. Hvee only grew on its home world, in all the galaxy – but Arlo tried it anyway.

He succeeded. The planet rooted and thrived. It was evident that the conditions it required for propagation existed here in the bright cavern, as well as on its native planet. In fact, his lone sprig had fissioned into twins, then four, and Arlo had rooted new plants and grown them to seeding maturity. Now they were radiating, becoming separate varieties, some larger, some greener, some hardier than others. He was trying to crossbreed them with the cavern glow moss, to achieve a glowing of hvee unique in the universe, and was having some success. Arlo was not experienced enough to realize how remarkable this achievement was, or how it reflected on Chthon's ability to control the processes of life within the caverns.

He stopped beside his most promising alcove, where a new variation grew. This plant was blue, and – yes – it did glow slightly! The first blue-glow crossbreed! He held out his hand to it, and the plant shied away from him. It did not actually move; this was an emotional thing. The leaves nearest him dropped subtly, signifying negation.

Shocked, he retreated. Never before had any of his plants rejected him! What did this mean?

He approached another hvee, a more conventional green one. It, too avoided him. Thus it was no peculiarity of the hybrid, but something between him and the hvee. And because of what the hvee was, that was awful.

Chthon! he cried mentally. But even the god rejected him. There was no contact.

This shook him fundamentally. Suddenly it was too much. Arlo ran from the garden, into one of the round exit tunnels following it up to its intersection with another, and on in an intricate ascent. He did not know exactly what he was running from.

Then he realized that he was headed toward the cave of the Norns. Yes – they could explain this. His subconscious had guided him truly. He continued on through the intricate network, avoiding pitfalls and dangers that would have wiped out any person or creature not completely familiar with these bypaths. He maneuvered through canyons and corkscrews crossing the paths of caterpillars and the labyrinth of a small dragon, and came at last to the cave.

It was a ledge behind the tall waterfall, about halfway up the cavern wall. Here the river was comparatively narrow, for it was falling rapidly. It formed a flattish translucent sheet that screened the ledge, wafting cool spray-mist across it. On the other side, he knew that spray dissipated in the air, helping from the clouds that occasionally added their rain to the plants below. Sometimes he wished he could fly among those clouds, penetrating their mysteries as readily as he penetrated those of the smaller tunnels. But such wishes were mild. He would have felt at peace here, were it not the lair of the Norns.

They came out of their dark hole, three human figures. They were zombies: two complete, the third half.

The half-woman stepped toward him. 'Yes we can tell you

Arlo, son of Aton,' she said. 'If we would.' She was actually rather sensual, with large, well-formed breasts, a small waist, unwrinkled skin, and flowing black hair. Arlo had no notion how old she was; it was impossible to tell with zombies. Probably fifty or sixty years, for her eyes were slits through which an ancient hunger shone.

Arlo drew up to the edge of their ledge and waited, not speaking. It did not surprise him or alarm him that Verthandi should know his mission without being told; that was the nature of the Norns. Their visions derived from Chthon, who of course knew everything. Yet they were not entirely of Chthon, for some human elements remained, especially in Verthandi. Their perspective differed.

The half-woman reached out her hand to intersect the waterfall. Spray shot out to douse Arlo. She had uncanny aim! 'My sisters will answer you,' she said, 'but they must touch you.'

Because they were blind. Something in the zombie process had destroyed their sight and much of their hearing, so that they were largely dependent on tactile input. Probably the myxo – a thick enough coating of that gummy stuff . . . ugh! Arlo knew that, and had sympathy for their plight – but he did not like being touched by those wrinkled grasping hands.

'Then talk to your hvee,' Verthandi said, turning her back.

She really *did* know! And so she must know the answer. He would have to submit. He knew they would not hurt him, in fact he could probably pitch all three over the cliff if he had to. Except that would anger Chthon. By the same token, they would be careful of him, for they were more dependent on Chthon than he was.

He stook, and the three came to him. Urder reached out a thin hand and laid it on his chest. From her mouth poured a dribble of gibberish as her fingers slid across the muscles of the chest.

'Child of malice,' Verthandi translated. 'Incestuous issue, but very strong.'

'I'm the child of *Coquina,*' Arlo said, irritatedly. 'She was never malefic.'

Urdur poked her jugged fingernail at his masculine nipples

and emitted shrill laughter. Arlo realized he had been duped by some sort of pun or joke whose meaning only the Norns comprehended.

Skuld now put her cold hands on his right leg. She burst into her own gibberish. Again Verthandi translated: 'How soon this flesh carries us all to Regnarok!'

This time Arlo kept his mouth shut. The prophecy made no . sense, but he didn't want to provoke more insane mirth.

Now Verthandi herself touched him. Her hands were smooth and strong, and they took hold of his genital, kneading, stretching, forcing a reaction that was not unpleasant. 'This hardening rod transfixes your sister,' she said.

'I have no sister!' Arlo cried, jerking away. 'Why don't you answer my question? Why does Chthon hide from me? Why does my own hvee turn against me? Who is this child Ex?'

Verthandi looked calmly at him. She was breathing with greater volume now, and had the shape of a remarkably fair woman. But her words remained zombie. 'We have answered; past, future and present. Your angry incest destroys life and death.'

Arlo backed away. 'This is crazy! What is your price for a fair answer?' For he knew they *could* tell him, if they only *would*.

Verthandi squinted at him a long moment. 'You are sixteen, very nearly,' she said.

Arlo started to correct her, then realized that he could not be really sure of his age. It had been a couple of years since he had asked Coquina about it, and perhaps he was older now.

'That may be considered an age of consent,' the Norn continued.

Now he understood her well enough to become uneasy. She had massaged his body, arousing a certain urgency in him, a certain mystery. Surely she knew more about this matter than he did, and wanted more of his body than a mere touch. And because there was a strong, confusing element of desire in him, his repulsion was greater. 'Not that!' He did not know what or why not;

perhaps it was a fear of being initiated into mysteries that could make him part zombie himself. 'What other price?'

She gestured. 'Stand in the water.'

He looked at the falls. It would be suicide to attempt to stand in that down rushing wall! But she extended her gesture to the side, and he saw that further along there was a smaller shoot that splashed off the ledge, forming an arcing spray over the chasm. There was a footing there—barely.

'I would be swept off,' he demurred.

She held her open hand toward him, offering to steady him. Arlo did not feel at ease, but decided this was the best compromise he could make. He walked toward the lesser falls.

From up close, the situation seemed more precarious. He felt an apprehension verging on terror. Therefore he proceeded, knowing the Norns were testing him. They expected him to fail, to back off – and then to have no pretext not to obtain his answer their way. Or give up the quest. As he would not.

He inserted the toes of one foot into the water. It was icy cold, and the force was such as to bounce his foot out again, throwing him off-balance. His arms flailed wildly, and Verthandi caught his hand, steadying him.

Perhaps she had as much of him as she required, merely grasping his hand, controlling his life physically. She could easily tip him into the gulf. So be it; he would not yield. He put his foot back in the water, setting it firmly on the slippery rock, then wedged his leg in slowly.

The numbing force of it traveled up his leg to his waist, than on up to his chest. At first it was as though he would be swept entirely away by that current; but as he came in wholly, the force steadied, and the water flowed all about him, containing him. The center of the falls was hollow; there was no strong beat upon his head. He withdraw his hand from that of the Norn and stood there, encapsulated in the descending chill.

Perhaps this was what it felt like to be a zombie, contained in Chthon's benificence.

Soon his confusion and annoyance with Ex faded. She was a young girl, a child banged on the head; naturally she reacted irrationally. He would take care of her, and she would recover. He liked that notion: taking care of her. He had never had a human companion before, especially not a female. A *real* female; the zombies didn't count, for they were only shells, their minds buried somewhere in Chthon. Being encapsulated might be nice—but only if it were possible to break out at will.

Now he was able to approach the hvee problem. Why had his plants shied from him? Did they resent the presence of another person in the garden? Yet old Doc Bedside came often to the garden. Arlo resented this but could do nothing; the man was another creature of Chthon – like the Norns, but different. The hvee did not like Bedside – but this had never affected the plants' reaction to Arlo. Why whould it be otherwise with Ex?

The reason had to be in Arlo himself, as the Norns seemed to have suggested. *He* must have changed in some way, making him foreign to the hvee. For the plants were mindless; they could not lie. They reacted only to what was in the person they were near.

This was difficult thinking! Arlo had seldom explored his own motives deeply, but now he had to try. He had to make it right with the hvee because the emotional plants mirrored his self-esteem. In this sense he was incestuous, perhaps destroying himself: his emotion breeding within their own family, not truly interacting with the emotion of other people. The Norns' message was coming clear!

How had he changed? No way—except that he had taken care of the girl. Would the hvee have liked him better if he had let her die? If he had let Chthon make her another zombie? No—he had done what seemed right, because he needed a companion.

A companion other than the hvee? No, the hvee was not jealous. In fact, it was the nature of the plant to cement the love of a man and woman. Once a given hvee fixed on a man it would die in his absence – unless in the presence of the woman who truly loved him.

Man? Woman? Love? What had any of this to do with him?

But he had to explore it honestly. The girl Ex fascinated him at the same time as she annoyed him. That was confusing. Perhaps that confusion extended to the hvee.

Well, all he had to do was to get to know the girl better. Then there would be no confusion.

Suddenly a feeling of dread infused him. Arlo grabbed for his spear and almost overbalanced himself. For an instant his face poked through the tube of water, and he gazed into the abyss.

But there was no immediate threat. He was safe here, as long as he kept his balance. As safe as it was possible to be in the caverns.

No—the menace was not to him, but to someone else. His father Aton? No, not directly. His mother Coquina? No.

He stiffened. Ex! She was alone and unguarded in the garden below, and something huge and awful was moving toward her. He felt it in that part of him attuned to the life of the caverns. That talent Chthon had taught him.

Arlo stepped out of the shower. The water wrenched at him again, and his feet slipped out from under. He sat down hard on the rock, his legs going out over the edge, his gaze fashioning a precipitous plunge through the glowing vapors of the middle space of the garden ... and again Verthandi's hand caught his and held him steady.

'You have saved me. You have also answered my question,' Arlo told her. 'I will remember that. But now I must hurry.'

She only nodded. She surely knew whether he would ever return to her, and was willing to wait. Zombies had extraordinary patience.

He left the cave of the Norns, impelled by his new urgency. He made his way down through the labyrinth of passages, again reminded how formidable they would have been for anyone who did not know their idiosyncrasies and dangers. His father could not pass here—at least not with any speed or security. But Arlo had had years to explore them, with Chthon's protection and help.

This particular region had only one safe exit: a corkscrew tunnel barely large enough to let a man pass. All other routes led past potwhales, caterpillars, and other predators. Arlo could traverse them when Chthon was with them, but not alone.

As he approached the corkscrew – the term derived from an artifact mentioned in LOE, a metal wire spiral used to remove the ancient stoppers from bottles – he stopped. A salamander was there.

The best way to deal with a salamander was to avoid it. Normally they did not stray from the hottest wind-tunnels. Which suggested that this one's presence in this key location was not coincidence. Chthon could have summoned it to bar the way.

Why?

Arlo froze, a prickle of dread traveling up him spine. Ex was alone; only his determination had spared her from Chthon's siege, before. She was imminently threatened by something vicious. A wolf thing. Now—

He had to get past the salamander! But the creature was aware of him, alert – and the very touch of its tiny tooth meant death.

'Chthon!' he called automatically, knowing that was useless. One lesson this experience with Ex had already taught him: he could no longer rely on his friend and god. Not completely. And what was untrustworthy part of the time was uncertain *all* of the time. He had depended on Chthon to protect him from cavern predators, until he had come to think of the caverns as safe. That had been a dangerous complacency!

Now he had to handle the salamander himself – and quickly, for the menace to Ex was growing. Chthon, balked from direct attack was now using an indirect approach, sending a monster to kill Ex while the salamander blocked off Arlo. Had he remained longer with the Norns, the deed would have been accomplished before he could return. The Norns, governed by another aspect of Chthon, had not informed him. They had sought to distract him longer.

Arlo scowled. One day, when he had nothing better to do he just might see about making them regret that.

Suddenly a new, ugly connection formed in his mind. *The hvee, too, had worked Chthon's will.* It had sent him to the Norns, rendering Ex vulnerable. The hvee was able to grow in the caverns only because of Chthon's ambience. Chthon could make anything happen. Chthon had wanted Arlo to be happy, so the cavern god had provided him, through Doc Bedside, with the ultimate in contentment: successful hvee. But by that token, the hvee was but another zombie, or at least a partial zombie, like Verthandi and Bedside. It seemed independent, but at the root it was not.

Arlo realized that he had complicated his life phenomenally when he had set his will against that of his god.

But the salamander: let the theoretical implications go, in the face of the specific. He did not dare put his hands on it. The thing was less than the span of his spread hand from thumb to little finger, but its virulent poison could kill within minutes. He could not risk hurdling it, for the thing could jump as high as he could. He could bat it aside with a stick—but he had no stick or stone, and no time to fetch one.

He did have his stalactite spear, still tied to his body. If he could stab the thing . . .

No time to debate. The salamander started for him, for these creatures always attacked, never relented. He had to fight or run. He could outrun it, and ordinarily *would* have – but there were no tunnel loops here that would enable him to circle beyond it and escape in the direction he required. Not in time.

He leaped toward it, stabbing with his point. The creature cooperated by opening its jaws to bite the weapon – and the point of the spear rammed right down its throat. Lucky thrust! Arlo threw the spear to the side. The salamander was not yet dead, but it could not dislodge itself from its impalement, or move while anchored by the heavy stone spear. The way was clear.

Then he hesitated. He might have need of his spear again. In fact, he surely would, to balk that menace closing in on Ex. Gingerly he picked it up by the end, lifting the salamander into the air. Its beady eyes stared at him with consummate malevolence, and this gave Arlo an odd thrill. He *liked* the hate of this little monster!

He moved on, carrying the spear horizontally and to the side, so that the poison would neither roll down the spear to his hand nor be carried to him in droplets on the wind. He could scrape the salamander off against a suitable rock, then rinse the spear carefully in running water. When he had time. Right now he had to carry it awkwardly.

The corkscrew was a special problem. If he slid the spear down ahead of him, poison might drip to the stone to be picked up by his body. If he held it above him, drops could fall on him. But he found he was able to carry it behind in such a way that it was never actually above him. Drops did fall on the stone, and he knew it would be long before he dared travel this way again. Well, the Norns could wait!

He ran on through the wider, lower tunnels. Soon he would reenter the gardens – and he had gained on the menace. The animal was very large, he knew, now that he was closer to it. It could not take the most direct route, but had to find passage for its girth. So it was slow.

'Arlo.' A man stood in his way. He was shorter and slighter than Arlo, and he was old: in his middle sixties, Arlo knew. This was Doc Bedside.

Arlo knew the man was up to no good. In fact, he represented another barrier interposed by Chthon – a more more formidable one than either Norn or salamander. For Beside was not only mad, he was intelligent.

Still, perhaps he could bluff his way past. 'I have speared a stray salamander. I must dispose of it. Be careful of the poison.' And he poked it suggestively at Bedside.

'Ah, yes, the episode of the salamander,' Bedside said, not yielding the right-of-way though his eyes seemed to glow within the sallow crinkles of his face. 'Had your father but known . . . "

'*I* killed it, not my father,' Arlo said. How could he move the man? The wolf was getting closer to the sleeping girl; now he felt both her slumbering innocence and its malice.

Malice – what had the Norns said?

No time for that! He had to get by, but he could not simply

shove the old man aside. Bedside had peculiar powers of his own, as the most cunning of all Chthon's minions. In many cases he actually spoke for Chthon. A direct attack on him would be like a sally against Chthon: despite everything, unthinkable.

'Aton was physically balked by the salamander,' Bedside said. 'But he was emotionally balked by the minionette. His death reflected his life, could he but have read the parallels in time.'

'Minionette? Death? My father *lives,*' Arlo said, perplexed.

'All men sent to the prison Chthon are officially dead,' Bedside said. 'The caverns have taken the place of capital punishment. There is no release; it is like the mythical underworld. I died in §394 by that definition; Aton died in §400. I was sentenced to prison Chthon because I am mad; he because he loved a minionette. Much the same thing.'

Arlo was growing desperate because of the looming approach of the cavern menace, yet his thirst for information about his parent's situation compelled him to follow this up. He knew Bedside was holding him here, just as the salamander had, just as the Norns had. But the hunger the old man had roused was more compelling than that the Norns had touched and harder to combat than the salamander's threat. He knew Bedside would speak only while his terms were met, again like the Norns he resembled.

Ah- but the wolf seemed to have mislaid the scent of the prey, temporarily. Chthon could not guide it all the way, for that would overtly break the covenant they had so recently made. The wolf had to find Ex itself. So a little extra time had developed. Arlo had to delay – or lose, perhaps forever, his chance to acquire this knowledge. Restricted as he was to the caverns, his sources of outside information were invaluable. So he listened, though simultaneously angry about being controlled this way.

'What's a minionette?' he asked.

'A female of modified human stock inhabiting the planet Minion. Your grandmother was a minionette; you are quarter minion.'

'But you said my father was imprisoned for loving a minionette! My mother—'

'Coquina is human, or close to it. She is native Hvee. The minionette is death.'

'The *salamander* is death!' Arlo said, looking at the creature on his spear. It still lived, struggling every so often.

'Precisely. Aton sought the incalculable wealth of the blue garnet, but what he found was the salamander. In the equivalent episode of his life he sought the lovely siren – or shall we say Valkyrie – the minionette, but that quest only brought him here to the nether world. Siren, Valkyrie, minionette: all are mere conveyances to death. All his life was like that.'

'All reflecting his death? That makes no sense—'

'His life reflected his death, and his death his life. All he had to do was interpret the parallels, and he would have known his future.'

Arlo remained incredulous. 'The salamander like the minionette? Did she have poison fangs?'

'In her fashion. Your life, too has parallels – if you can read them. The hints are all about you.'

Arlo smiled, looking again at the salamander. 'If I meet a minionette, I'll poke my spear through her belly.'

'Undoubtedly. That would certainly be best.'

If Bedside agreed with him, Arlo knew he had better reconsider. But suddenly an unbearably intense sensation passed through him. The wolf had recovered the scent, charged Ex, and had her in its teeth!

Arlo held the salamander before him and sprinted. This time Bedside, alert to the menace, got out of his way. Arlo would gladly have impaled him along with the salamander!

Moments later he burst into the garden. But his approach had already alarmed the monster. All he saw was its huge haunch as it fled. He hurled the spear after it, hoping to nick it with the poisoned end, but the range was too long.

Ex lay in blood on the stone. Her body had been torn open like that of a butchered chipper, exposing her innards yet she lived. Arlo took one horrified look and knew he could do nothing. He had to get help.

Where? Not from Chthon, certainly! Who else was there to turn to?

He was hardly aware of his rush home. Suddenly he was there, panting violently, drawing on his trunks as Coquina looked up in surprise.

She wore a dress, very like those pictured in LOE. She was always clothed, despite the stifling heat. Clothing was part of the home-cave ritual; it had never occurred to Arlo that things should ever be otherwise. She was a woman of about fifty, and whether she was beautiful or ugly was irrelevant. She was his mother.

Arlo had a hard time catching with breath, and the sweat seemed to be squirting out of his skin in this sudden oven. But Coquina never left her burning-wall premises, heated by a boiling stream. Not for more than a moment, certainly.

'A girl,' he cried. 'Attacked. By a monster. Dying—'

Coquina wasted on time with questions. 'Aton's questing in the upwind forest. Find him there. Take Sleipnir.'

'I can't ride Sleipnir!' Arlo protested.

'Hang onto his tail; follow him. He can find Aton immediately and carry you both back.'

She was right: this was the fastest way. 'Thanks, Mother! She hadn't even shown surprise over Ex!

He left the oven-cave and ran to the pasture. This was a closed minor network of passages reserved for the animal, barricaded not against his escape but against the intrusion of dangerous predators. He located Sleipnir by the sound of the animal's grazing: a steady chip-chip-chip. Sleipnir was another glow feeder, his great front teeth chipping off flakes of rock to chew for their coating of lichen. It was a tedious chore, requiring much time and effort – but the creature had time, and strength, and imagination for little else. In fact, Aton had to pasture him in a suitable section each time, or the chipper would work over a recently deglowed stone, and starve.

Sleipnir had a bulbous, long-snouted head, a segmented body, and eight powerful legs. He was low and long, able to run through

fairly tight tunnels without pause. That was what made him such
a good steed – for Aton. Sleipnir had little wit but he knew his
master and tolerated no one else upon him though he was strong
enough to carry several people at once.

'Come, stupid,' Arlo said.

The animal ignored him.

'Sleipnir!' Arlo cried loudly. Now he perked up, hearing his
name – but when he saw that it was only Arlo, he returned to his
repast. CHIP! CHIP!

Arlo grabbed hold of the creature's spike like tail. 'Find Aton!'
he bawled, making his voice sound as much like his father's as he
could. 'Aton! ATON!'

That registered. Sleipnir looked about, searching for his master. When he did not see him, he sniffed the floor. 'Aton! Upwind
forest!' Arlo cried, jerking on the tail. With Ex dying, he had to
struggle with this moronic beast!

Sleipnir could not understand the words, but now the need to
find his master had been invoked, and he began to move. His
brain was minimal, but his nose was sophisticated. In a moment,
he had located the freshest spoor. He pursued it.

Was there really such a difference between man and animal, Arlo wondered. Norns, salamander, and Doc Bedside
had evoked particular responses in Arlo, just as Arlo had
evoked this response in the pseudo-horse. Intelligence was
not of itself sufficient to circumvent such responses, or he
would have been able to save Ex by ignoring the distraction
placed in his way.

When Sleipnir ran, he *ran*. Arlo hung to the tail with both
hands and sprinted, but the steed was too swift for him. Soon he
was reduced to bouncing: putting down both feet together in a
kind of sliding hop, to support himself while the creature's head-
long pace carried him along. This was rough exercise – but it was
getting him where he wanted to go!

The passing caves became a blur. Some were dark, some light;
some small, some huge. Some were straight, with the wind rush-

ing through; some curved and recurred intricately. An outsider would have been amazed at the variety of shape and color; Arlo took it all for granted.

At last they reached the upwind forest. Here the stalactites extended down from the ceiling to connect with the stalagmites below, forming columns. But many were not vertical; the force and eddies of the wind had taken the dripping fluids slantwise, and the rock formations had followed. At times over the centuries, natural forces had shifted the wind, causing the structures to change direction, and the growing presence of upwind columns had interrupted the air stream and affected the downwind columns. Slow accretion had been replaced by wind erosion. As a result, the stalactites had irregularly descending branches, and the stalagmites had roots that twisted in widely varied configurations. The colors, too, were divergent, with glowing blue and pink stripes augmenting the green moss. Even Arlo could see that this represented a kind of history of the cavern: the glow had not always been green, but only in the developing columns were the prior types recorded.

'Father!' Arlo cried. His arms and legs were numb, his body sore from the bruising run, but that hardly mattered.

Aton turned. He was fifty-two years old, dark-bearded and powerful, with a certain aura of determination or ruthlessness about him. He punched his fist into Sleipnir's nose, his way of patting the animal. The creature was so tough it could not feel a light touch. Aton's single eye looked inquiringly at Arlo.

'Girl. Wounded. Dying. Blood. Help.' Arlo said between gulps of air.

Aton put one hand on Sleipnir's back and vaulted aboard. This vigor did not seem strange to Arlo; his father had always been an active man, and only recently had Arlo outgrown him. Aton leaned over, caught his son under the arms, lifted him. And deposited him on the rear segement of the steed. Sleipnir didn't notice; all he cared about was that Aton was riding him.

There had never been another human being in this region of the caverns other than Aton, Coquina, Arlo, Doc Bedside, and the zombies. Yet Aton hadn't hesitated. 'Where?' Aton asked.

'In my gardens.'

Aton had never been to the gardens, though he knew where they were, because the way was blocked by so many animate and inanimate threats. Aton did not have the aid of Chthon on that route; it was as though the god wanted no one but Arlo there. But of course Arlo had explored al the tunnels and knew his way through safely, regardless of Chthon's influence.

Aton guided Sleipnir according to Arlo's instructions, and they thundered toward the gardens. Even on this fleet mount, it took some time because the safe route was circuitous. Afraid to contemplate what they would find there. Arlo talked with his father: a thing he seldom did. It was not that there was any bad feeling between them, but that there was inadequate feeling. Arlo really did not know his father well. 'What is a minionette?' He had asked this question of Bedside, but received no satisfactory answer. Of *course* a minionette came from planet Minion; why should that be significant? Why did she equate with sirens, Valkyries, and death?

Aton's back stiffened, and Arlo knew that he had made a mistake. As the second son, substitute for the favored firstborn, he dared not presume. He had supposed this to be a special case. 'Who spoke to you of that?'

'Old Doc Beside.'

Aton grunted contemptuously, but he relaxed a bit. 'What did he tell you?'

'Only that I was quarter-minion. My grandmother—'

'Enough!'

Arlo was glad enough to let it drop. Aton was a man of violent temperament, and he had a sadistic streak . It was evident that Bedside had been sowing dissent, in his subtle fashion. Time for a change of subject.

'How did you get Sleipnir?'

Aton relaxed again. 'That was Bedeker's doing.' He always called Doc Bedside that. 'He and I went exploring in the early days, but we were careless and got trapped by a caterpillar. He tried to distract it while I pounded a hole in the wall, but it stabbed him with its tail and incorporated him.'

Arlo knew how that worked. The long caterpillars rammed their tail-spikes through the quarry, impaling the victim through the middle. In moments, special substances or nerves extended into the victim's body, and instead of dying, he was reanimated as a segment of the creature, marching in unison with the other segments. In due course, the segments of the latter end of the creature were slowly drained of their resources, going to sustain the forepart, shrinking until they were little more than walking lumps. · The caterpillar never ate with its mouth; its face was a huge façade intended to frighten potential prey toward the tail. There was little defense against a caterpillar except avoidance, as with other Chthonic menaces. But it could readily be avoided with suitable foresight. On occasion Arlo had scrambled over a caterpillar's mid-portion since only the tail could attack.

Then the other meaning of Aton's words penetrated. '*Bedside* was incorporated? But he's alive!'

'That took you while, son,' Aton said with a brief laugh. 'Bedeker is only half-alive. He's a creature of Chthon, a mad doctor, a golem, an animated stick. A *good* doctor, though, especially with Chthon's assistance. You should have gone to him for help first.'

'I couldn't. Chthon wants the girl dead.'

'I thought as much,' Aton said. 'Chthon wasn't in on this particular scheme, it seems. You're beginning to appreciate that the god of the caverns is not necessarily beneficent.'

'Yes!' It had been a hard lesson, as most cavern lessons were. Yet Arlo realized that his father was pleased. Aton hated Chthon – yet he stayed here in Chthon's demesne, and Chthon tolerated him. Why? Arlo dared not ask – yet.

'An ordinary man would have been lost,' Aton continued after a moment. 'But Bedeker belongs to Chthon, and Chthon controls all life in the caverns. Except the three of us. The human mind is too complex to control without an enormous special effort.'

'The myxo!' Arlo cried.

'Right. And those of us with minion blood are capable of re-
sisting the myxo, so that if Chthon prevails, the result is not a
controlled human mind but a zombie. So it isn't worth it. Still the
mineral intellect has ways of making its point. Chthon could have
stopped the caterpillar – but maybe it wanted to teach us a lesson.' He always referred to Chthon as 'it,' signaling his smoldering antipathy. 'So it let Bedeker get caught. I escaped – only because Chthon let me – but for a week Bedeker marched in the
caterpillar. Several more segments were incorporated behind him.
I thought I'd never see him again, and I wasn't sorry.'

Aton shook his head, his dark hair waving with the motion.
'Until that episode, I never really appreciated Chthon's full power.
Maybe I still don't. Well, Chthon showed me! A predator attacked
that caterpillar – some huge wolf like thing and—'

'Wolf!' Arlo cried. But he shut up as his father paused. He
wanted to hear the rest of the episode.

'The wolf severed it just in front of Bedeker. The main caterpillar escaped, but Bedeker survived as an independent segment.
He wasn't a real caterpillar; he couldn't use his tail to incorporate
new segments. He was just a ten-legged fragment walking around.
But now he had control. Maybe it was really Chthon-control; I'm
sure *I* would have died in that situation. But in due course the
predator attacked again, this time cutting off the last four segments. And still Bedeker lived. He returned almost to normal –
it's hard to tell, since he is half mad, half Chthon anyway – while
the remainder of his former body carried on by itself. Again, no
death. The new head assumed control and started eating. Those
last segment had been pretty strong, so the thing was stupid but
powerful. Bedeker gave it to me to take care of, and he named it
Sleipnir, after eight-legged horses of Norse mythology. You'll find
that in LOE.'

Aton fell silent, and Arlo asked no more questions. The story
was incredible – yet he had to believe it. Chthon *did* have such
power, and Doc Bedside did have huge scars on his body whose
significance suddenly manifested. But how amazing, for the old

mad doctor had almost literally birthed this fine cavern horse – a
four-segment caterpillar fragment! Where else could such a thing
have happened?'

They entered the gardens. Aton looked around with interest,
blinking in the unaccustomed yellow light, for he had not had
opportunity to inspect this region before. 'Nice,' he said apprecia-
tively. 'I seem to remember something like this, vaguely. I think
the first time Chthon guided me through the caverns, using the
half-woman . . .'

'Black-haired?' Arlo asked.

'Yes. Half-zombie. Don't tell me she's still around?'

'Yes. She's one of the Norns.'

'Norns!' Aton exploded, laughing. 'Chthon must have quite a
sense of humor, deep in its stone circuits. She was a Lower Cavern
bitch, when I knew her.'

Bitch. The female of an Old Earth dog, evidently a term of
disrespect. But now they were coming into Arlo's particular green
near the falls, where the girl lay.

Ex remained as she had been. Arlo had difficulty looking. It
was not the sight of wounds and blood that bothered him. But the
fact that he had so recently known this person, and in fact had
some responsibility for her condition.

'She's been gutted, but she lives,' Aton said. 'That's remarkable. Are you sure she's not zombie?'

'She's *human!* Chthon tried to take her – and then sent the
wolf.'

Aton looked up. 'Wolf?' he asked sharply, evidently making
the same connection Arlo had. A wolf had freed Bedside from the
caterpillar . . .

'That's what it felt like. Its mind. Bedside blocked me off, so I
came too late and hardly saw it. Big – big, like a wolf.'

'You've never seen a wolf!'

'I've seen the picture in LOE. But it's only the feel I mean.
The malignancy. It doesn't matter what it *looks* like. It's a wolf.'

'A wolf,' Aton repeated. 'You're right: in the caverns, feel is more important than appearance.' Then he shook himself. 'So you've got a girl! She must have strayed from the prison.'

'Yes. She said so.' But now Arlo was aware of a certain devious-ness in his father and knew he was concealing something. Aton should have been surprised, perhaps angry – but he was neither. He could hardly be in collusion with Chthon. So what did he know?

'We can't save her,' Aton said regretfully. 'Her guts have been spilled. I don't know what keeps her alive.'

There were times when his father lacked tact. Yet it was true. There was no explaining what kept Ex breathing. 'We have to try,' Arlo said.

'All we can do is tie her together and see what happens. Only Chthon can save her.'

'But Chthon *won't.*

The man's eye looked at him, and Arlo knew the question was rhetorical. 'Why not?'

'Because Chthon sent the wolf to kill her!'

Aton nodded. He gathered strong vines from the native flora of the garden 'Don't you think Chthon could have arranged to kill her outright, instead of leaving her hanging by a thread?'

'I—'But his arrival could not have had much effect; the wolf had already been departing. 'Chthon *wanted* her – this way?'

'It is possible to bargain with Chthon. That's how I saved your mother.'

Arlo was torn by hope and incredulity. 'You—'

'She had the chill.'

'The chill?'

'I forgot. That's not in LOE.' He sighed. 'I hate this business. I think your girl is going to die, so I'm talking about something else. But maybe this will help.' He paused, finding his mental place as his hands worked, preparing the vines. 'Most of what I know about the chill I learned from fat Hasty. That's Hastings – a fellow prisoner, a quarter-century ago. Hasty, Framy, Bossman, Garnet, the black-haired bitch – I never did know her name—'

'Verthandi.'

Aton snorted, but continued: Two hundred forty-one deni-
zens of the nether caverns, and as many more in the upper prison.
But Hasty was special. He knew everything except how to mine a
garnet. He died stuck in a hole, chopped in half by Bossman's axe.
Had to be done, because the jelly whale was coming . . . ' He
trailed off.

'You mean a potwhale?' Arlo asked.

'Hasty did a marvelous presentation. He phrased the mystery
of the chill as though it were a parody of the earlier quest for the
nature of light. He talked about the particle theory and the wave
theory, and showed how the first was exploded and the second
swamped. He had fun with his puns! He also took his digs at the
obtuseness of military doctors who suppose that no person without a fever can be sick, even though he appears to be dying. And
the scholastic "publish or perish" system that has always kept pro-
fessionals too busy with irrelevancies to attend to their legitimate
work.'

Arlo shook his head. 'I don't understand.'

'No, of course you wouldn't. The prisoners didn't grasp the
nuances either. But the essence was this: the chill comes in ninety-
eight-year cycles – waves of it spreading out from the center of the
galaxy. Where it strikes, more than half the population dies. Each
infected person becomes colder and colder until he can no longer
sustain the bodily processes necessary to live. There in no cure.

'Coquina caught it when it crossed planet Hvee the last time,
in §403. I knew she would die. She had stayed in the path of the
chill only to take care of me in my madness, and in that manner
she showed me what true love was. I knew I loved her too. So I did
what I had resolved never to do, and I made a bargain with Chthon,
agreeing to come here to stay provided Chthon enabled her to live.
As long as Chthon keeps its bargain, I keep mine. Honor between
enemies, you might say. She stays in a cave so hot her body temperature cannot drop, and Chthon's ambience touches her to keep
her sane and functional, and so she survives. It isn't much of a life

for her, but if she ever leaves that heat, or the presence of Chthon, she will die.'

Arlo was stunned. In one speech his father had clarified life-long mysteries – yet how many new mysteries unfolded in that telling! What was the real cause of the chill, and how could Chthon nullify it as though Coquina were merely another hvee plant, existing by the god's will, yet no zombie? How did the minionete relate to this? And why had Chthon *wanted* Aton to live here? Arlo knew better than to inquire; his father, like Bedside, volunteered information only when he chose. This had been an unprecedented windfall, but that was all.

Aton wrapped the vines around Ex's torso, pulling the great wound together and poking her intestines inside, one link at a time, gently. Even Arlo could see that this was extremely crude surgery, bound to be futile; but there was little elso to do.

'At least there are hardly any harmful microbes here,' Aton murmured. 'Wounds don't suppurate here, and there are no contagious diseases. Outside, even a scratch could kill you, or the air exhaled by a sick man.'

'A scratch by the salamander kills,' Arlo said. 'And the breath of a dragon, too.'

'Something like that,' Aton agreed, with an obscure smile.

'I bargained with Chthon,' Arlo ventured. 'I threatened to kill myself if it didn't stop the myxo.'

Aton looked up at him eye widening. '*You* experienced the myxo?'

'It was trying to take over Ex, and she was crusted with white, so I put the spear to myself and—'

'And so you bargained with the nether god, because it had either to make you a zombie or let you die. And you won!'

'I guess so. But when I left Ex, the wolf attacked—'

Aton put his hand on Arlo's shoulder. 'Son, you are a man. You fought Chthon itself to save your girl, as I did. But you did not go far enough.'

Arlo was immensely flattered by his father's statement. But he looked down at the bound body, still slowly leaking blood, and knew that he had lost what he had fought for. 'I guess not.'

'You stopped Chthon from using the myxo. But so long as it controls the animals of the caverns, it can kill the girl. You cannot save her without coming to terms with Chthon.'

Arlo shivered despite the warmth of the gardens. 'Should I try to kill myself again?'

Aton closed his eye. 'Son, I have neglected you. Aesir was my son, and when he died it was as though I had no child. You were there, later, but you were hardly real to me. It is the same mistake I made when I clung to the minionette in preference to your mother. But now you are a man, and I know that though you came second, you are every bit as much mine as is Coquina. The second is *not* inferior to the first! I would not have you die.'

Again Arlo was amazed. This was the strongest expression of affinity he had ever heard from his father. And now he had heard the name of his lost brother: Aesir. And he had Aton's admission that he had loved the minionette. But Arlo kept his voice steady. 'I am glad. But how can I protect Ex from Chthon?'

'Only as I protect Coquina. Tell Chthon you will not oppose it so long as your girl lives. *Really* lives, not a zombie! Chthon wants your cooperation, even as it wanted mine. In fact—' Aton paused momentarily, a strange expression passing across his face— 'In fact, I suspect Chthon only wanted me here in the caverns so that I could beget a child. A human creature conceived, birthed, and wholly enclosed by the caverns. It is possible Chthon killed Aesir because he was not suitable for its purpose. Now you are here – and Chthon wanted you whole. I don't know why. But I think you can bargain. It would take many years to produce another like you – and I doubt Chthon wants to wait that long.'

'Chthon wants me . . .' Arlo echoed. 'It must be true. Chthon has always been my friend. Until Ex came.'

Aton smiled. 'Evidently Chthon wants no child from you! And certainly no corruption of your mind by any outsider. There is your bargaining point perhaps. Tell it you will have no child by Ex and will cooperate as before no matter what she may tell you, so long as Chthon makes no further move against her. And repairs the damage already done.'

'But I don't know how to have a child – or how not to! Arlo protested.

'You'll find out how. And Chthon can prevent conception, so long as the two of you remain here. I think it's a fair bargain. See if Chthon agrees.'

Arlo turned inward – and Chthon was there, his friend, as before. 'Chthon agrees,' he said, wonderingly.

Aton raised the eyebrow above his good eye. 'Just like that!' He had no direct contact with Chthon and wanted none.

Arlo looked at Ex, who seemed to be resting easier now, 'What is conception?' he asked, suspecting it had something to do with the curious crease between her legs.

Aton turned toward Sleipnir. 'The girl is young yet. Do not force her. Let her recover, let her grow a couple of years. Get to know her well. If she is good, she will fill your life as Coquina fills mine. She will convert the animal into a man.' He climbed onto his steed.

It came to Arlo that his father had to have known that Ex was coming: company for a boy who had not realized he was lonely. But Chthon had not agreed to the arrangement, and here was the consequence: the wolf's attack.

'You asked about the minionette,' Aton said. 'When you go home, ask your mother. She will tell you as much as you care to know.' Then, to Sleipnir: 'Any route home. I believe Chthon will protect us this one time.' And he was gone.

Arlo felt Chthon's confirmation. The god had known what Aton would say and do, and thus had permitted his visit to the gardens. This once.

He sat beside Ex for a long time, mulling over what his father had said, watching to see if the girl got better.

Finally Doc Bedside came. ''So you have made peace with Chthon,' he observed. 'Let me see to the child.'

Now it was all right. Arlo let the man remove the vines and leaves and explore the great wound. 'She has astonishing vitality,' Bedside remarked. 'And marvelous good fortune. No internal organs ruptured, bleeding minimal, considering. A few stitches and Chthon's beneficence will see her through, I suspect.'

'But why did Chthon want to kill her?' Arlo asked. Aton had suggested a reason, but now the notion of sacrificing a living human being merely to prevent her from being a companion seemed less credible. Surely there were less strenuous ways!

'Chthon's ways are inscrutable. But you have made your bargain; Chthon will honor it. No creature of the caverns will harm her so long as you and Chthon are one.'

'What does Chthon want with me?' Arlo cried.

Bedside studied him in his disquieting fashion. 'I am mad. By that I mean I do not conform to the norms of your society, though I can approximate them when necessary. Your father is half-mad. You are sane. You are Chthon's chosen. Your destiny is huge.'

'Chosen for *what?*'

But Bedside only smiled.

Ex recovered. It was amazingly rapid, considering the severity of her injury, but it did take time. Arlo brought her food that Coquina made: glow-bread, fermented vine sap, dried chipper meat. He carried her regularly to a narrow, deep crack above flowing water so that she could defecate cleanly. He supported her as she practiced walking. And he talked with her.

Arlo told her all about the caverns: the rivers, the potwhales, the ice tunnels, the caterpillars, the forests, the chimera, and Chthon. He told her how his father mined gold and precious garnets and other stones to make beautiful rings that Doc Bedside took outside to trade for civilized goods: clothing, tools, books.

She in turn told him of the great outside world. How the wonderful § spaceship traveled from Earth all over the human sector of the galaxy and even traded with sentient alien species: the Xests, Lfa and EeoO. (She had to pronounce those strange names several time for him: *zzest, fla* only with the L and F reversed, one syllable, and EE-e-o-O with accents on the first and last syllables, the whole run together so that it sounded more like an exclamation than a name.) How mankind had fragmented into planetary sub-species, each adapted for its particular world in subtle ways though all looked completely human and could interbreed. (Interbreed? Arlo inquired, interested. How is that done? But she seemed not to hear him.) How the stars came out at night, just as described in LOE: pinpoints of light too numerous to count, especially in the 'Milky Way' region of the planetary sky. How there were rocks floating in orbit about individual stars, called 'planetoids'- some only a few miles in diameter, so that a visitor could hardly cling to their surfaces. 'But excellent for mining rare ores,' she said. 'Because the deep strata are all exposed and accessible. Gold, iridium – all sorts of things just there for the taking, and almost no energy required to get them into space. Ore-shuttling is a big space business.'

'It must be,' Arlo agreed, entranced with this vision. LOE had nothing like this!

'And some of them are made into holiday stopovers. Spotels. Sealed in, completely private, with all the comforts of home.' She winked confidentially. 'I was conceived in a spotel.'

'But how-'

'My father's dead now. So's my mother. Must've been some romance, though, while it lasted!'

That balked further question about the nature of human breeding. But the two became intertwined in Arlo's imagination: ore-mining, planetoids, and romance.

They didn't talk all the time. They played games ranging from hot-hands to chess. Ex was good at all of them, as she had excellent physical and mental coordination. For a young girl, she knew a surprising amount.

As she grew stronger a strange thing happened. Her body, thinned drastically by the rigor of the injury, filled out to more than its original from. Her legs grew rounder, especially in the upper thighs. Her chest swelled into two humps. Hair grew under her arms and between her legs, concealing that cleft that had so intrigued Arlo. Her body came to resemble, to some degree, that of Verthandi the Norn. And her face changed subtly, becoming less childlike. She was, in short, a golden-haired little beauty.

But her manner changed most of all. She remained highly irritating, but she also became highly suggestive. And, oddly, it was when she was most infuriating that she was most intriguing.

'Where do these lead?' Ex asked, gesturing toward an irregular series of openings in the wall. She was almost better now, and eager to go everywhere.

'Only to the big gas crevasse,' Arlo said, 'No way to pass that. It's the largest canyon in the caverns, hundreds of miles long.'

'Oh let me see!' she cried, and ran for the nearest hole.

'Wait!' Arlo exclaimed, pursuing her twinkling bottom. Part of his mind noted how much fuller her buttocks were than they had been; perhaps it was because she had sat for so long, recovering. 'It isn't safe!'

But she scurried on through, bending over to clear the low tunnel ceiling. This had the effect thrusting out her posterior further, making it an object of increasing interest to Arlo, though he was aware that there really was nothing there. Still, the immediate danger alarmed him.

'There's a drop-off!' he called. 'No safe way down, from here – and the gas would choke you anyway.'

She scooted on around a bend. He followed. Beyond it was another turn, and here the passage narrowed so far that her hips caught against the sides. He knew the drop was close ahead, so he grabbed her where he could. One hand passed inside her legs, catching the front of the thigh, his fingers sinking into the smooth flesh. 'Stop!' he cried.

'You're doing it!' her voice came back 'Goosing me!' She wriggled, and her hips slid through the construction.

He tried to hold her, but first her thighs pressed tightly against his hand, then spread wide, and his fingers slid out. Again he experienced that mixed excitement and alarm, wanting to hold that thigh because it excited him, and to protect Ex from danger – and losing that hold despite everything.

He dived after her – but now his own hips caught in the construction. He ripped free, scraping skin on both sides, for the rock was very rough. Annoyed by the burning pain, and by her escape, he accelerated again.

'Oh!' she cried ahead, and for a moment he feared she had plunged into the chasm. But she had stopped in time, and now was sitting on the cliff edge, dangling her legs down.

'Why didn't you wait?' he demanded angrily. 'You could've gotten killed that way! I *told* you it was dangerous!'

She looked out into the mist before them as though nothing had happened. "What is it, Arlo? I've never seen anything like this!'

'It is the gas crevasse, as I said,' he said tightly. 'The gas vapors drop down from the ceiling, there.' He pointed to the distant, lofty roof, not actually visible from this vantage. 'they drift into the bottom, maybe a mile down, maybe more – I don't know how to judge it – and get sucked into tubes. At the other end, way across the caverns, there's fire. It blows into the passages and makes the hot upwind tunnels where the prison is. The wind finally expands and cools and slows and comes back here, to pick up more gas and repeat the cycle.'

She peered down. 'I can't see anything.'

'Course you can't. There's no glow down there.'

'Then how do you know about the gas?'

'My father told me.' On one of those few prior occasions when Aton had talked freely. He was more apt to tell about things than about people.

'How does *he* know?'

'Fat Hasty must have explained it to him, when they were on the Hard Trek.'

She sniffed. ' That's a myth.'

'What?'

'The Hard Trek. It's just a prison story. There never was any such thing.'

'My father was *on* it!' Arlo protested hotly. 'They had nothing to eat, so they ate their own dead. The chimera stalked them, and the myxo, and-'

'It's a lovely story, anyway,' she said. 'And you've lovely too.' She leaned over to him where he squatted beside her and kissed him on the mouth.

She had not done that before. The effect was potent. Arlo's whole being seemed to funnel into the meeting of their lips, and he felt as if he were turning, around and around and end over end. It was sheer, confusing bliss. LOE had described kissing many times, often shortly before the ellipses that annoyingly concealed the mechanics of reproduction – but the reality was beyond his expectations.

Suddenly the falling and twisting were literal. Ex pushed herself off the ledge, and almost took him with her. Arlo found himself clinging to the rough rim by the one hand, his other arm about her, while his feet scrambled for some toehold.

In a moement his experienced toes found that lodging, and the terror of his incipient fall abated. 'What were you *doing!* he cried in fury.

'I slipped.' Her attitude was blithe.

'You did not! You—'

She scrambled up, treating him to another view of her newly mysterious bottom, and ran down an adjacent passage. Again he pursued, furious.

This tunnel was even tighter than the other. Ex wriggled through just ahead of him and finally emerged in the main passage. But Arlo, flowing too closely, blinded by mixed lust and anger, got jammed again. This time he has really wedged, his hips so tight against the stone that he could neither advance nor retreat without exquisite pain. He was stuck upright, facing into the passage.

Ex looped back when she found he wasn't chasing her. 'What's the matter?'

'I'm caught. I can't move,' he said hotly.

'Really?' She sounded pleased.

'Well, what does it look like!'

She leaned forward to peer closely at his midsection. Her newly developing breasts assumed more form in this position. In time, he knew, they would resemble those of Verthandi, large and full. Later perhaps, they would become pendulous, like those of the other Norns, and less stimulating. But this nascent quality was now immensely provocative. 'I think it's rising,' she said.

'My *hips are what's stuck!*' he said. Help me out!'

'Yes, it's definitely getting big.'

'Shut up about that!' he exclaimed in a fury of embarrassment. Though he had scant sexual shame and was proud of the erection he could muster, he did not want it in this particular situation. It tended to show his ignorance, and it reminded him of the touch and interest to the Norns. What had they said about it? 'This rod transfixes . . . ?'But he had no control.

Ex danced very close, turning and thrusting out her rear so that it almost brushed him. 'Why don't you. . . . '

Arlo suffered an abrupt clarification of motive. He knew where to put his hardened organ! He lunged at her, uncertain whether he intended rape or mayhem or both. But the rocks held fast, and he got a searing bolt of pain in the flanks. He was so angry he could hardly see her, yet he lusted for her with an intensity he had never known could exist. Yes, he knew what to do – when he had the chance!

'Kootchie-koo!' Ex sang, this time actually touching his member.

Arlo got smart. He twisted instead of pushing straight forward. Skin scraped from him on either side, and the very bone seemed to be compressed – but he wrenched free, sliding out of the constriction.

But Ex was gone. She was now as fleet as he, and she knew the caverns well enough to hide from him indefinitely. He could not catch her.

Perhaps it was just as well, he had bargained with Chthon to preserve her life, but in that moment he would gladly have killed her himself.

'The minionette?' Coquina repeated, and now the stress lines showed on her face, making her look older.

'Father said I could ask you now,' Arlo said, his muscles tightening nervously. Now, for once, he was glad of the required clothing that helped conceal the tensions of his body. 'Doc Bedside said the minionette was death like the salamander – that they were parallel, like all his life and death. He—'

'Dr Bedeker is mad,' she said.

'Yes. He says he's all mad, and that my father is half-mad. Only I don't think he means the same thing by the word that we do. But Bedside has always spoken truth to me, in his fashion, and he says my father was imprisoned for loving the minionette. Yet he also said my grandmother was a minionette, and I am quarter-minion. How can a man be imprisoned for loving his mother? I love you-'

Coquina put her hand to the hot wall to steady herself. Arlo grabbed her other arm, afraid she would fall. 'What's the matter?'

His mother got a grip on herself. 'How are things with you and Ex?'

Coquina had met Ex only once. It had been a disaster. Coquina had shown no jealousy, but instead had extended her arms in welcome – and Ex had run away. Arlo had reacted with familiar fury, but he could not get Ex to return or explain. She associated with Arlo, Aton, and Bedside, making them all angry in little ways – yet Coquina, who had nothing but love to give, was shunned. That was just one of the things that aggravated Arlo – but despite it, he was drawn to Ex with increasing passion. It was as though he *liked* perversity, as though part of him wanted to hurt and be hurt – and that disgusted him. On the off-chance that something in his heritage could account for this, he had finally gotten up the nerve to put the question to his mother.

'She's a damned nuisance,' he said. 'But sometimes she's awfully sweet. Half the time I want to kill her, and the other half-' he
hesitated, uncertain how much he should admit. He doubted that
Coquina would be pleased to hear about the misadventure of the
gas crevasse, for example. Nothing had happened, really; but had
he been just a little faster . . .

'She is a young female, and you're a young male,' Coquina
said. 'It's natural for you to desire her sexually. There is no shame
in this.'

Then why had his mother never told him how to implement
the sex act? Obviously there *was* shame, some there. 'But I desire
her most when I hate her most!' he exclaimed.

Coquina sat down on her rock chair. Because it was stone, it
conveyed the heat of the wall and floor to her body Arlo was sweating from the ambient temperature, but his mother never sweated.
Her whole temperature-control mechanism had broken down, apparently. 'Yes, it is time for you to know. But I have to warn you:
There is pain in this – for your father, for me, and even for you.'

'Because I am quarter minion!' he said, catching on.

'Yes. I had hoped this element would be suppressed, but it
seems it is not. So it is best that you know the truth, so that you
can deal with it, as your father did.'

'He loves and hates *you*?' Arlo asked, horrified. No one could
hate Coquina!

She smiled wanly. 'No. He has never hurt me. But until he
conquered his chimera, it was very bad. There was much blood on
his hands, much that must be forgotten, because he didn't know.
I pray there will be none on yours.'

'He didn't know *what?*' Arlo cried in frustration. At times his
parents were as bad as Bedside or the Norns in their obscure an-
swers, tantalizing him.

'It began with your grandfather Aurelius Five, Aton's father.
Aurelius married a daughter of Ten, by all accounts a wonderful
woman the hvee loved. But in two years she died in childbirth, for
Planet Hvee is primitive in some ways. In anguish he went to

space, and there fell into the power of the minionette. It was his terrible sorrow that attracted her to him – even his guilt at loving her.'

'I don't understand! Why should he not have remarried?'

'Minion is a proscribed planet. He broke galactic law by going there, and broke it again by taking Malice home with him. So—'

'Malice!' The Norns had used that word! 'What kind of a name is that?'

Coquina put a restraining hand on his shoulder. 'That is difficult, son. Bear with me.'

'I'm sorry.' She was trying to explain something vital, and he had no right to keep interrupting. He could save his question for later. 'All the minionettes have names like that. Fury, Agony, Torment, Wrath, Misery-'

Arlo started to interrupt again, but turned it into a cough . He had to listen, not argue!

Coquina smiled, and he saw in that expression the aspect that had made his father love her. 'Yes, it seems strange at first. But they are true to their nature, as we are to ours. You see, the emotions of the minionette are reversed. What we perceive as love, beauty and delight, they perceive as hate, ugliness, and revulsion – and vice versa. Because they are emotionally telepathic, they receive these emotions directly. A man's hate is divine to them, but his love can be fatal. In fact, they are virtually immortal; hardly anything can kill them and they remain young-seeming and beautiful for centuries. They all look alike, too, until you get to know them well. So they live until someone's love reaches them – and then they die. Their names are actually endearments.'

She took a breath, as though marshalling her strength. 'The men of Planet Minion are more nearly normal, but they have learned to hate those they love. They beat their wives and even try to kill them – knowing that only in this way can they preserve them. So the minion male has a strong sadistic streak associated with his love. That is why the planet is proscribed; that kind of love has made too much mischief in the history of Old Earth and would wreak devastation among the civilized cultures of the galaxy.

'Malice stayed with Aurelius one year – long enough to bear him the child Aton. By that time Aurelius's grief over the loss of the Daughter of Ten was fading, and he was coming to love Malice without guilt. He did not understand – perhaps did not allow himself to understand – that this was what drove her away. So Aton was raised without a mother.

'But there is one other thing about the Minion culture. The women live for centuries, but the men normally die by the age of fifty. Apparently it takes that long for their hate to turn inevitably to love, for their sadism to weaken, and when that happens, they are executed by their own kind. It is a sad but honorable demise, known by the euphemism "carelessness." But the minionette is not widowed; she takes her son as her next husband.'

'She *what?*' Arlo exclaimed. All that he had learned of human culture indicated that incest was taboo.

'It is their system, natural for them,' Coquina continued, though he could see that she herself suffered fundamental misgivings. Coquina was a Daughter of Four, Planet Hvee, innately conservative, a child of the land. Yet she had adapted to her extraordinary situation – for love of the half-minion Aton. She had mastered tolerance. 'The minionette is wife to her son, and after him her grandson who is also her son, and all her male descendants, though she is the literal mother to them all. She bears only boys until at last she grows old; then she bears the girl who will replace her.'

'But if my grandfather-' The implication almost over – whelmed him.

'Aurelius was human, not Minion. He could not accept the Minion system. But Malice came in quest of her son, Aton.' She paused as if gathering strength again, and this time Arlo well understood why. 'You have to understand. She had the aspect of a young beautiful woman, and she came as a lover not a mother, and he did not know-'

Young and beautiful. That abated his revulsion somewhat. But the other matter could hardly be similarly dissipated. 'My father Aton – married his – *mother*?'

'Yes. There was no ceremony, for she had to conceal her identity from the authorities. Technically, he was betrothed to me, but—'

'I will kill her myself!' Arlo cried, filled with a new kind of range.

'No. She is long dead – and she was not a bad woman. I met her. I knew her. What she was, what she did, was in her genes and in her culture. We are all creatures of our ancestry! There is no right and wrong, objectively.'

'There *has* to be,' Arlo said.

'I have never known a more intelligent, lovely competent and loving woman, apart from that ironic inversion of emotion. What I see today in Aton is that half-share he possesses of the minionette, and I love him as much for that as for his human side – which is also excellent.' Again she paused. 'Yet I would love him regardless . . . '

'But he would not have married you, if she had lived,' Arlo carried. 'How can you—'

'It is no bad thing to be the second love,' she said. Arlo felt a tingle, remembering the very similar thing his father had said. These two, so different on the surface, had certain community of nature underneath, and were well matched. 'First love may be wild, inadvised, difficult; second love is based on experience. I regret only that the minionette had to die to make our marriage possible.'

'He would not marry you until his mother died? I will kill him!' Arlo cried, shaking with fury, yet knowing it was bravado. He had neither the power nor a real desire to kill his father; he had merely to express his support for Coquina. Actually, he was getting repetitive – but the idea of requiring one's mother to die to make way for one's wife had an unholy fix on his mind.

'You are quarter-minion,' she said. 'To kill one's father—that too, is the way of the minion. The men who live too long are killed by their sons, who are impatient to assume their conjugal duties.'

That stopped Arlo cold. All his recent furies and passions came into focus now: the minion blood in him craved sadistic love. No wonder his romance with Ex had been turbulent! He would have to change that.

'I hope there is more of Aurelius in me than of the minionette,' Arlo said. 'I would have liked to know that bold old man.'

'His brother Benjamin still lives. Doctor Bedeker still has occasional dealings with him. He is very like Aurelius.'

'Oh?' That was most interesting! 'Will I ever get to meet Benjamin?'

'You would have to leave the caverns, or he to enter them. Either is unlikely.'

True. Intriguing as it was, it was a dead end. Arlo returned to the primary matter: 'Still, you sould have been Aton's *first* choice, not his second.'

'No. It was an arranged marriage between us. First son of Eldest Five, Third Daughter of Eldest Four. Highly expedient, socially – but we had never met, and did not meet until after his liaison with the minionette. And of course he had known her since his childhood. She was his first – and I would have been satisfied to have been his hundredth, so long as I was his at last. After knowing her, he chose me – that is the greatest compliment of my existence.'

Coquina would not speak against the minionette! 'Who killed her?'

'Aton did.'

Once again, Arlo was stunned. '*He* killed his wife – his mother? Why? How?'

'By loving her.'

Arlo sought out Ex, wanting to explain, to apologize. But she avoided him. Her golden tresses flew out behind her as she ran down the cavern passages. No doubt she thought he was going to hit her again. She feared no creature of the caverns since his pact with Chthon, but Arlo himself could hurt her.

'Wait! Wait! he called. But she would not listen.

He pursued her far beyond and garden, across the great river whose finned predators would have torn apart anyone else, and into the chill ice caverns. He seldom ventured there because the footing was treacherous, and he quickly became uncomfortably cold. But he could not relent until he made her listen.

Ex swung around a stalagmite. 'Whee!' she cried as the warmth of her hand melted its sheen of ice and eliminated her support. Her feet went out from under her and she took a graceful fall, unhurt. 'Whee!' she repeated, as she slid on down the winding river of ice on her bare bottom, feet and hands lifted, spinning slowly around.

Arlo flopped on his belly and followed. A thin layer of water flowed over the ice, making it frictionless. The heat of his run made the chill contact stimulating. Seeing Ex rotating blithely with elevated but attractively disposed limbs stimulated him another way. First he would explain: Then—

The ice river debouched into an ice lake. Hairy cavern ice-fowl fluttered out of sight as the two humans shot into the center. Broken ice stalactites littered the surface. Arlo swept them out of the way with hands and feet, and watched them skate in their fashion until they crashed tinkling against the vertical ice-slick rock of the shore. It was fun – but that was not what he was here for.

Ex's forward progress slowed. Arlo, heavier, had more momentum. He reached out a hand and caught her foot as it passed by him, and hauled her into him. 'I just want to tell you about the minionette,' he gasped.

Her mouth popped open prettily. 'You *know*?'

'Yes. I am quarter minion. My grandmother was Malice, the minionette. It is from her I inherited my sadistic streak. But it can be suppressed. My father suppressed it – and so will I. I love you.'

For a moment he thought she misunderstood him. Her face froze in seeming pain.

'What's the matter with you?' he demanded with a flash of the old irritation. 'I said I love you!' And inside he wondered whether this could really be true, or whether Coquina's remark about the wildness of first love had really been a warning. He had not before experienced this type of love . . .

Suddenly Ex smiled. She reached out and pinched him in a most indelicate region. 'Prove it!' Then she braced both feet against him and pushed off, hard.

She sailed across the ice in one direction, he in the other. In one sense her reaction was funny; in another infuriating. Either way, a challenge. Grimly he set out to prove his love – aware that he was catering more than a little to his minion quarter, but nonetheless determined.

He reached the rock wall, braced his feet, and shoved off. He shot back across the lake, toward Ex. But she bounced off the opposite wall and passed him on the bias. 'Yoo-hoo, stupid!' she cried waving gaily.

Growing hotter as his posterior grew colder, Arlo reached the wall and pushed off again, angling directly toward her. But she avoided him again, maddeningly. 'You're not trying very hard!' she called.

Determined, he planned a better strategy. He watched her push off just before he struck his wall, then angled his own thrust to intersect her line of travel. She was unable to change it in the middle of the ice, being essentially in free-fall, and so he was able to grasp her long hair as they passed each other.

He yanked cruelly, letting her hair transmit the full shock of the cancellation of their inertias. Then he was sorry, as she spun about, mouth open, eyes staring. But she only laughed, and he was angry again.

He drew her in to him. She came willingly, her legs spread, droplets of cold water falling from her heels. Her buttocks were white where the ice had cooled them.

She kissed him, again arousing his instant passion for her body. Then her feet came up against his stomach, and she shoved him away again.

But he was not to be caught twice by that device! He still had hold of her hair. Her legs flung out, but she could not get away from him. He hauled her back in, trying for the embrace her open arms and legs had invited. There was no traction. Ex laughed as he attempted to put his torso adjacent to hers. It was like trying to write the old Earth script, in one of his mother's lessons, while holding the sheet of paper in air. Without firm backing, the effort was useless. Ex was anything but firm; in fact she wriggled like a rockworm, finding his ineptitude hilarious, all the time showing him tantalizing glimpses of the target. When she laughed, she quivered right down to her crotch. 'You're not much of a lover!' she cried cheerily.

They had retained a net impetus across the ice. Now they fetched up against a wall. And Arlo had an idea. Here was his backing!

He maneuvered to get her backside against the wall, her feet and hands forward so that she could not push off again. He found rough edges, crevices in the stone, and pressed his fingers hard against them so that the thin sheathing of ice melted. That provided him with a firm grip. His arms and legs formed an enclosure against the wall, and she was trapped within it.

Now, he thought, the key maneuver. It was as though he were one of the spaceships she had described: an ore-shuttle, bringing iridium ore up from the surface of a planetoid. Now he was in orbit, aligning with the hanger, the ore-storage facility. He had to dock precisely, extend his jettison-chute and pump his cargo into the sealed hopper. The pump would trigger automatically as the connection was made, for this entire operation was automatic: no human hand controlled it. That way the ships did not have to be pressurized or carry life support systems, or shielding against radiation. It was very efficient.

But this shuttlecraft had suffered a malfunction, with the result that he could not grapple the receiving mechanism properly. He had to make ties to the outlying wings of the hanger, and swing the center in to make contact. With proper care and judgment, this could be accomplished. The conveyor hydrant had been primed for immediate delivery; rigid, it nosed toward the hopper-tube. The crushed ore was already rising along the internal conveyor, building up pressure for the release. Slowly, slowly , toward the target . . .

The aim was off; a correction had to be made. Nudge to the side—too much, compensate! *Now* it was dead center. Time for the decisive forward thrust –

Contact! The hydrant triggered, jettisoning the ore.

And something at that instant shoved the nozzle to the side. Too late for correction! The invaluable cargo missed the hopper and spewed out into space, wasted, irrecoverable.

Arlo woke from his reverie amidst a climax of pleasure-pain. Ex was laughing so hard she could hardly catch her breath.

Arlo's own hands had been occupied, gripping the rock behind her. He had forgotten that hers were free. She had used them at the critical moment to foil his purpose.

Arlo's hands let go of the rock and closed about her neck. He squeezed, at the same time banging her head against the wall. But there was not much force in it because of the lack of traction. Once more they drifted out into the center of the lake.

'I'm sorry,' Ex said contritely.

'*Sorry!* You—'

Dubiously, still smoldering with disappointment, he took her back to the garden. There he picked a fine blue-glow hvee plant, holding it until it oriented on him. Then he presented it to her knowing that it would shrivel and die, for her love could hardly be true. Yet part of him hoped that wouldn't happen, not only for the human relationship, but for the same of the unique blue hvee.

And the hvee retained its health as she placed it in her hair. Its glow, if anything, increased. Silently she faced him, needing no words, suddenly no teasing gamin but a beautiful. Girl.

She *did* love him; the hvee proved it by its brilliance. And by this token they were betrothed, after the style of his ancestry.

CHAPTER II

Death

Two men sat in the passenger lounge of the FTL ship. They looked out at the simulated stellar view: it was impossible actually to *see* the stars while in Faster-Than-Light travel, but the simulation was accurate and probably more effective than the reality would have been.

One man was old. Pacemakers and inducers attached to his major organs forced them to function, however reluctantly, and a portable lung gave him breath and oxygen. Nevertheless he seemed ready to die, for his whole body was wasted by the ravages of some hideous malady.

The other was a minion: a small, sour-looking man of indeterminate age, bearded and garbed in the traditional loincloth of his culture.

'Shall we celebrate with wine, Morning Haze?' the old man inquired, showing an ancient bottle.

'Is it permitted for your health, Benjamin?' Mornign Haze inquired in return.'

'Naturally not!'

'Then by all means! What is the occasion?'

'Today I am one hundred and eight years old,' Benjamin said.

'Well! For that we should make it a party and invite our pilot.'

'Yes. And – your wife?'

'Not yet,' Morning Haze said meaningfully.

'I beg pardon. In my infirmity I sometime forget . . . '

'How well we know the cause of that infirmity! Make no

apology.' And the man of Minion smiled as he rose to fetch the pilot.

Benjamin poured two glasses of wine with a slightly trembling hand, then rested the stringy muscles of that arm.

In a moment Morning Haze returned with the pilot. This was a Xest: eight-legged with a globular body, like the center of a compact galaxy. Ship's gravity was maintained at a quarter Earth-normal in deference to the needs of the spider-like creature—and that level did no harm to old Benjamin, either.

The Xest had no vocal apparatus, so the humans augmented their dialogue automatically with galactic sign language. 'We are celebrating my one hundred and eighth birthday, this day in §460,' Benjamin said.

'You have been hatched one hundred and eight times?' the Xest inquired, twitching two legs in far more facile Galactic than any human could manage. It had associated with Benjamin for more than thirty Earth years, yet still seemed to have no clear notion of human reproduction or aging.

Benjamin laughed as heartily as he dared. 'It is merely our measurement of time. I was born in §352, Second Son of Eldest Five. My brother Aurelius was born four years prior, so took the A designation, leaving the B to me. Thus I am not of the first rank of Five, and never sought to marry; perhaps that was fortunate. I am indubitably the oldest surviving Five. *The only* surviving Five, as my old friend and companion Morning Haze knows. Since all such humble vanities are soon to end, I celebrate. Do you imbibe?'

'It is a festive matter?' the Xest signaled.

'Indeed it is. Be merry, for there will be no tomorrow.'

The Xest made a syncopated quiver with four legs, indicating some alien emotion. It well understood their mission, but had not until this moment realized that the truth was to be acknowledged openly. 'Then one may be permitted the Taphid?'

'Taphid?' Morning Haze inquired.

'How fitting!' Benjamin exclaimed with such vigor that the

warning indicator on his portable lung swung into the red. 'I with my wine, you with your wife, the Xest with its Taphid. This will be the mightiest party ever!'

The Xest brought out a small box. It lifted the lid. Frost formed: the interior was refrigerated. Then the creature paused. 'Do you both know the meaning of the Taphid?'

'I do not,' Morning Haze said.

'Not really,' Benjamin said. 'But I assure you, it is permissible on this occasion, if it is your desire. Anything is permissible, save deliberate discourtesy. My alcoholic beverage is an example: It will surely kill me.'

'Death we comprehend,' the Xest signaled. 'Yet there are differing modes. Why does the minionette remain alone in her cell?'

'Her presence would not enhance our celebration,' Morning Haze said. 'In due course I shall go her and initiate a private celebration, in that way avoiding a demonstration that could be offensive to others.'

Benjamin set down his drink. 'This may be out of place – but I suggest, with no disrespect intended, that she *should* be with us now. I doubt that any offense will be taken – on this occasion. It is right that our friend be enlightened – as the Xest shall enlighten us.'

The minion signaled directly to the Xest. 'You realize that though our definitions of beauty may differ, this may not be pretty for you?'

'The Taphid is not pretty, by your definition. In fact, there will be some risk to you.'

'You aren't fooling – either of you,' Benjamin said with a smile. 'I have no such telepathy as you do, but my smattering of information – I say, let's indulge ourselves, each in his fashion and perhaps in his companion's fashion. We shall none of us have another chance!'

'Very well,' Morning Haze agreed, touching a stud on his wrist band. 'I have released the lock. Misery will join us presently.' He leaned over the table and picked up an ornate whip.

Benjamin poured himself another drink, though the minion's

drink remained untouched. 'Odd isn't it, the diverse mechanisms we invoke on behalf of individual demise,' he said. 'I am taking sweet poison; the minion takes the minionette, the Xest takes the Taphid. Does it not show how very similar we really are, at the root?'

'We are all sentient life-forms, therefore similar,' Morning Haze remarked, flexing the whip experimentally. It was evidently an instrument he was well familiar with. 'The Human, the Xest, the Lfa, and EeoO – superficial distinctions at Regnarok, as we discovered.'

The Xest lifted out a frozen cube. It steamed as the heated air of the ship touched its surfaces. 'There well be perhaps half a unit of your time. Is this sufficient?'

Benjamin looked at his watch, which was built into the master control of his digestive regulator. 'Half an hour . . . contact is in forty-two minutes at present velocity and azimuth. I believe that is a satisfactory margin.'

'Quite satisfactory,' Morning Haze agreed. 'If one of you will be so good as notify me when only five minutes remain . . . '

'I expect to be too drunk to speak, if my liver has not already failed,' Benjamin said with regret. 'I have shorted out my alcohol-neutralizing circuit, so that the raw element can reach my old brain.'

'One, too, will be incapacitated,' the Xest signaled.

'In Old English that would have been a pun,' Benjamin observed. 'One, two—'

'I will notify you,' the minionette said from the doorway.

Morning Haze peered over his whip at her. 'Thank you, my dear.' He elevated his weapon. 'Step forward, please.'

She stepped into the room. Misery was a tall figure in a voluminous cloak, veiled; yet her motion conveyed the suggestion of extraordinary beauty.

'Let me see your hair,' Morning Haze said.

She hesitated. 'There is little luster.'

'Because I have neglected you, my love,' Morning Haze said.

The whip cracked loudly. Misery's veil flew off her face. Her hood fell back to reveal dull brown tresses. A streak appeared across her cheek where the whip had struck. But she smiled radiantly.

'Misery, meet my old friend Benjamin,' the minion said. 'And my other friend the Xest, who is nameless as is the custom of his kind. Smile for them, bitch.'

The minionette smiled dutifully at each, and such was her facility at this expression that Benjamin paused in his imbibing to smile back while the Xest's leg-joints spasmed together.

'Will you now commit mergence?' the Xest signaled. 'Excuse it if one's curiosity transgresses propriety. Our kind has never properly comprehended the complete nature of your kind.'

'And never will,' Benjamin agreed. 'There is no transgression this hour.' He stood unsteadily, his pacers shifting across his body like so many decorations. 'Friend minion, my brother died in §402 of the minionette. Malice was her name, I believe. I have harbored for decades an insidious urge that only rising intoxication permits me to vent now. May I?'

Morning Haze handed him the whip. 'It would gratify me, friend. Who has a better right than you?'

Benjamin raised the whip. 'You see,' he explained to the Xest as well as he could with only one hand left to signal, 'the emotions of the minionette are reversed. Our pain is her pleasure. I feel extremely guilty about this, therefore—'

He cracked the ship, inexpertly. The lash caught the woman across the shoulder, more or less harmlessly. 'Damn Chthon!' Benjamin swore as his lung-unit swung out and banged into his side, in effect punishing him instead of the object. The minionette smiled.

'You lack practice,' the minion said, also smiling – and now the minionette looked pained. 'I was not addressing myself to you!' Morning Haze shot at her, and her smile returned.

'This is most interesting,' the Xest signaled. 'There is a certain similarity to the Taphid. One begins to comprehend.'

Benjamin clasped his glass left-handed, took another gulp of wine, steadied himself, checked to be sure his pacers were clear, and raised the whip again. 'When I strike her well, I cause her pain, and so she is happy. It is my guilt at causing the pain that affects her, not the injury itself, which she is well equipped to endure. When I miss the mark, I am angry at myself for my inexpertise – and again she is happy. That is the beauty of it. Not for a century have I had such a chance to exercise my suppressed antagonisms!'

'Execpt at Ragnarok,' Morning Haze murmured.

'Ah, yes. Chthon . . . '

'Nevertheless, it does seem to have a tonic effect,' the minion added. 'You are moving more spryly than hitherto.'

'Yes! By such expression of hostilities I might extend my life indefinitely, were it not to end well within the hour regardless.'

'This one would like to comprehend,' the Xest signaled. 'This concept of inevitable destruction – it relates to our mutual destiny.' The cube before it was melting.

'Since this is proper occasion for the exposition of the unfortunate,' the minion said, 'I shall explain about Ragnarok while my friend beats my mother.'

Parent?' the Xest inquired. 'One had supposed she was your mate, such as one comprehends the term.'

'She *is*. Mate *and* mother – and, for many fortunate minions grandmother and on up the ancestral line. In the normal course she would also be my daughter-in-law, mate to my son, and so on down the line. After my demise, of course. This is the way it is on my planet.'

'Then you reproduce by fission!' the Xest signaled, as it were a great light dawning. 'Your individuality continues from generation to generation, as does ours.'

'Congratulations,' Benjamin gasped, made breathless by his rather ineffective exertions with the whip. 'Man of Minion, you have at last made clear the riddle of the centuries: the Nature of Human Reproduction.' He chuckled, bringing up morsel of spittle. 'Fission!'

The Xest paused, contemplating its dissolving cube. 'But why, then your two aspects?'

'Two sexes,' Morning Haze said patiently.

'Two species?'

'Two variations, male and female. Both unite to form a new individual.'

'Yes,' the Xest agreed, understanding anew. 'As do the EeoO! Yet your female aspect is continuous, parent, mate, offspring. This is fission, as well as fusion.'

'Marvelously well stated,' Benjamin said.

The minion shook his head. 'Surely the sexed species have been over this ground with your sexless species many times! Perhaps it would help if you explained your own system of reproduction – and how the Taphid relates to it.'

'Gladly. We fission involuntarily, as when an appendage is accidentally severed. It regenerates a new Xest. So there are two where there was one. Since we are overpopulated, a debt to society is incurred. We do not enjoy debt. So we employ the Taphid.'

Benjamin was getting the hang of the whip, despite his debilitation and advancing state of intoxication. Strips of cloth were falling from the minionette, bringing her splendid body into view. Her hair was turning red, as though a flame were playing in it.

'It is hard to believe you are over eighty years old!' Benjamin murmured.

'I am older than you,' Misery said. 'I birthed three sons before Pink Rock. He broke the chain by turning awful before I could conceive by him, and my tribe had to terminate him for his carelessness. Thus I was widowed. Had Stone Heart not come at that time—'

'Amazing!' Benjamin gasped. 'Your face, your breast – a human girl in your condition would be a full century your junior.'

'Do not neglect the whip,' she reminded him.

'Sorry.' He cracked her again, exposing a bit more of that torso he so admired. 'What a crime I am committing – sadist and voyeur! And I too far gone to utilize any of her, were it permitted.'

'In our experience,' Morning Haze said meanwhile to the Xest, 'the Taphid only consumes. Plastic, flesh, wood – anything remotely edible. What is the specific use you make of it?'

'The same,' the Xest replied. 'The Taphid is the most efficient consumer we have located – better than anything native to our planets. Therefore it is in great demand and accounts for the majority of our trade with other galactic species.' It examined the cube again, passing one leg over it. 'The grubs will emerge soon.'

'Do not tax yourself unduly, sir,' the minion said to Benjamin. 'We do want you with us at the finale.'

'Perhaps that is best,' the old man agreed, turning over the whip. 'This is marvelously restorative, but there are limits. Most of my pacers are now in their warning zones.'

Morning Haze lifted the whip and efficiently cracked off the remnants of the minionette's clothing. She had a breathtakingly (in a convenience of speaking, for the Xest did not breathe) voluptuous figure: neither slender nor exaggerated, but crafted as though by a master artisan to represent the feminine ideal.

Benjamin watched, sipping more wine. 'I begin to understand why my brother took up with Malice,' he said. 'had I been subjected to such temptation, I would not have remained celibate. Yea, even though I *knew* the doom that awaits those who become enamored of her kind!'

'The doom that awaits all minions,' Morning Haze said. 'Except *this* one, for a reason uniquely galactic. Now let me see – how can I climax her in the most humiliating manner?'

'That requires no intense concentration,' Benjamin said. 'Remember my nephew.'

'How could I forget? *I* am your nephew.'

Benjamin sighed. 'Ah, it is indeed the time of the unveiling of ancient secrets! But yes, let the record be acknowledged before the end! You are my kin, and the heir to the fortune of Eldest Five.'

The minionette moaned.

Benjamin smiled. 'See how our gladness hurts her! Are we not sadistic?'

'If one may inquire,' the Xest signaled. 'In what manner may the two of you be related? One becomes confused again.'

'Humans have foolish pride,' Benjamin explained. 'When we transgress our social bylaws, we attempt to conceal it, thinking to protect the reputation of our families. Disloyalty to our legal mates is one such transgression.'

Morning Haze looked across. 'The minionette never transgresses,' he said. 'She is always loyal to her inherent mate, of whatever generation. Even the whipping you gave her, she tolerated only at my directive, and only in my presence.'

'True, nephew, true! Though I wonder at times what would happen if one of them thought her natural mate dead, so took another – than discovered her natural one alive after all. How would she resolve such inadvertent transgression?'

'The most natural mate is always preemptive. The intruder would have to step aside.'

'Even if he were legally, galactically married to her, or shared a blood relation?'

'In such a case, the two mates would have to meet in mortal combat—'

'But normal humans are not always so strong. My nephew Aton, betrothed or married in his fashion to Malice, sought information by visiting Planet Minion in §401. There he tarried with a recently widowed native girl—'

'Stone Heart!' Misery cried, smiling brilliantly.

'Perhaps that is what he termed himself.,' Benjamin agreed. 'And so he impregnated you, Misery, and departed the planet. In due course you birthed Morning Haze, who matured to become your husband. And so he is my grandnephew, and his quarter-human blood is the blood of the great Family of Five. This is the secret reason I sought him out, and facilitated his entry into the galactic culture. Though I violated our law in the doing of it. I have not been disappointed!'

'How fortunate your nephew Aton was able to impregnate her so readily,' the Xest signaled, though obviously it was using a term it was still vague about, and hardly agreed with the 'fortune' of such ready replication.

'No fortune,' Misery said. 'We conceive when love is strongest. Stone Heart's love was more powerful than any I have known.'

'Even than mine?' Morning Haze inquired wryly. 'remember, I am kin to you, as my father was not.'

'He had supreme emotion,' she insisted. 'He very nearly killed me with the violence of his passion. If only he had stayed—'

Morning Haze struck her in the face with his fist. 'I would have killed him, to possess you, bitch that you are!'

'Ah, now you almost approach his love,' she murmured, pleased.

Benjamin turned to the Xest. 'So your kind has a problem of surplus goods?'

'No. Our problem is a chronic brevity of resources.'

'But then why the Taphid, this efficient consumer?'

'You must understand our debt system. Each entity must maintain a favorable balance, returning as much or more to the species as one consumes. If one fissions recklessly, one multiplies one's debt.'

'Even when fission is involuntary? The leg-regenerating-the-individual sort of thing?'

'Correct. Such accidents are disastrous. We cannot permit promiscuous multiplication of entities, whatever the pretext. Therefore, the Taphid.'

Benjamin shook his head. 'I am inebriated and my reasoning powers are minimal. Somehow it seems that the efficient consumption activity of the Taphid would only aggravate your problem.'

'Not so. It's essential that fission-control be practiced.'

Benjamin shook his head. 'No doubt all will come clear in due course.'

'Your own situation,' the Xest asked politely. 'How did you come by it? You seem to be well on the way to complete cancellation of debt.'

Benjamin stared into his drink. Most of the indicators on his pacers had reverted to near-normal, but he was obviously not in

ideal condition. 'The situation is galactic. My own part in it originated with my brother Aurelius, who bore a son by a minionette,
as we have already noted.' He glanced up. 'We *did* note it? My
ancient brain fogs—'

'It is understood,' the Xest said diplomatically.

'When that son Aton took up with his mother – this is referred to as the Oedipus complex in our annals, as contrasted with
the Electra complex in which a girl takes up with her father – he
was in due course discovered and sent to the terminal prison
Chthon. He escaped, but in the process discovered the cavern entity Chthon, a mineral intelligence, who maintained an abiding
antipathy to all living things. It became apparent that this chthonic
entity intended to eliminate all life in the galaxy. To prevent this,
we mounted a preemptive attack against Chthon, using our base
on the surface of Chthon-Planet, called Idyllia. Fitting symbol-
ism, that: Heaven above, Hell below, both warmed by the same
fiery winds. As though there is no concrete distinction between
the two . . . but I drift. I – where was I?'

'Preemptive attack,' Morning Haze called.

'Thank you, nephew. I found myself there in the front ranks,
as it were. At least, I was on the surface of that planet because I was
considered to have the best chance to reach my nephew Aton and
convert him to our side. And because the distant Earth-govern-
ment did not take the threat seriously enough, I had to act myself.
I believed I succeeded, or would have – but I found myself en-
meshed in mortal combat with the insane Dr Bedeker.'

'Surely there was more than that!' Morning Haze objected.
He had tired of whipping Misery, and now was banging her face
against the wall, using her luxuriant hair as a handhold. She looked
more beautiful than ever, and her happiness seemed to radiate
from her. Benjamin, drunk as he was, found this masochism fascinating; never had such loveliness been so brutally treated!

'Of course there was more; I did not realize it was of interest.'
He glanced at the Xest as he signaled, and saw the grubs emerging
from the thaw. Quickly he returned his gaze to the nude woman,

noting how her breasts moved up and down as her head was forced back. She offered no resistance to any of this.

'My nephew Aton, half-minion, killed his mother, then took up with his arranged bride, a daughter of Four named Coquina. Coquina the shell. A lovely girl – lovely.' But it was Misery the minionette he saw, not the Hvee girl. 'However, she came down with the chill, and he had to take her to Chthon caverns, where controlled environment could preserve her life.' He paused again. 'There must have been more to it that that. They tried heated chambers before, during earlier chill sieges, and that didn't work. I – now wait, I can find my own place this time! I – I was present when Dr Bedeker made the contract. " I will pray to your god," Aton said, "If only she lives." And they took Coquina away.'

Benjamin closed his eye. 'There was nothing I could do. But I had seen my nephew – a man of incalculable potential and unbreakable will , who could stand up to the chthonic power itself – I had seen him broken. Bedeker had won. In that awful victory he made me his enemy, and I swore to myself that I would kill him. But I had no way to reach him – and even if I could, Aton and Coquina were hostage. And so my hate for the destroyer of the great Family of Five consumed me, from that moment in §403 until the war of §426.

'Yet it was my enemy Bedeker who kept me informed, for he alone had free access to Chthon. I never betrayed him to the authorities, for then I would have lost all contact with my nephew and his wife. I learned that Aton had two sons, Aesir and Arlo; the first died young and the second lived to about fifteen, when Ragnarok came and all life on and in that planet was exterminated. I, virtually alone escaped. If you could call it escape.'

Benjamin paused for yet another drink. 'This is not as much fun as I had hoped,' he said, setting the first glass down. 'I can't get high enough to forget what I remember! Well, all that was thirty-four years ago. I was seventy-four at the time, Bedeker perhaps a decade younger. It was a phantasmagoric battle, there at the fringe of the nether caverns; there were monsters like none

known to man. But I knew somehow that if I killed Bedeker, nothing else would touch me.

'Well, I killed him. But in his expiration he wounded me, and
infected me with some chthonic malady, a botulism-type infec-
tion or something remotely akin to it, not quite familiar to our
medical science. It ravaged my nervous system and God knows
what else. You see me now! Oh, I had very the best medical care –
but after all, Chthon had won, and all they could do was extend
my life artificially. It has not been a pleasure – and now I am glad
to let it go.'

'Forgive my insistence,' Morning Haze said as he labored over
a reverse lock on one of Misery's elbows. Such pressure should
have broken a normal woman's arm, but had no apparent effect on
her. 'But I feel that there is yet more to this matter, and I am of a
mind to plumb all secrets. There was an emotional intensificiation
when you spoke of Aton's sons. I lack the sensitivity my wife has,
yet—'

'Yes,' the minionette agreed. 'He has not yet expressed his full
love. It is very deep and large, yet from a small avenue, like a great
lake filling a caldera, fed by a tiny stream.'

Benjamin chuckled ruefully. 'By "Love" you mean "hate." Yes.
Very fetching imagery, that stream-fed caldera, suggestive as it is
of some prior volcanic eruption. It is the time of deepest confes-
sion. Yes, Bedeker told me of Aton's two sons. The first was Aesir,
named after Norse mythology. The Aesir were the gods of – but
that is irrelevant. By the mad doctor's account, Aesir was a thoroughly charming lad. I believe Bedeker spoke truly, for he de-
lighted in tormenting me, and he knew the truth was the most
cutting weapon of all. How I hated him!

'He told me how Aesir, a bright, friendly boy even as a tod-
dler, captivated the entire caverns. He was, if I may use the expression, favored of Chthon. No creature would hurt him – not even
the demonic salamander, whose venom meant certain and almost
instant death. Hitherto only Bedeker had possessed immunity from
cavern danger, thanks to his affiliation with the cavern sentience of

Chthon. Apart from what he termed the zombies, that is; I believe those were mindless women. I never grasped their purpose in that scheme. At any rate, Bedeker was insanely jealous – no pun! And resolved to eliminate the child. Oh, yes – he told me this and I believed him. I *still* believe . . .

'He could not kill Aesir directly because the lad was Chthon's chosen tool, destined to do what Bedeker could not. Because, unlike Bedeker, Aesir was wholly sane. The only sane, intelligent entity able to communicate directly with Chthon, to do the cavern entity's will willingly. Bedeker was completely dependent on the mineral entity; had he antagonized Chthon directly, he would have died. So he schemed . . .

'I don't know how he arranged it, deceiving Chthon as well as the lad's parents – but Bedeker did kill Aesir. All others thought it was an accident. *Me* he told, for he had to brag to someone. I alone knew the dreadful secret – as much as anyone but Bedeker himself knew. I alone had motive for revenge. But I, too, was limited.

'And so I bound him to his deep cave. I used certain connections I had to put a galactic intercept on all his available assets. He could not make any purchase, draw any credit, without immediate alert and arrest. That meant his coded spaceship was useless. In fact, he was effectively barred from space.'

Banjamin smiled, and the minionette smiled with him. 'Bedeker was, as he termed it, half-mad—but the sane, or shall we say human portion of him, longed for galactic society. He used to travel to Earth just to browse around the planetary library or gaze upon the ancient oceans. He was an educated man, a scholar in his fashion. He understood artistic things; perhaps one has to be made to have that ability! I deprived him of all that. Only with my collaboration could he emerge from his caverns, and only where and when specified. Then he had to bring the beautiful handcrafted bracelets and rings my nephew crafted, accepting in trade my gifts to Aton and Coquina. He was my messenger boy, my servant! And so I was avenged for Aesir, though I never knew the boy directly.'

'Beautiful!' Misery said. 'Such love . . . '

The minion looked up from his project. He was trying to blind the minionette by poking out her eyeballs with his fingers, but she seemed invulnerable. 'So that was the true manner of our meeting! I had supposed you were merely recruiting competent personal for the campaign against the mineral entity—'

'I was, I was!' Benjamin agreed.

'So I became the commander of the backup forces. But you returned to tell me that the battle was lost, and to withdraw immediately, because the killchill was starting. Only that timely warning saved me and my complement; we escaped ahead of that wave-'

'The wave we are now returning to,' the Xest signaled. 'I was the pilot of your ship – and now I, also, understand.'

'Ragnarok,' Morning Haze repeated. 'The great encounter between the forces of good and evil – and good lost, as it was fated to.'

'Yet to Chthon, *life* was the evil,' the Xest signaled. 'And it may have been correct. Much of life it knows only through Dr Bedeker. Are we not now unified in seeking death?'

Benjamin looked at the Xest, in order to read the signals. He blinked and looked again, temporarily sober. 'Minion!' he whispered.

Morning Haze paused, and Misery also looked. All three people were astonished.

The Taphid grubs had emerged from their frozen hibernation and now swarmed around the Xest, who stood balanced on the deck. At each foot the shiny white bodies clustered, their sandpaper tongues rasping avidly. *They were consuming the Xest's legs.*

'You asked to be notified of the time,' The Xest signaled with the stump of one leg. 'It is a fraction early, but one may not be able to—'

'So I did,' Morning Haze replied. 'No need to worry – my wife agreed to remind me. I thank you nevertheless.' His eyes remained fixed on the Xest. 'Are you aware—?'

'One is being consumed,' the Xest said. 'After one, the Taphid will come for you. However—'

'You import the Taphid at great expense to consume *you*?' Benjamin demanded.

'Of course, This guarantees eradication of debt.'

'But suicide – death by torture—'

'Beautiful!' the minionette said.

The Xest settled another notch as its legs were shortened. It was now only half its original height, and signaling was becoming awkward. 'We knew . . . would comprehend.'

'*I* don't comprehend!' Benjamin said.

Now the minionette turned to him. 'Ordinary death is impossible for this creature. Were it to be cut in half, both portions would regenerate into complete entities, doubling its societal debt. Were it sundered by an explosion, every fragment would regenerate, even single-cell debris, multiplying its debt a hundred –or a thousand fold. The only certain way to terminate potential debt is to undergo complete consumption.'

Morning Haze shook his head. 'Bitch, how do you know this?'

'She . . . telepathic . . . as one,' Xest signaled with difficulty. 'Receives . . . pain of demolition . . . appreciates properly.'

Benjamin dispensed with his glass and tilted the bottle to his mouth. He choked, but got a good swig down.

'You . . . killing self,' the Xest pointed out. 'You . . . coming . . . comprehend.'

'Yes,' Benjamin agreed. 'I comprehend at last.'

'Come, love,' the minion said. 'It is time.' He kissed her.

Suddenly the minionette writhed in pain. 'No!' she cried.

'I have waited fifty eight years to love you,' Morning Haze said. 'Now that we are all about to die, what difference can it make to you?' He kissed her again and ran this hand across her shoulder and over her breast: not roughly, but delicately. 'Your very presence thrills me. Your aspect is beyond description, mother mine. Never have I known a creature so lovely—'

'Causing pain,' the Xest signaled. 'She . . . mercy!'

'Let me possess you truly,' the minion said, ignoring all else. 'Not with sadism, but with utter joy and respect. I love you!'

The minionette screamed. She twisted violently, trying to free herself from his embrace. 'Xest, help me!' she cried as if deranged.

Now the Taphid had reached the Xest's globular body. Yet the creature managed one more series of signals with the last short stump of one leg. 'One transmits . . . agony . . . you.'

And the minionette relaxed. 'What bliss you send! Now I can endure . . . '

The hunger of the Taphids seemed to grow as the body of the Xest shrank. The last of the leg-stump diminished and disappeared, and the globe of the body ground into the collective maw of the voracious grubs. The Xest, facing certain death anyway, still preferred to utilize its familiar mechanism, canceling all potential debt.

Morning Haze clasped Misery to him in an expression of passion that would surely have been fatal to her in other circumstances. But the Xest was dying as the Taphids ate out its innards, transmitting exquisite agony. And the smile on the face of the minionette was beatific.

'I never thought I'd see the like!' Benjamin said, his head swiveling from one event to the other. 'It is now thirty seconds until—' Than he clasped his chest. 'Oh-oh – one of my gimcracks failed at last—'

Benjamin staggered forward, tripped over the boiling mass of the Xest, and fell. He landed on one desperately outflung arm, and the brittle bone snapped instantly. But this was the lesser horror. The Taphids swarmed eagerly over him. The effect was so stimulating that he was able to function without the defunct pacer. He wrenched himself out – but now there was no escape.

The old man crawled on three limbs across the deck, slapping feebly at the rasping grubs with his dangling arm. He lost his fragile balance and rolled into the vibrant minionette. The Taphids spread out to attack this new, delicious prey.

'Aahhh!' Misery cried in renewed ecstasy, as Benjamin's death agony joined that of the Xest, and the minion's climax was augmented by the devastating appetite of the Taphids. Her outflung arm convulsed, bringing Benjamin's staring face into her breast.

Taphids fell wriggling from his punctured eyes and began their demolition of her mammary. The minionette had found paradise at last.

Then the kill chill struck. There was no immediate effect on the metallic or ceramic parts of the ship, but everything either living or of organic origin began to disintegrate. The wood paneling sagged and powered out; the plastic fixtures melted.

All life dissolved. Human, Xest, and Taphid melted into a common goo, its liquids flowing across the deck, its gases bubbling out. Then a kind of flame played over it, as the fundamental proteins that made life possible were destroyed.

The husk of the ship continued, truly dead – as was all the galaxy where the wave had passed. The remainder of the galaxy was following at the speed of light. The ramifications of the forced interaction between fluorine and oxygen made the process inevitable.

Chthon had won.

CHAPTER III

War

Arlo snapped awake. Beside him, Ex sat up too. She was more beautiful than ever, despite the rather sadistic turns their love seemed to take. He had found himself striking her, reviling her, despite all his efforts to suppress his quarter-minion sadism. Yet she accepted it with singular grace, making him ashamed, angry at himself.

'What is it?' she asked, stretching languorously.

'I had a dream . . . '

'A lovely one . . . ' she said. 'Was it of me?'

'A nightmare!' Then he had to fend her off as she bashed him with a fistful of moss. 'But that isn't what woke me. Something's in the caverns.' He looked about, seeing beyond the bright garden. 'I sense tremendous conflict.'

He had told her about his minion blood that made him partially telepathic. It was that ability, he realized now, that had enabled him to communicate with Chthon. The cavern god was virtually omnipotent within its sphere, but the ordinary human mind was deaf to that power. Coquina could not perceive Chthon at all, and Aton *would* not; but Arlo had associated with Chthon from the time he was conceived, and developed his ability right along with his human speech.

In fact it was Chthon who had awakened him. 'Stay here, Ex,' Arlo said. 'I have to go investigate.'

'C'mon, stay,' she said, taking his hand and holding it against her body.

Arlo was torn by indecision. Was she offering cooperation, a really willing liaison? That was too good to turn down! But Chthon had called, and he had agreed to cooperate with Chthon. What should he do?

Now the summons became more urgent. Chthon was really concerned! But Ex spread her legs, invoking his masculine reaction in the way she knew so well how to do. Such an invitation was compulsive.

A warning mood came from Chthon. Arlo had a brief vision of Ex suffering from the myxo, or torn open by some great wolflike beast, and decided: he could not risk breaking the contract. 'Chthon summons; I have to go.'

'If you do, I'll make you sorry,' Ex said.

'Not as sorry as Chthon can make me,' he said. Better her bitchiness for a few days, than Chthon's ire! He went.

He ran easily through the caverns, following Chthon's cell. It was a long way. He left the cool, scented passages of the garden region and entered the extensive, sloping tunnels that conveyed air to the gas crevasse. But he moved upwind, away from the crevasse. Though these tubes gradually descended, the wind became stronger, requiring increased output of energy to maintain his pace. He would have slowed, but Chthon infused strength into him, alleviating his fatigue. Gradually the air became hot, and the sweat of his exertion made him thirsty. He had to detour briefly to seek a river. It was sucker-infested, but Chthon held the leeches back while Arlo drank deeply. Then onward.

As he approached the prison region, he became cautious, warned by his friend. He slowed, then concealed himself in a cave aperture.

None too soon. People were marching down a passage, bracing themselves against the stiff hot wind. At first he thought they were prisoners, for they wore the waterbags; then he saw that they were clothed.

In fact, they were women, strange not only in their apparel. They were all young, quite pretty, and distribingly familiar. They carried what he recognized as weapons: spears, clubs, and others he recognized only from descriptions in LOE: swords and bows. Much of it was incomprehensible to him, however.

These were Amazons: fabled female warriors. What were they doing here? Never in his memory had humans from Outside invaded the caverns. They could not be prisoners; they were an army.

Chthon surely knew what this meant, but Chthon could not convey such a concept directly. Arlo waited until the troops were past, then did some stalking of his own. He could locate Doc Bedside and ask him – but Bedside was far away, and anyway Arlo preferred to do his own research. If he could isolate and capture one of these intruders . . .

He followed the detachment down the wind passage. He knew the caverns as evidently they did not; some of these women were bound to get lost. For one thing, this passage terminated in the river – and down the river was a potwhale. A large one. That would disrupt their formation!

Sure enough: in the next hour they found the river and followed it down.

And when they came to the potwhale pool, they set out to swim across it, like total fools. He ascended to a passage crossing above the dome, located in crack in the floor, and peered down into the pool from directly above.

They stripped, laying their uniforms, weapons, and water bags carefully on the surrounding ledge, showing their marvelously voluptuous torsos. In a reaction that was becoming so frequent as to be an embarrassment, Arlo's member stiffened. The sight of any female body had an effect on him, but these were exceptionally stimulating bodies!

Naturally the potwhale came up and started taking them in. Its bulk filled the pool – for of course the potwhale itself had widened the pool over the centuries to accommodate its slow growth – and its ropelike tongue slapped about, coiling around any swimmer it touched, hauling her into its maw. Such a waste of beauty!

The amazons tried to fight, but they were at a disadvantage in the water. Nevertheless they performed creditably. They stabbed their spears into the blubber of the potwhale and hacked off its tongue. After a while it had had enough. It submerged.

One of the Amazons had fled into a confusing tunnel-loop. Rather, she was exploring for she did not rush. She had a queenly bearing, and evidently had some authority over the detachment. Perhaps she was looking for other dangers, so that the women would not fall into any more such traps. That was an intelligent thing to do. Already Arlo heard the measured tread of the caterpillar of this territory, and he knew other predators would soon converge. Meanwhile, this was his chance. Arlo dropped silently into the tunnel and cut her off in a pocket, holding his spear ready. He had no doubt of his ability to subdue her, for he was a man, she a woman.

'Why are you here?' he demanded in verbal Galactic.

She whirled, seeing him in the green stone-glow. 'Why hello, Arlo, she said.

He pushed, startled. How could this strange Amazon, new to the caverns, know him so readily?

'Of course we know you,' she said. 'You are the only independent cave-boy in Chthon. I spotted you back in the wind tunnel as we marched by, and saw you following us, and then I glimpsed your face in the ceiling fault. I hoped I could finally approach you if I came alone. I did not wish to frighten you.'

'I am not frightened!,' he said indignantly.

'True. Forgive my ill choice of words. We know you will help us. As you have seen, we desperately need help, for we do not know the dangers of the caverns.'

'You are telepathic!' he cried.

'I am a minionette' she said, standing straight.

The minionette! The word conjured a confused host of images, angry and enticing. Now he saw how beautiful she was despite her clothing; lovelier than Ex or Coquina or Verthandi, lovelier even than her nude companions of the Amazon detachment. Her hair was like a living flame as it billowed about her face and shoulders, and her eyes were deep garden pools.

So this was a living, semitelepathic minionette, like that of his recent dream. It was suddenly very easy to appreciate why his human grandfather and half-human father had loved one. She was so absolutely gorgeous it almost hurt his eyes to look at her.

Arlo felt a tinge of guilt, for he was betrothed to Ex and thought he had set aside casual lust. Not at all, he now knew!

'You are handsome yourself,' she said. 'Your guilt pleases me.'

It was true! Not only could she read his emotion, she received it inverted. She *liked* his self- condemnation, the bitch!

'Yes,' she agreed. 'That is why Planet Minion was proscribed, until this mission. Normal humans did not want us among them, though we are really quite human ourselves.'

'Who are you?' It was all he could think of at the moment.

'I am Torment. Once I met your father Aton. What a rare lover he was!'

Baffled rage flooded him. 'My father never loved you!'

'No. He loved my sister Misery – but all of us felt the rampant emanations of it. Lovely!'

'It was *Malice* he loved!' Arlo cried. 'His—mother.'

'He loved us all.'

Oh—he had allowed himself to be confused. She meant Aton had *hated* them all. But who was this Misery she mentioned? It was as though he knew her . . . from his dream?

'You possess the secrets of Chthon,' Torment said. 'Chthon is wonderful; Chthon loves us all. Help us win Chthon.'

Translation: Chthon hated them all with a mighty hate. Thus they all became bright and beautiful and sought to come closer to the cavern god. What a devastating army!

Chthon! he cried inwardly. *What do I do now?*

And Chthon replied: *Leave her.*

Arlo jumped. He had comprehended the words—as words! Always before it had been a general, nonverbal comprehension. His linkage with Chthon had abruptly improved.

'So you are in direct contact with the cavern entity,' Torment said. 'Excellent. Take us to its home base.'

'So you can destroy Chthon?' Arlo asked angrily. 'Get out of here!'

She looked at him, unafraid. 'Arlo, you are of *us*. You are human – and minion. Chthon is out to kill us all – and you too, when it no longer needs you. Its promises are worthless, for it is the ultimate enemy. Chthon means to wipe out all life in the galaxy.'

'Chthon is my friend!' Arlo cried, stabbing his spear at her. If there were evil in beauty, or beauty in evil, the minionette personified it. Surely Chthon had brought him here to show him this!

Torment parried the thrust easily, smiling. 'Better learn to fight, young man.'

Enraged. Arlo struck at her with the fist. She took the blow on her shoulder, unflinching, unaffected. 'Very nice. Arlo. You are strong. But you pulled your punch. And did not aim for a vital spot. Try it again.'

The bitch was right. His misadventure with Ex, that had almost killed her before he really knew her, had made him cautious. But now he was beyond caring. He struck Torment on the cheek as hard as he could.

• The blow rocked her back against the wall. But she smiled dazzlingly, still unhurt. 'You are not the man your father was – but you have good potential.'

Arlo struck at her again. This time she caught his hand, spun about, and threw him over her hip. But he did not land hard on the rock floor, for she held him up. She leaned over and kissed him on the nose. 'Tempting as it is, I may not dally with you, cave-boy. Take me to Chthon.'

'Chthon is here,' he said.

'I don't see it.'

Then she stiffened. Chthon was applying the myxo siege on her. This time Arlo had no objection. 'You wanted to meet Chthon,' he told her mockingly. 'How do you like it?' And while she was struggling, he took her weapons: the short sword, a bright metal knife at her hip, and a tube of some sort that was lodged in the front of her uniform, vertically between her remarkable breasts. He sighted down it, but the tube was blocked: evidently not a weapon after all.

The white slime was forming on Torment's face, arms and legs, staining her uniform. Arlo pulled up her brief metallic skirt to verify that the myxo extended all over her body. He discovered that even under the awful white coating, her torso was exquisitely shaped. Apparently this was the heritage of every minionette: incomparable figure that no coating or clothing could make repulsive. She would become a zombie – but an extremely attractive one. Verthandi would be jealous!

He had to smile at that. Jealousy in zombies?

Then Torment smiled. The myxo flaked off, a very shallow layer. 'Love me some more, Chthon!' she cried. 'I am in ecstasy!'

And abruptly the myxo siege halted.

Arlo stared. The minionette had fought off Chthon!

Torment opened her eyes. She spat out a lump of yellowish pus. 'We believed we would be effective against the cavern entity because of our nature. Obviously it used telepathy, and we—' she shrugged. 'This is the reason Life's army has been largely recruited from Planet Minion. It is good to have this confirmation. It would be sad to destroy so loving a sentience.'

'You must not!' Arlo cried.

'It is either us or it,' She said. 'We are of the living, it is of the dead – and Ragnarok is at hand. All living sentients support our effort, human and nonhuman alike. The Xests and Lfa and-'

'Not Hvee!' Arlo cried. 'Not the Family of Five!'

'Your granduncle Benjamin commands this task force,' she said. 'And your brother Morning Haze pilots our ship.'

'I have no brother!'

'You have more than you know' she said. She paused momentarily. 'Actually, I misremember. A Xest is the Pilot; Morning Haze commands the backup troops.'

Her very mismemory argued strongly for her sincerity – yet she was speaking nonsense!

'Please return to me my weapons,' she said.

Numbly, Arlo handed back her sword and knife. Again parts of his dream haunted him, for it had involved Benjamin and Morning Haze. Had it really been a dream, or was it in fact a vision? Could Torment have read his mind and fed his fancies back to him as supposed facts? Yet this vision had indicated that Regnarok was long over, and that Chthon had been victorious. If it were false, she should hardly have advertised it; if it reflected truth, why should he be concerned?

'Keep the blowgun,' she said. 'You may need it.'

'Blowgun?' He looked at the tube.

'You blow hard in this end. The dart shoots out to strike the target. Careful – it's poisoned.'

'Poisoned?' Events had dazed him.

'Pseudo-curare. Will stun a creature your size in seconds, kill in minutes if not antidoted. Here – You'll want some more darts, and here is the nullifying agent.' She brought out several more and pressed them into his head, along with a little cube. 'Oh – you don't have anywhere to carry them, do you!'

'In my mouth,' he said.

She laughed musically. 'What a delicious thought! You'll carry them right to heaven that way! In approximately five seconds. Your saliva would dissolve the protective coating on the tips, releasing the poison.'

'In my hand, then.' His brow wrinkled. 'With this – you could have killed me.'

'None of us would kill you, cave-boy,' Torment said. 'You are our ace in the hole.'

'What?'

'Archaic slang. These verbalisms continue so long as they are useful. Look it up in LOE.'

Arlo realized that this beautiful woman was not only stronger than he, she was smarter. He turned to go.

A dozen other minionettes blocked the passage behind him. Each was exactly like Torment: firm, round legs made alluring by the shadows of the short skirts, projecting breasts, firesmoke hair, lovely, even facial features. It was as though copies had been made. He could not have told any of them from Torment, had he met them alone.

They parted to let him through, smiling as they picked up his dismay. Disconcerted, Arlo left.

Near his home region, Arlo spied a young chipper about his own size. On a sudden notion he raised the blowgun, took a breath, aimed and blew. There was a satisfying release of pressure, a swish, and the dart was sticking in the furry back of the animal.

The chipper turned to him, surprised at the slight pain of the dart. Then it fell over.

Arlo went to it. 'Hey, chip – I didn't mean to hurt you,' he said. 'Get up.'

But the animal was dying.

Arlo looked at the blowgun, then at the darts. He shuddered. He contemplated the little curative cube, wondering how it worked. It had nothing but a button on one side. Finally he set the cube against the flank of the animal and pushed down the stud.

There was a ping! from the cube, and it jerked slightly in his hand. Arlo dropped it. But nothing happened, and after a moment he picked it up again.

The chipper revived. It raised its head, then hauled itself to its feet. Evidently the cube had done its job; the victim would live.

Arlo inserted a new dart in the tube and went on.

A stranger sat in the garden: small, short-haired, feminine.

'Don't you recognize me Arlo?' she demanded, rising.

The voice! 'Ex!' But she looked so changed! Without her flying golden tresses, her head seemed small, her neck long. Her breasts were suddenly much lower and larger, more like those of the minionette. In fact—

'Bedside did it,' she said. 'He snuck up on me while I was asleep and—'

'You weren't asleep!' Arlo cried. 'You *let* him. You threatened to do something to make me sorry, if I went-'

'All right. I let him. Bedside can't hurt me, not while you have the pact with Chthon – but he surely doesn't *like* me. He thought you'd kick me out if I weren't so pretty, but I know better. So I accepted his gambit, and-'

'You – you're a minionette!' Arlo whispered, seeing the flame and smoke in the ragged stump of her hair, the dawning perfection of her torso, the comeliness of her features. Not a perfect miniionette, but a close approximation. Had he not spoken so recently to Torment, seen her identical sisters, and had the vision-dream, he would not have been attuned, not recognized it in Ex. But the traces were unmistakable now that the distraction of the golden hair was gone.

'Yes, she is a minionette,' a man's voice said. It was Doc Bedside. "Her name is not Ex, but Vex. They have this intriguing code of nomenclature – but surely you know of that, being the child of Malice. *Now* what do you think of her, Arlo?'

Suddenly a mystery was resolved. No wonder Ex had been so perverse, especially at the point of love. Her emotions were reversed! It had not been his latent sadism, but her masochism that brought out the worst in him. She had had to make him hate her, at least temporarily, so that she could love him. Every act of irritation had been her courtship.

Angered by the man's assumption, Arlo reacted oppositely. 'I think I want to possess her.' And he took her in his arms, his member rising. Let Bedside watch; let the old, mad zombie, murderer of Aesir, suffer open defeat! Arlo had not been repelled by his experience with the warrior minionette Torment, but rather intrigued – and he had his own minionette. So, with mixed lust and ire, he took her down – and she cooperated, chuckling. She didn't like Bedside either, and in this manner she won her wager.

'She is twice her apparent age,' Bedside said, unruffled. 'She looks twelve – or did, before she bloomed for you. But chronologically she is twenty six – a generous ten years your senior.'

At the point of entry, Arlo stopped. 'You lie,' he muttered. 'Ask *her.*' And now Bedside chuckled. 'The minionette cannot lie to her beloved.'

'It is true,' Ex/Vex admitted. 'I was birthed in §400. But it doesn't make any difference. See, the hvee still glows.'

'§400!' Arlo cried, his member dwindling.

'It is the minionette way,' Vex said. 'Until we have a man, we remain young. A widowed minionette even regresses somewhat: first her hair fades, then her form diminishes. We are creatures of love, Arlo. Until I loved you, I *was* a child; and my development is just one of the proofs of my love, along with your blue hvee. Soon I shall be fully beautiful – and it is all for you, my lover, my beloved, my husband, my all.' She shot a momentary snarl at Bedside. 'Ask *him!*'

'True,' Bedside said, accommodating smoothly to this new aspect of debate. Arlo realized the man was keeping his hate controlled, to not give Vex any pleasure in it. 'The minionette loves only her lover truly, until she bears a son. Then she discards him for that son.'

'But not before he wishes,' Vex fired back. 'While the father lives, the father has priority.'

'Exactly,' Bedside said. Vex's eyes went staring for a moment, and her body tensed. Arlo realized that the doctor had in some clever, subtle way scored heavily.

Still clasping her exciting body, still halfway at the point, Arlo understood that he had become a pawn in the battle between Chthon and the minionettes. The invaders wanted his help, so they had sent in an advance scout to convert him. Chthon had known this and had sought to eliminate her at the outset. Now the fight was verbal, informational, but just as vicious.

Still, the hvee showed Vex's love was true, and he did not object to her being a minionette. Even her age became irrelevant: she *had* bloomed for him. And he still could spite Bedside by completing his act of love in the man's presence. In fact, it would be best that way, for Bedside's hate and frustration would cancel out Arlo's love and keep Vex sweet. His member stiffened again. Oh yes, he knew why she was cooperating so nicely, and he was glad of it! She even felt his background anger at the situation, that it should have to be this way, and enjoyed that too. What a complex of adversities, combining to build a positive structure!

Her legs spread wider, and she wriggled to accommodate him.

'I'm glad you know,' she whispered. Now we can really do it. Love me!'

Viciously he thrust, trying to make her hurt.

'She called you her lover, her beloved, her husband, her all,' Bedside remarked. 'But she omitted something. She should have added-'

'Shut up!' Vex screeched, pulling Arlo's face down to her. 'Kin.'

'Don't listen to him!' Vex whispered fiercely in Arlo's ear. She half-smothered him with frantic kisses.

'Don't worry,' Arlo reassured her. 'Nothing he can say can—'

'She is also your sister,' Bedside continued imperturbably.

'She—!' Arlo froze in mid-stroke, shocked. The ban against brother-sister relations pervaded LOE.

'Damn!' Vex murmured as she smiled beatifically and moved to take him in. 'You feel so new and wonderful.'

Suddenly his confusion resolved. 'All minionettes are sisters,' he said. 'It is a convention between them. I am quarter-minion, so in that sense—'

'Ooo, you hurt!' Vex protested, reacting to his resolution of conflict. She tried to withdraw, but he held her tight.

'Via the human connection, no figure of speech,' Bedside said.

Intellectual dialogue was difficult in the present circumstance. 'I have no sister!' Arlo snapped, and felt Vex soften and warm, inside and out, as his ire manifested. Yet what had the Norns said? *This hardening rod . . .* 'Only a brother – and he's dead.'

'More precisely, half-sister,' Bedside continued. 'The truth is, Aton Five has three living children by three separate women.'

'He is loyal to Coquina!' Arlo flared. What oddities of dialogue had he gotten into, amidst this attempted act of love? 'I know all about it. Malice is dead.'

'You are the youngest, birthed in §410,' Bedside said. 'By the minionette Misery he conceived Morning Haze, birthed in §402 on Planet Minion, heir to the Eldest Five fortune. At such time as his status is acknowledged – which may be never, for he is a bas-

tard, a crossbreed of two cultures, both of which disapprove bas-
tardy.' Bedside scowled, thinking of Benjamin, his abiding enemy. 'But do not be concerned: it was but a momentary dalli-
ance.'

'So maybe I do have a half-brother,' Arlo said, for this coin-
cided with his vision and therefore became believable. 'He is ille-
gitimate. *I* am the named heir to Eldest Five; I bear the A designation.'

'But you are legally dead, as is your father. Aton died in §400,
in eyes of Galactic Law. The dead do not inherit.'

'Neither do they conceive bastards,' Arlo muttered. But he
found he did not care for this technicality. 'Then let Morning
Haze inherit! He is a good man, kind to his minionette. I have
things to occupy me here.' And he resumed operations with willing Vex.

'By his mother /lover, the minionette Malice, Aton conceived
his firstborn, birthed while he was in prison in §400,' Bedside
continued. 'This one was legitimate.' He held up a hand to fore-
stall Arlo's outburst. 'Stay your wrath – Aton did not know of this
child either. Malice had no real chance to inform him before he
killed her. But the infant was returned to Planet Minion by your
granduncle Benjamin, to protect the name of Five, and I have black-
mailed him since. He is the very model of discretion; never once
has he spoken of this matter to any outsider, and he never will. But
there are no secrets from Chthon. Now, If you do not behave, I
shall inform Aton.'

'He will never credit such lies!' Arlo said.

'Is it a lie? Ask Vex whose child she is, then.'

Arlo, his attention split between the bitter dialogue and the
most stimulating physical interaction with the girl, had not made
the obvious connection before. 'Not—?' he demanded with dawning horror.

'I am the child of Aton and Malice,' Vex said. 'I am daughter
and granddaughter to that minionette.'

Stunned, Arlo tried to reject it. 'The minionettes bear only boys!'

'Not so, else their line would perish,' Bedside said. 'When a minionette is old, or sees herself near death, she births a girl. Malice knew she would die when Aton came to her again, for he lacked the discipline of a native minion. So—'

'Impossible! A woman can't control—' Arlo said.

'A minionette can,' Vex said. 'Her body can choose between the male and female seed of her lover, accepting only the appropriate type. Soon I shall conceive a son by you, unless death approaches me. Then I would give you a girl to replace me.'

'Electra!' Arlo said recognizing another concept from LOE. Then: 'My sister!' Actually, Chthon would not let her conceive, but that hardly changed the picture.

'Isn't it beautiful?' Vex asked. 'The mad doctor thought the truth would drive you away from me, like the cutting of my hair, and I feared it too, but our love remains true. Doesn't it?' And she made a flexing motion inside that brought Arlo to an unwilling, guilty, but powerful climax.

'My sister!' he gasped, horrified by the reality of Minion's system and the prediction of the Norns. In that moment he hated Vex – yet he loved her, too. He knew he would be unable to resist her blandishments in future – for however angry he became, her love would always match it. And the guilt of the association carried its own spur; forbidden fruit *was* attractive. He was quarter-minion, she three quarters, and the trap had sprung.

Now at last he understood what had motivated his father to such acts of desperation and incest.

The war proceeded. Day by day the minionettes advanced along the passages spreading out from their base at the old prison. Resistive to the myxo and ever more sophisticated about the assorted menaces of the caverns, they routed out the underworld creatures Chthon sent against them. One specimen of each was sent to the surface of the planet for study.

'I don't think I like this,' Arlo said to Vex as they relaxed in the garden. 'Those animals are innocent; they should not be wiped out.'

'Caterpillars? Potwhales? Dragons? Chimeras?' she retorted derisively. 'Innocent? What about that wolf thing that laid me open?' She paused, reflecting. 'Actually, that was sort of fun. You know, we minionettes are almost unkillable by normal means, but that thing – I'd like to meet it again.'

Arlo remembered the massive malevolence of the wolf. 'You have a death wish,' he said. 'Bitch or bride, I don't want you dead. I'll help the Amazons track it down and kill it.'

'As you wish,' she said diffidently.

He reached for her, but she avoided him, responsive to his positive emotion. 'Remember, I'm your sister!' she reminded him teasingly. 'Your culture says you shall not raise your penis to me.'

'Hell with the culture, sister!' he cried, grabbing for her leg.

'Sister!' It was Aton's voice.

Aton and Doc Bedside stood at the entrance to this bright inlet, blinking in the daylight illumination of the high gas jets. Arlo had never expected such a visitation – but of course Bedside could guide Aton in safely, if it were Chthon's will. There was about to be another facet of the Chthon/minionette struggle.

'As I informed you,' Bedside said to Aton. 'Your daughter – by your mother.'

Aton stared – and Vex stood up straight, smoothing her flanks, inhaling. Her figure had filled out completely now, and except for her short hair and certain human touches, she was every inch a minionette. Even the hair showed it, for it formed a crown of rolling flame.

'My daughter . . . ' Aton said, his eyes fixed on Vex. 'So like Malice . . . '

Arlo stood still, watching it unfold. What was his father going to do? Kill the minionette? Arlo could not allow that. Obviously, Bedside had done it to get rid of Vex. The revelation of her relation to Arlo had not eliminated her, so now the battle had been widened to include Aton, who had killed Vex's mother. By loving her.

'An abomination!' Aton said. 'That she should come here to tempt my son—'

Arlo raised his blowgun, uncertain whether he had the courage to use it against his father. But Vex took more direct action. She walked across the path into Aton's arms. 'Father!' she said passionately.

Arlo saw his father's hands clench as though to crush her. Again he raised the blowgun. But he remembered how very difficult the minionette was to kill. Barehanded, Aton could not do it. The stronger his hate, the less chance he stood.

Then Aton kissed his daughter. Vex kissed him back. By appearance alone, they were an ideal couple, and Arlo knew in that moment how Aton had been with Malice. This was as close a duplication as possible.

Doc Bedside appeared at Arlo's side. 'You realize, of course, where this will lead,' he said.

'No!' Arlo said angrily.

'He hates her – but he loves her, as you do. For she is Electra, and he is dead because of her mother.'

Arlo shook his head. 'What?'

'Electra, in Greek legend, was the daughter of Agamemnon and Queen Clytemnestra. The Queen killed her husband, and Electra was so outraged that she hid her young brother Orestes from the Queen's wrath, and enabled him to grow up to avenge his father. Later, the Electra complex was designated as a girl's sexual love for her father, in competition with her mother. It is in many ways parallel to the Oedipus complex : a boy's sexual love for his mother. How fitting that Aton should enact *both* roles.'

'Both?' Arlo was still bemused.

'The mode of the minionette is of course Oedipal, with the woman mating, successively, her spouse, son, grandson, and so on down the line. But—'

'I know this!' Arlo snapped.

'But when she passes, she leaves a daughter to carry on – and naturally that young girl's attraction is to her family line. She thus is the willing consort of her father, the first man in her life and her nearest of kin. By him she bears his successor.

And so Electra complements Oedipus in a beautiful, continuing relationship. It will be so satisfying to see it enacted here – don't you agree?'

Slowly the awful concept hammered its way through Arlo's skull. Bedside had hinted at it before: the father took precedence over the son, until the son killed the father in the recurring oedipal pattern. This was the hell Vex had brought into their lives. 'My father – the minionette. . .'

Suddenly Aton threw Vex aside, cursing. She fell to the floor and lay unmoving, though of course she was not hurt.

'Naturally he resists the concept much more violently than you do,' Bedside continued. 'He was raised on Planet Hvee and received the finest galactic tutoring. He has civilized reservations. He *knows* it is forbidden – knows it right down through his subconscious. Which means he is genuinely, violently angry about the temptation. That of course makes him doubly attractive to the minionette. See how she lures him.'

Indeed, Vex presented a remarkably fetching picture of romantic innocence, half-supine on the floor, legs spread, palms flat against the stone to her right, arms supporting her twisting shoulders so that her breasts hung partly forward, her head drooping. Never had she been more lovely, this angel in distress.

Aton whirled and strode into the darkness of the tunnel, almost radiating fury.

'He will return,' Bedside said. 'Inevitably – for she is his daughter, child of his beloved mother, the minionette.'

'But she is my betrothed. . .' Arlo whispered. 'The minionette is always true.'

'True to her nature,' Bedside said. 'True to her closest kin. You are her half-brother, only quarter-minion. Aton is her father, half-minion. *He* is the one.'

Arlo looked at Vex and saw her looking after Aton. He knew he had lost her. No human law or scruple could prevail against the combined tides of minion blood and minion nature. 'What re-

mains for me?' he asked Bedside, almost as if in this extremity the
mad doctor were his friend.

'Chthon loves you,' Bedside said. 'Chthon sought to spare
you this. Chthon can fulfill you.'

'As a zombie?' Arlo flashed.

'As a god.'

Arlo, his heart numbed, acceded – as he knew his father had
before him, when Coquina was dying. Doc Bedside had prevailed
again, this time destroying Coquina and perhaps the whole thrust
of Life's invasion. But Arlo hardly cared. 'Chthon was always my
friend,' he said.

'Always!' Bedside agreed warmly.

CHAPTER IV

Tree

Doc Bedside conducted Arlo to an unfamiliar section of the caverns where the stone was a strange gray, with portions bare of glow. The passages diverged and rediverged in grotesque loops, and there was no wind at all. Stagnant pools filled the declivities, and the glow had settled in them, providing what scant light there was. This, surely, was a place of dying. The normal small sounds of cavern animals were absent.

'This is the lowest portion of the caverns that man has trodden,' Doc Bedside said. 'See, there is my marker.' He indicated a cairn, a pile of stones. Beside it was the crude outline of a human skull, scratched in the soft rock of the floor. Beneath that were four jagged letters: MYXO. 'Undisturbed these thirty years. I made that as a warning for any fools who might follow, back in §395.'

'But the myxo can strike anywhere,' Arlo said. 'It is Chthon's weapon, his zombie-device.'

'Back then, Chthon was just developing it,' Bedside said. 'I was Chthon's first human subject.'

'But you're not a zombie.' Arlo paused, reconsidering. 'Not completely.'

Bedside smiled. 'I am half-zombie, half-mad, half-human. Chthon overlaps my madness, so all you witness is near normality. You will comprehend my rationale shortly.'

'I don't want to be like you!' Arlo protested. 'Or like the Norns.'

'On the failures of the past are built the successes of the future. The zombies are complete failures; Verthandi the Norn and I are half-failures. Your father might have been a success, but in the end resisted too strongly. Your brother Aesir was closer yet.'

'So you killed him,' Arlo said.

Bedside's composure was momentarily broken. 'How would you know of that?' he asked tightly.

'Uncle Benjamin told me.'

'You never met Benjamin!'

'No?' Arlo did not choose to explain about the vision. 'He said you were jealous of Aesir, who was closer to Chthon than you were, so you killed him. How can I be sure you won't kill me, too?'

Bedside slumped, very much the way Coquina had when she told him about the minionette. 'I did kill him – and suffered the double vengeance of Benjamin and Chthon. I need no further lessons of that nature.'

Mad as he might be, Bedside always spoke truth. 'What happened?'

'The cavern creatures all loved him, for he was beloved of Chthon. None would harm him. But I initiated a game, a blind hunt, and in their confusion they destroyed him. Yet Chthon became aware, though I had not touched him myself, and Chthon put me into a caterpillar. . ."

'Sleipnir!'

'It is not a process I recommend. I assure you I would kill you only if Chthon directed it. I am the servant, not the master, not the chosen. You will not be like me; you will be the first living chthonic god. Chthon does not need or desire any more partial successes. You must believe that, or this is useless. You must come to Chthon voluntarily, with no reservation in your mind or soul.'

'I can't be sure of that,' Arlo said. 'I'd have to know what I was getting into.' Chthon was his friend – but there were limits to friendship.

'Chthon will show you. Your mind will not be touched, only our perceptions. Then you will return to your garden, alone, where you will meditate upon the options with full knowledge. Thereafter, you will walk either to the claws of the minionette, knowing how that 'must end, or to the comfort of Chthon.'

'Nice phrasing, that,' Arlo remarked dryly.

'Phrase it as you will. *Your choice will be free.*' Bedside's words were augmented by a mental projection from Chthon, doubling and more than doubling the effect.

'I believe it,' Arlo agreed. 'Chthon has always been fair with me. How do we proceed?'

'Lie here. Be comfortable, relaxed. Open your mind to Chthon,' Bedside said. 'Do not resist; Chthon is your friend. Chthon will assuage your wounds.'

Arlo lay on the rock. It was not uncomfortable, for he had often slept on stone before. His gaze traveled to the ceiling.

Above him was a massive stalactite, crystalline, translucent at the fringe. It resembled, in its gross fashion, an open hvee flower. From it a thin mist descended, like that of the gas crevasse. Was he now to discover what happened in the suffocating depths of that chasm? To be sucked through a network of pipes to be consumed in the flames? Would his essence emerge as a precious blue garnet, forever inaccessible?

No. He trusted Chthon. More than he trusted the minionette!

Arlo opened his mind. And it was like walking down a long dark tunnel. Yet, as he traveled down it, the way became opaque. The walls wavered and his footing became unsteady. 'Relax; let the irrelevancies bubble off,' Bedside said from somewhere outside. 'You are seeking to extricate yourself from the prison of your senses. Let the body go. Don't force it. Just let it pass in its own way.'

Arlo relaxed – and the tunnel in his imagination firmed. He walked down it to meet his friend and god directly. Now a light manifested far ahead, and he knew that light was Chthon.

As he went, the way became easier, the obstacles fewer and less formidable. The tunnel widened and finally opened out in a vista of dazzling beauty. It was an explosion. From a pinpoint source, bright plasma thrust outward in a multidimensional sphere. Fire-radiation and matter-smoke, like the hair of a loving minionette, it expanded at an awesome velocity.

'This is the nascent universe,' a voice said. 'Eclat quintessential.'

And it was. Arlo had never imagined such splendor. He watched it blossom, form rifts and internal swirls, fragments. The fragments sundered in turn, their main parts coalescing and turning, swirling, throwing off sparks of matter in the form of gas. Glowing segments developed, thousands of them, millions, filling the universe with their secondary light. Then these faded, becoming smaller as their aggregate formations became larger. Motes appeared within them as they paled.

'Quasars,' the voice said. 'Prototype galaxies – masses of energy and gas, forerunners of more solid matter.'

'I don't understand!' Arlo protested. But how he wanted to!

The focus centered on one quasar. It wavered and changed as it spun through the great emptiness around it: chaos without and within. Parts of it were fire, and parts were ice; where they met they steamed and hissed and formed into – a giant man.

But the giant died and fell apart, and his flesh tumbled into soil, his bones became stones and mountains, and his hair took on independent life and became vegetation. His blood ran out and pooled into a great sea, turning green. His skull exploded, the dome of it forming the sky; its brains became clouds.

Maggots bred in the decaying hulk, ancestral Taphids, and these stood up and showed themselves as animal life of diverse kinds, including men and women.

Arlo watched, shocked. Life was infestation, corruption of the perfect body of the world! Even humankind, even Arlo himself – maggots!

Now he saw the formation of inanimate sentience. While the maggots riddled the fallen giant's body, the molten metal beneath formed into the solid globe of the planet. Natural forces acted within it: bubbles of gas pushing up, water percolating down, molten rock spreading sideways. Caverns formed as the more volatile substances melted and vaporized, leaving their strata empty. Uneven heat-expansion and cold-contraction forced the layers to buckle and crumble. Amidst this rubble crystals formed, growing enormously in favorable situations and shattering when conditions changed. Some succumbed to slow pressure, transforming into other substances. Some generated substantial electric and magnetic potential; lightning flared, arcing across differentials of charge, remelting metals in spot locations, causing them to flow in myriad rivulets, only to harden abruptly in place. As the shifting pressures and heating continued, new currents were generated, traveling along the metal circuits. Some formed transformers, funneling broad, slow charges into high, narrow ones, producing new currents in the old channels, currents that possessed new properties. Recirculations, juxtapositions, and feedbacks occurred, intensifying the effect, until a portion of it became self-sustaining, like a fire. Then it spread slowly, replicating itself with variations throughout the planet. In some regions natural fires raged, feeding on combustible gases; these provided a steady source of heat energy which translated into constantly moving air. In others, the formations were so constituted as to refrigerate themselves, for the air expanded and cooled quite rapidly. These temperature differentials enabled diverse processes to operate. After billions of years of random, inanimate experimentation, one of the complex feedback circuits achieved the ultimate condition: sentience.

This occurred wherever conditions suited – and there were many such planets in the universe. But these inanimate sentiences were largely immobile; they could *think*, but not *act*. And so, constant, they functioned – until the maggots of life intruded destructively. The chemical processes of life had already transformed the atmospheres of all planets they infested, developing corrosive properties that prevented any surface expansion of mineral organization; now they burrowed down into the deep rock itself. The war between the living sentiences and the dead sentiences began.

The forces of the living were multiple. On thousands of planets in the adjoining reaches of the galaxy, the maggots squirmed.

But on only a few did they achieve the power to infect neighboring systems. They accomplished this by using machines: truncated, limited versions of mineral intellect, adapted to provide not superior thought but superior physical force. The mineral sentiences, in contrast, adapted truncated versions of living entities, also used for mechanical force rather than mental. Neither side possessed the sophistication to develop its use of enemy fragments thoroughly, but each side soon became largely dependent on those fragments. It was an ironic impasse.

The main sources of Life's contagion were four: Lfa, EeoO, Xest, and Human. Each originated on a single planet, festering there for a prolonged period before bursting out.

Arlo watched the spread of life to planets across the galaxy. First the Lfa, who resembled animate piles of refuse, dismantled themselves and formed, after millennia of unsuccess, a viable space-traveling format. Wherever they landed, they formed new Lfa entities by contributing from each entity a part, until the new individual was complete. Then the parent entities would regenerate the missing parts. It required the presence of fity to a hundred parents to form one offspring in this manner, but the new entity was able to function effectively almost from formation. There was no limit to the number of times this assembly tax could be invoked, and it was possible for each parent entity to contribute to several offspring simultaneously. Thus the Lfa expansion through the galaxy was limited largely by the velocity of their space-travel assemblages and the availability of suitable worlds. In a few thousand years they had colonized half the galaxy.

The EeoO, in contrast, replicated largely by pooling. A minimum of four entities – one each of E, e, o, and O – melted and merged in a common puddle, and from this four small EeoO's coalesced, or more if the pool were larger. As the infants grew, they sundered, first into twin Eo and eO entities, then into mature adult individual E's, o's, e's and O's. They were now ready to pool, at will or need, preferably with individuals from other parent-pools, for the sake of species-unifying exogamy. However, they were vulnerable when pooled, for any dilution or draining of the pool would interrupt the process, prevent replication, and terminate the contributory entities. Thus the EeoO accounted for only one-fifth of the galactic colonization, though the initiation of their expansion may actually have predated that of the Lfa.

The Xests reproduced by fission – any fragment of their bodies, when separated from the whole, formed into a new entity, complete and functional from the outset, possessing the entire mentality of the parent entity. Therefore, their potential for replication was greatest in the galaxy. But they believed in economy and fiercely defended their resources by controlling their population and eschewing all but essential contact with other galactic species. So they came to occupy only another fifth of the galaxy.

The Humans were the last to exploit space, but their expansion was explosive even in the volatile framework of Life. Their form of replication was not remarkably efficient, but they had accumulated a tremendous population on their home-world before achieving space. They were sexed entities, with the coupling of one male and one female required for genesis of a new individual. The male inserted seeds into the body of the female, who subsequently fissioned into two: an adult and an infant. The adult protected and fed the infant until it became adult, a time-consuming process involving as much as a third of the normal Human individual-entity lifespan. However, it was possible for one or two adults to conceive and care for several infants in overlapping sequence, and infant losses were minimal. The result was inevitable growth of population, with strong cultural continuity. The Humans colonized a full tenth of the galaxy in less than four hundred of their years.

The initial encounter between life and nonlife sentience occurred in that small Human sector of the galaxy, perhaps because this species was most prone to raid the mineral interiors of its planets. Therefore Humans predominated at first – but soon the other three living galactic sentiences joined the battle, recognizing a common threat.

Arlo reeled. There was too much illumination, too much information. More than he had ever imagined! 'But – but –' he started, and halted, surprised to discover he did have a voice, here in this vision. 'How – how—?' But he could not formulate his question; the concept would not compress enough to be compassed for a query.

And Chthon was with him, an immaterial presence, benign and ambient. The scene shifted, and it was a laboratory on the surface of Planet Old Earth, spawning ground for the Humans. 'Here is a holographic transcription, authenticated,' one man said, drawing a cube from a pocket of the white vegetable-fiber clothing he wore. 'There is no longer any question – yet no answer either. This device has accelerated until its velocity is beyond our capacity to measure directly.'

'Locked in a closed orbit about a magnetic core?' the other inquired, lifting a hairy eyebrow skeptically while his fingers toyed with one of the shiny metal buttons on his dark animal-skin jacket. 'Where did it go?'

'It's still there – it has to be – but nevertheless out of our ken. Why don't you watch the transcript for yourself? I don't really believe it myself, yet.'

'Hmph.' They watched the holograph projection, seeing the experiment-sphere within its vacuum torus. The sphere was about the size of a man's fist, and the torus was a transparent donut (Arlo had read of this delicacy in LOE and pestered his mother to make one once: it was a disappointment, nothing but sweetened cooked dough) fifty feet in diameter. The outer rim was braced by a twelve-inch-thick steel girder backed by twenty feet of reinforced concrete, and the whole thing was set into bedrock. The center of the torus was a giant electromagnet, its elements surrounding the vacuum chamber on three sides: top, bottom, inner. Chthon explained it all in nonverbal concept, for Arlo could hardly have grasped the significance independently.

The metal sphere would be attracted by a magnetic force so great it could theoretically remain stable at 99 per cent of the velocity of light. The magnet would not be turned on until a significant fraction of light speed was achieved, for the sphere would have no chance to move otherwise.

'Self-powered,' the white-frocked man said. 'Slow to begin.'

'So I notice,' the black-jacketed one said. The ball was traveling, thanks to the initial rolling impetus of introduction to the torus, at a velocity of approximately one inch per second, or five feet per minute. Slowly it accelerated.

'I'll jump the tape forward one hour,' the white-frocked one said. 'It does start slowly, but as you'll see –'

Suddenly the sphere was moving at about a foot per second, sixty feet per minute.

'Great!' Black-Jacket said derisively. 'In one hour it accelerated to substantially less than one mile per hour. Great in rush-hour traffic!'

('Rush-hour traffic?' Arlo inquired. 'The press of Human machines through clogged apertures: a standing source of personal irritation,' Chthon's voice explained.)

'Here is another hour.'

Now the sphere was doing ten miles an hour. 'Its acceleration, without a doubt, is improving,' Black-Jacket said. 'But frankly at this rate –'

'Don't you see – it's a geometric rate. It accelerates to ten times its former velocity – every hour.'

'Sure – so far. Let's see the *next* three hours.'

The image changed. Now the sphere was rolling around its channel at a hundred miles an hour. Another jump – and it became a blur, invisible.

'Back off!' Black-Jacket exclaimed. 'That's-'

'One thousand miles an hour,' White-Frock said smugly. 'We're too close and it is too small to make out comfortably at this velocity.'

'Pick it up from one hundred per, and let me watch it straight.'

They did. The sphere accelerated smoothly from one hundred to one thousand miles an hour, then continued on rapidly to two thousand, four thousand, and ten thousand miles per hour.

'You aren't getting input from the magnet?"

'Magnet was off. No exterior input. That's why it's *rolling*, owing to friction with the outside surface. The magnet would maintain it in a kind of orbit, no contact with any physical surface. The thing appears to draw power from *some* exterior reservoir – but not our magnet or anything else we can detect. A *lot* of power. In fact, there seems to develop a transfer of power the other way: from the test sphere to the magnet, later in the program. Otherwise the sphere would have broken free—'

'Sounds to me as if you're talking perpetual motion!'

'Perhaps we are. Actually, perpetual motion exists, as with an object hurtling through deep space. But—'

'All *right*!' Black-Jacket mopped his brow. 'You know what I mean.'

'It all depends on how great the reservoir of hidden power is. If, as we suspect, it is fundamental to the structure of the universe – perhaps the inertial velocity of the original cosmic explosion –'

'You mean if we use up this power, the universe will stop expanding and begin to collapse?'

'A few seconds sooner than otherwise, yes. Considering the tens of billions of years in that time scale, the effect would be infinitesimal, and not even detectable until long after our species has passed from the scene, even if we caused a differential of eons.'

'Free power, then.'

'It does look like it, sir.'

Black-Jacket nodded. 'We'll look this gift horse in the mouth very thoroughly, very soon.

('Gift horse?' Arlo inquired. 'A four-footed mammal –' 'I know what a horse is, from LOE. But what's this business of—' 'An Earth horse commands a good price unless defective. Advanced age is a defect. The teeth in its mouth indicate its age by their wear. Therefore-' 'I see,' Arlo said dubiously.)

'If there is any fakery involved . . .' Black-Jacket continued, trailing off meaningfully.

'We welcome your investigation,' White-Frock said. 'The civilian wants to know as badly as the military, I can assure you. We frankly don't understand this thing, and don't trust it – but we suspect its effect on our economy will be profound.'

'Profound! If true, it's nuclear!'

'More than that. We're frankly scared of it.'

'How fast does it go?'

'Measurements are necessarily imprecise. But if the observed ratio is maintained –' He made a little flourish with his hand, resembling a figure 8 lying sideways.

'Out with it, man! *How Fast?*'

'In approximately ten hours, it should match the velocity of light in a vacuum.'

'Um. We brasshats are not entirely dull. You realize what you're saying?'

'I realize what I am implying. Relativistically –'

'Paradox. So let's look for the flaw. How long did you run the test?'

'Three days.'

'Seventy-two hours? Why didn't you turn it off?'

'We were unable to activate the unit's control system.'

'What kind of tests do you run? Everything's supposed to be fail-safe!'

'Theoretically, yes. But –'

'So just turn off the switch!'

'We tried.'

'Look, doctor –'

'Our switch seems to have become inoperative.'

'Well, repair it! Considering the billions dumped in this sump —'

'It is in working order. The problem is, our remote control is limited to the speed of light. Of the electromagnetic propagation of energy.'

Black-Jacket paused. 'You're telling me that the sphere didn't level off at light-speed? That that thing's going too fast to – *faster than light?*'

White-Frock nodded. 'That seems to be the case. We are picking up Cherenkov radiation –'

'What?'

'Cherenkov radiation. An impulse that manifests when some
other energy exceeds the velocity of light through a medium. Light
slows as it passes through certain substances, you see. Only in a
vacuum does it maintain full speed.'

'And you have a vacuum in your test-torus?'

'Yes. Not perfect, of course, but quite good. Never before has
Cherenkov radiation been observed in this hard a vacuum. It appears that our sphere had exceeded the velocity of light in a vacuum
– the fastest theoretical velocity possible – or so we once thought.'

'I'm no physicist. But if what you say is true—'

'Precisely. We may have found the means to conquer space
itself.'

Indeed they had. From this discovery the § system dated, and
in the course of the next century it replaced the conventional cal-
endar entirely. Just as Newtonian physics had become a special
case of relativistic physics, relativistic physics became a special case
of §. All were valid – in their terms. Since the details of the break-
through were shrouded in secrecy, legends grew up to fill the
vacuum –

('Vacuum!' Arlo chortled. 'That's funny!')

—naming a 'Professor Feetle' as the serendipitous inventor of
§. Large models of the logarithmic § accelerator were constructed
and placed in space ships. Within the field of the sphere, space
and time were normal – but the sphere traveled through galactic
and intergalactic space at velocities that made light seem virtually
stationary. The universe was available to man – in hours. The species Human was the fourth – and last –of the galactic sentients to
achieve §.

The first substantial Human interstellar colonization com-
menced in §20. Since time and power were no longer limitations,
only the costs of construction, organization, and selection of per-
sonnel governed emigration. Thus the novalike expansion of the

Human demesnes. Within a century the volume was as extensive as was reasonably possible without infringement of the concerns of the other galactic empires. Only intensifying settlement within that volume remained, utilizing less and less ideal planets. §50 to §100 were popularly regarded as the golden years of colonization, during which the best available planets were discovered and settled. In §71 the heaven planet of Idyllia; in §79 the garden world of Hvee.

One entrepreneur of special note was Jonathan Reginald Point, §41—154. Not only was he a top-notch stellar scout, he was alert to the private potentials of his discoveries. In §75 he discovered an ideal star – and made a fortune by selling it to a private group. This was of course against Human law, but he had a lawyer back on Earth who was equivalently industrious and unscrupulous; the deed was shrewdly finessed. He named the star after himself, Point, and the planets after units of type: so many 'points' to the inch. Thus the planets of that system were designated Excelsior, Diamond, Pearl, Nonpareil, Minion, Brevier, Bourgeois, and Elite – the names corresponding to their positions in orbit, counting outward (the closest two being unusable and unnamed), and also to points. Excelsior was 3 point, Diamond 4 point, and the best one, Minion, seventh and 7 point.

The group that settled Minion was working on genetics: a secret, largely illicit project. It was their notion to achieve wealth by breeding the most beautiful, intelligent, and acquiescent of Human females in the galaxy, for sale to rich potentates as houri or hetaerae. They would be semi-telepathic, to respond better to their masters' hidden desires, and would remain lovely and faithful as long as their masters survived, having no object in life except to please them. The physical model used was the most beautiful woman of the day: a green-eyed, red-haired, ideally proportioned creature obviously built by nature for love. A thousand clones were made, virtually identical, and these were closely inbred to perfect the refinements.

But the substantial modifications resulted in one spectacularly unfortunate side effect: emotional reversal, or the appearance of it. The hetaerae's actual feelings were similar to those of normal Human women – but the telepathy, like a photographic negative, reversed it. Thus the market for such women was extremely limited, with the chief appeal being to incorrigible sadists. This gave the brand a bad name in the trade. Soon Planet Minion was closed off, and later proscribed and forgotten. The inhabitants were left to fend for themselves, deprived of both the controls and the advantages of civilized technology. They survived by adapting to their established nature: completely incestuous, sadistic monogamy. A horrified, fascinated mythology grew up about them: the fatal romance of the minionette.

(Arlo called another halt. 'The minionettes – they are people like us! They don't intend any evil – they're just the way they are!'

'*They are the enemy*,' Chthon replied, in thought and voice. '*That emotional inversion subverts the myxo, abates our power. Unchecked, they will destroy us.*'

'But they could destroy you anyway – by blasting apart the planet from space!'

'*No.*' And Chthon explained this, too:)

The first really formidable problem the Humans encountered in space was what they termed the chill. It decimated their populations, unamenable to any treatment. Yet this was coincidental, for the chill was merely the side effect of a signal message. When the chill reached Chthon – not directly, but in the form of Coquina, who had contracted it – Chthon recognized it as the handiwork of its kind: mineral sentience. Others like Chthon, in other galaxies, had succeeded in generating this impulse, to alert their own kind.

Given the hint, Chthon set about doing its part. It generated a band of radiation that prevented chemical or nuclear explosions. This did not inhibit the § ships – but they were far too costly to use as simple shot against a planet. This prevented the forces of Life from attacking Chthon with modern technology. Lasers and blasters could be used, but these had very little effect on solid rock, and so became less efficacious than simple hand weapons. Meanwhile, Chthon was preparing a modified chill radiation that would expand at light-speed to force the compounding of all life-related forms of fluorine with oxygen, wiping out all life in its presence. Both fluorine and oxygen were ubiquitous in life, and those few organisms that did not require oxygen could hardly escape its effect since it was common in both air and water. This destruction would take time, for the galaxy was large, but within a hundred thousand years the sterility would be complete. Chthon would have restored this region of the universe to the purity of its origin and would be ready to join the fellowship of the mineral intellects of the other galaxies.

The killchill would actually be a modification of the chill. It could not be initiated until triggered by the arrival of the chill at Chthon in §426, since the extragalactic entities were more advanced in radiation technology than Chthon. The code for its magnification into completely killing intensity was buried within the chill wave itself, and Chthon could not anticipate that secret. So it prepared its basic circuits and waited for the formula.

But somehow the forces of Life, perhaps alerted by Benjamin, had fathomed this threat, and mounted an invasion of the caverns just before the chill wave arrived. This caught Chthon by surprise; never before had life-forms come voluntarily to the caverns. Deprived of most power weapons, the invaders had adapted other hand instruments – and sent as shock troops the subspecies most resistant to Chthon's internal weapon. Thus the army of minionettes, who perceived the myxo siege as the utmost delight. It was a savage, sophisticated campaign, with an advance agent whose mission was to subvert the human element of Chthon's defense.

'Vex!' Arlo exclaimed, aware now how well she had succeeded.

A disturbance developed as he spoke that name. 'What's happening?' he demanded, seeking the return tunnel.

An encounter between Chthon's minion and Life's, Chthon explained mentally.

Arlo grasped the references immediately. 'Bedside and Vex! She must have tuned in on me when I thought of her, and come—' For he still loved his minionette, desiring her beyond all else. If she should return to him—

What she offers is not for you, Chthon warned.

'I'll judge for myself!' And Arlo wrenched himself back to his physical body. With great effort, he cracked open his eyes.

Bedside and Vex were fighting, literally, physically. Bedside had a scalpel in one hand, its point orienting steadily on the girl, but he did not attack. Vex seemed not to watch the blade, but she stalked him carefully, never laying herself open for a thrust.

Vex made a feint to her right, then suddenly whirled left, grabbing the knife-wrist with her left hand while her right came across to catch under his right shoulder. Her knees bent as she continued her turn, and she heaved the man up and over her shoulder.

, Arlo recognized the maneuver. It was one of the throws his father knew, part of the spaceman's judo, which skill derived from older martial arts of Earth. No doubt there existed a volume somewhere, similar to LOE, but instead of covering the Literature of Old Earth, this would be COA: Combat of Old Earth. If it were as rich as LOE, it would be a devastating text!

For a moment he saw Bedside flipping over her shoulder, his feet flying up as his body came down face-up on the cavern floor. A bruising landing! But Arlo's anticipation deceived him, for Bedside did not take the fall. Instead he jerked to his left, stepping forward, his right elbow looping over her head – and Vex was left straining at nothing.

Instantly she attacked again, and he whirled to face her, the knife on guard. Her attempted throw had been very pretty – but it was as if he had expected it, so readily had he foiled it. Perhaps Chthon had read her intent and guided the doctor's response. No – Chthon could not enter the mind of a minionette! Bedside, though he talked rationally, was actually largely directed by Chthon. Surely Vex had been well trained in combat, and had accepted Arlo's first blow, back at their first meeting, merely to instill in him that initial guilt and remorse that had so undermined him. But her antagonist was not a normal man. Bedside was more and less than human, and under Chthon's directive he could accomplish things that the man alone could not.

Yet Bedside, however directed, did not seem to be trying to kill her. Arlo realized that the key lay not with Vex but with him, Arlo: because of the contract he had made with Chthon. No direct attack on the minionette. The man was merely balking her; Vex was doing the attacking.

Why? She had gone to Aton, her father, in the minionette fashion. Or *would*, eventually, inevitably. Why should she come here to Arlo, however much he might long for her? Not to kill him, certainly; his hvee still rested in her hair, glowing brightly blue, distinct from all other plants. Had she changed her mind, renounced the compelling call of her ancestry, returned to her brother? Or had Aton rejected her, absolutely? It hardly mattered, so long as she did return!

Vex moved toward Arlo. Bedside blocked her way with the scalpel, warningly. That was his mistake. She knocked the arm out, then caught the wrist and shoved him back with a twisting motion. Bedside scuttled back and to the side, regaining his balance – but she shoved him into the cavern wall, half stunning him before Chthon could guide his defense. Because she had reacted to his thrust, instead of initiating a planned attack, Chthon had been unable to anticipate her. She had reflexes like those of a salamander: a dangerous opponent, especially when mindless.

Vex clubbed Bedside on the wrist, jarring loose the blade. Then she jammed her fingers into his neck, interrupting the supply of blood to his brain. Even Chthon could not reanimate him immediately – and seconds were all she needed to win through to Arlo.

'Arlo, beloved – I know you can hear me,' she said.

Her telepathy informed her he was conscious, of course. He didn't move. He could see her also, but deemed it inexpedient to let her know if he didn't have to. She had fought her way to him; what was her intent?

'I've been thinking,' she said, kneeling beside him so that her breasts were almost above him. 'You know my mother – your grandmother Malice – is dead. I am destined to take her place, in the minion fashion. It isn't that I don't love you – it's that I can't go against my nature. Arlo, believe me, I didn't know my father was still alive. . .'

Arlo waited. She certainly hadn't offered him much of an inducement to respond; she had only confirmed what Chthon had warned. Nothing for him here.

'I came to subvert you, as you know. But they did not tell me who you were, that you were my father's son. I thought you were a stranger until you talked of Malice. And even then, though I had met Aton, I did not realize that he was *the* Aton Five, whom I thought dead. Maybe I didn't want to know. I accepted you as my brother without following the obvious reasoning through, perhaps because it was obvious that Coquina, your mother, was no minionette. Until Bedside forced it on me. On Minion there is never a brother and sister; our minds simply do not work that way. So I erred and made you a promise I could not keep; therein is my crime.'

He could accept that much. Aton had legally died when he was sent to Chthon – and the minionette birthed only one child at a time. Aton's connection with two minionettes and a human woman was extraordinary, in Minion terms. There would naturally be much resistance to these concepts, to one raised on Minion. And it would not be easy to change one's concept of a man legally dead to actually alive, unless a specific issue were made of it.

There were tears on her face, evidence that Vex was suffering in exactly the way a normal girl would. She was not receiving his emotion, which was deadened at the moment; she was experiencing her own, and it did her credit. 'But I know this hurts you, Arlo, and though I am what I am, I would not hurt you voluntarily, because you were my betrothed. . ."

Were. . .

'But we have forgotten that another person will be hurt, too. I don't want to hurt anybody – not that way. Minionettes have feelings just like yours – you're quarter-minion so you know that's true – only the telepathy inverts them. Your mother Coquina would be left out, and she has nothing because she can't even leave her cave. She needs to be considered; it isn't right to take Aton away and leave her nothing. She's not a minionette, not part of the scheme.'

So Vex had a human conscience, too! Would she renounce her minion heritage? She was right about Coquina; the shell did not deserve this treatment!

'So I've worked out a compromise,' Vex said, 'and I wanted you to know. There is no need for anyone to suffer further.'

Doc Bedside stood up, but did not interfere. What point? Arlo loved Vex; if she were his, Chthon could retreat into its rock and be forgotten – if that were the price of it. *If she were really his.* It would hurt him to renounce Chthon – but that very hurt would attract her more strongly to him.

Minion logic and custom differed from normal human, but the logic of the situation forced a common answer. Two could not steal their happiness at the expense of two others.

Arlo gathered his forces, preparing to step out of his trance the moment she said the word.

'When I go with Aton,' Vex said brightly, 'you go with your mother Coquina. That will establish two legitimate genetic ladders, and no one will be excluded.'

00

Arlo retreated to the world of LOE, the garden of his mind. He shied away from the Oedipus/Electra mythologies, seeking something less painful, yet applicable. A framework for his situation, buried in the massed Human wisdom of the book.

Interlog : [00]

Yggdrasil   Sentience
Great World Tree   Galactic Habitats
Whose roots extend   Heaven/Purgatory/Hell
Into three realms   Idyllia/Prison/Caverns
The Gods   Aesir – Vanir
The Giants   Zombies
The Dead   Chthon
History of Aton Five's mergence with Chthon
Shape of a Hexagon
Garnet-faceted
Crafted by mineral intellect
History of Arlo's divergence from Chthon
Shape of a Y
Antennae marking bifurcate futures:
Victory of Chthon   Victory of Life
Center marking the decision.

∞

And found himself in Norseland.

Aesir – his dead brother. In the Norse mythos, the Aesir were gods who resided in Asgard, the great walled city that was the divine residence. Chief among these gods was Odin, he of the single eye, maker of golden rings.

Arlo paused, feeling a shock of recognition. He knew that figure! It was his father Aton.

Odin possessed an eight-legged horse named Sleipnir. Sleipnir had come about when the friend/ enemy god Loki took the form of a mare to distract the remarkable stallion of a giant – and had subsequently birthed Sleipnir. As Bedside had fashioned Aton's steed, by merging with the caterpillar. So Loki was – Doc Bedside. How well it fit!

Odin had two wives. The first was Freyja, a Valkyrie or warrior maiden, in one of her aspects. Malice the Minionette!

With climbing excitement, Arlo explored the other parallels available. Odin's second wife was Frigga, the mother of his two sons – though he seemed to have had other children on a less legitimate basis (Morning Haze) – and a somewhat less extravagant female than Freyja. This was Coquina, of course.

And the first legitimate son was – Balder. Balder was beautiful. But as Balder grew older, he became disturbed by nightmares. These gave him a premonition of impending doom and colored his whole outlook, making him melancholy.

Alarmed, Odin made a trek to the world of the dead to inquire about his son's prospects. He rode his eight-legged steed (Arlo paused: an anachronism here – but time was fluid and the parallels inexact) along the rough and dangerous road, crossing the bridge that spanned the river marking the boundary of the underworld.

Everywhere he saw preparations being made for a great celebration. When he inquired, he was told that the Underworld was making ready to welcome Balder. He inquired further about the manner of his son's death, but could learn no more.

But Frigga was determined to save her son from his fate. She set out to obtain a pledge from all things of the world that none would harm Balder. All promised – expect one she overlooked, a spring of mistletoe.

Now Balder seemed safe. The other gods made a game of throwing a great variety of things at him, knowing that none would hurt him. But Loki fashioned a dart from the mistletoe and got a blind god to throw that. It struck and killed Balder.

So that was how Bedside had killed Aesir!

Frigga sent an emissary to Hel, the goddess of the Under–world, to plead for the return of Balder. 'All nature mourns for him,' he said.

Hel told the emissary that if not even one thing did not weep for Balder, then she would have to release him. So they made a survey—and Loki changed himself into the likeness of an old woman and refused to weep. And so Balder was lost.

This was the signal of the beginning of the end, for the gods had been unable to preserve their most cherished one. It portended the extinction of the gods at Ragnarok, the final battle between Good and Evil.

(Again Arlo paused: In the old Norse framework, the entire pantheon of gods, giants and dead had been 'good' in that it was the established way of belief. All of it had fallen – to Christianity. In that sense, Christianity was the Evil that had triumphed – yet had the Christians seen it that way? How could any person really know Good from Evil?)

But the gods had discovered what Loki had done, and they punished him severely by binding him in a deep cave under dripping poison. He remained in that torture until Ragnarok.

Arlo worked it out. Benjamin's revenge had confined Bedside to the caverns. Chthon had put him into the caterpillar. He had paid for his crime both intellectually and physically!

Odin's second son by Frigga was Thor, red-bearded god of thunder. That could only be—Arlo himself! And Thor's wife was Sif, of the golden hair – considered in some versions to be another minionette, closely related to Malice.

Bedside had cut Vex's hair just as Loki cut Sif's. The parallels fell into place so neatly; he should have perceived them long ago!

Yet how did this help him to solve his problem with Vex? By whatever name, he loved her, though she was his sister. *Though*? His minion blood compelled the truth: *because* she was his sister! Sif might be an aspect of Freyja, and the gods might tolerate father-daughter marriage – but Arlo wanted Vex for himself.

He turned to his friend. 'You were right. The minionette had nothing for me. What do you offer?'

Chthon showed him. The power of the mineral intellect flowed into his being, and he was able to control the animals of the cave: to make them stop, turn, march – at his will, not theirs. He could perceive through their senses, individually or multiply. He could

station them on three sides of a stalagmite and see that pillar in
the round, holographically. Much better than his human eye! The
entire caverns became open to his comprehension, without physical travel on his part. Godlike power, indeed!

The minionettes were still advancing. Their minds were opaque;
they had not submitted to the myxo inducement and were not
part of Chthon's demesnes. They were a brutal, alien intrusion,
cutting into the heart of the living caverns, killing the eyes and
ears and noses of Chthon.

'If I were running this war . . .' Arlo murmured.

Run it, Chthon replied. *For this you were cultivated.*

So that was it! Chthon was not competent to combat the
massed minionette attack and needed a general. Chthon had fore-
seen the potential need for the generalship of a human mind to
ward off such an invasion by human beings – at least until the
killchill deadline had passed.

'But then I, too will die!' Arlo cried, realizing.

No. Even as I spare your mother the chill, I spare you the killchill.

'Spare my family, too!' Arlo bargained.

We spare all life within this planet, Chthon assured him. *All
other life shall be extirpated.*

Arlo hesitated. What did he care about life outside the caverns? His world was *here.* 'Fair enough'

He concentrated. He summoned the most mobile creatures of
the caverns: the large chippers, flying chimeras, small salamanders,
and others. The caterpillars, potwhales, and dragons were limited
largely to their private habitats; they could be useful, but not as
mobile troops. He moved his creatures into the labyrinth surrounding the most forward column of minionettes. Then he sent them
charging, in a many-sectioned wave, striking, biting, shoving.

The minionettes, attacked from all sides, fought bravely. But they
were overwhelmed. The poison of the salamanders did the most damage, for they infiltrated undetected during the distraction provided
by the larger beasts. Arlo didn't even have to direct them once they
spied the prey; they attacked savagely, for it was their nature. And –

the minionettes, enjoying the sheer hate of the salamanders' little minds, tended not to protect themselves well from the bites, though the poison had the same effect on them as on normal Human flesh.

'Organization and attack,' Arlo said to Chthon. 'Pick your site, gather your forces—and victory is certain. Don't wait for *them* to strike! They've never faced organized animals before and don't really believe it is possible. Wipe out every member of an attacked party, and it will be some time before they catch on. With luck, we'll get enough so they can no longer muster effective missions.'

Then something else claimed his attention. He focused – and found he was in the mind of Doc Bedside. This was intriguing; the man was only half-controlled, but he responded quickly to suggestions, and the human brain and experience was phenomenally more complex than the animals. If this were what half a human mind offered, how much better a full one!

And Arlo himself was that full mind. Raised, like the animals of the caverns, right here in the bosom of Chthon, so that communication was possible without the intercession of the myxo. Possible, but not assured; the human mind had to be amenable. Not a zombie, but a partner, drawing on Chthon's immense resources, contributing his own. The ideal collaboration!

He did not try to control Bedside. He merely drew from the mad doctor's senses. These at the moment were orienting on Vex; that was what had attracted Arlo's attention. He was surprised to learn that Bedside found Vex physically attractive – but what male *wouldn't*? The two were nevertheless enemies.

'Let me through, zombie, or I'll ram your head through a wall!' Vex snapped. 'I want to talk to Arlo again.'

'Talk to me,' Bedside said. 'Arlo is in conference with Chthon, and shall not be disturbed again.'

She charged at him. Now Arlo assumed control. He caught her lifted arm, put one foot against hers, shifted his weight to bring her off-balance, and spun her by him, panting – and Bedside's perception was as responsive to the heave of her perfect breasts as

Arlo was. 'So you want to fight!' she snarled. Even twisted by genuine rage, her face was a lovely thing.

'I am Arlo,' Arlo said through Bedside's mouth. The words were somewhat slurred, because it was the first try, but he knew it would not take long to adjust.

She stared at him, shocked, and despite the opacity of her mind he felt the fringe of her emotion: pleasant acceptance. That actually would be irritated incredulity, if the reversal held for her broadcasting as well as for her reception. But mixed emotion was difficult to interpret anyway. 'Why so you are! How—?'

'What did you have to say to me?'

Now she faltered. 'Could I talk to you, personally? I don't like him listening.' She meant Bedside.

'All the caverns are listening,' Arlo said, with moderate but intentional cruelty.

'But he enjoys it too much.'

Accurate assessment! Bedside would have been happy to have Arlo make love to her, using Bedside's body. That would have created a complex of emotions like that of Morning Haze, Misery, and the dying Xest. Arlo sent Bedside away.

Vex approached his body. Now he animated it, as he had Bedside's without actually reentering it. His mind was with Chthon; only his perception and control extended to the physical mechanism. Chthon was correct: the Arlo brain, sane, competent and compatible, was the finest instrument available in all the caverns. With that tool, Chthon could win the war with the Minionettes. But he merely listened, not responding overtly.

Vex knelt beside him, as she had before. ' I tried to compromise, Arlo, to make it right for you. But you wouldn't have it that way. I was thinking Minion, not Human, and I'm sorry. But it is time for complete candor between us. Your folks wanted you to have a human girl so you would not grow up alone. Without the chance for love, Bedside said he'd arrange it, with Chthon's consent. But your Uncle Benjamin outmaneuvered us all and substituted me. None of you knew I was a minionette until too late.

Chthon was first to realize, but you balked it from killing me. Then Chthon reversed the ploy by bringing me together with Aton. So it has been some tough infighting with you and I both pawns.

'But I do love you, Arlo. On Minion you would have killed your father to possess me, and it would have been all right. Aton killed *his* father, really, to possess my mother. But you don't have enough minion blood. Well, I have a mission to perform, and that has to override my nature. Because without that mission, there will be nothing, nothing at all—except Chthon. No love, no life, no nature. So I have to assume that my father is dead, and that you are the senior serving Five. Because we do need you, Arlo. You know the caves better than any sane man – and no man from the galaxy can resist the myxo. The minionettes must ultimately follow a man; it is the way we are constituted. Without the animation of a strong man, one with minion blood, our effort must weaken and fail, as it is doing already. You will have to prove yourself – but I believe in you, and not merely because I love you. I know you can do it.

'You have won, Arlo. I will be your bride, faithful to you. Only come back to us and command the forces of Life.'

She waited, but he did not respond. 'I won't even tease you, Arlo,' she added. 'Your love is my pain, but I am quarter-human. I can take it without dying. Do what you will with me; feel what you will. I will never bear a son to replace you, if that is your preference. Anything—'

It will not work, Chthon warned. *You do not want a broken woman. Torture is not your way.*

All I want is her, Arlo responded. *I will accept her offer without implementing it. It is enought that she came to me.*

But I offer you so much more, Chthon said. *Why give up all this for the sake of one girl you cannot be happy with?*

Chthon was right and Chthon was reasonable, and Chthon was making no threats. Chthon was his friend, even in this adversity. But Arlo was already sitting up, taking Vex into his arms.

CHAPTER V

Thor

The tide of battle had turned. The cavern creatures were now organized and on the attack, cutting off and surrounding segments of the minionette army and annihilating them by living-sea charges. Arlo recognized the strategy, for he had developed it himself. No doubt Chthon was now using Bedside's mind to organize the individual actions. Bedside would not be as creative – but Chthon had so many expendable animals that it could soon wipe out the entire forces of Life. All that was needed was that one spark of creative thought that Arlo had provided.

No wonder Chthon had let him go without a fight. Arlo had already provided Chthon with the key to victory.

According to the mythology of LOE, the forces of Good were to suffer defeat at Ragnarok. Setting aside the question of which side represented Good and which Evil – for Arlo was not certain himself whether Life could seriously be equated with Good – there remained substantial doubt. No matter what, the gods would not prevail; it was the end of the system. What use, then, to struggle?

'Chthon's winning,' Arlo told Vex as he surveyed the situation. "The farther our troops penetrate the caverns, the more difficult it becomes for us. Our supply lines get longer, and we encounter more controlled animals. It's the Hard Trek all over again. We can't sustain our present rate of losses. We'll be wiped out.'

'We are well aware of that,' she said. 'The moment you went to Chthon, we started suffering disasters. We have contingents from the four major sentiments of the galaxy, but can't coordinate them properly. That's why we knew we had to have you back. You are the key to victory – either way.'

'I doubt it. I have already given Chthon what it needed: organization of the monsters. I can't *un*organize them, now that I'm on the other side. And—it is written in LOE that the gods will be defeated at Ragnarok.'

'Nonsense!' she flashed, and he noticed with pleasure that her reactions on the intellectual plane were completely human by his definition. A minionette without telepathy would be like any other woman, only more beautiful. 'Don't you see, Chthon fed you that whole Norse mythos, knowing that if you accepted all the other neat little parallels – Aesir, the Norns, even that damned eight-footed horse, yet! – if you swallowed all that , you'd have to accept that version of Ragnarok, too. You're the key; if *you* believe we'll lose, then we'll lose, no matter which side you think you're fighting on. Why do you think Chthon let you go so easily? Because you're really fighting on its side – *so long as you believe!'*

'I don't know,' Arlo temporized, shaken by her logic. The cute, difficult child he had rescued had grown a mind as thorough as her body! 'There are so many monsters that no matter what I might think , the battle still would—'

'You have to believe in the victory of Life!' she cried. 'Your framework is reversed, like my emotions – but intellectually we both must overcome our handicaps. *And we can!* You have to lead us in the fight. You're Thor, ruler of the gods!'

Arlo chuckled. 'See? Even you believe in the Norse paralles.'

'I do not! It was just a figure of—'

'You're awfully pretty when you're mad'.

She swung about, showing her teeth in no smile. 'Are you going to get yourself a cart drawn by two billygoats, then, to be like Thor? And put on gloves and a girdle and—'

But Arlo kissed her. 'It's the minion way,' he said. "The madder you get, the more I love you. Let's make love.'

'The hell!'

He raised his forefinger to her nose. 'You have a short memory.'

She paused, and gradually the blaze died, 'Is that what it's like
– from your side?'

'Yes, actually. Didn't you know? You always had to make me
angry before you waxed affectionate. Turn-about—'

'I guess I *knew*. I didn't *feel*. If you know what I mean.'

'Serves you right.' He drew her to him, and she acquiesced
without resistance, as she had to.

'Wouldn't it be nice,' she murmured sadly, 'If we could reverse the telepathy. I mean, turn about so that we both perceived
love the same. So we'd be in positive phase – mad together, loving
together.'

'The whole history of Planet Minion would have been different,' he said, proceeding with his lovemaking. Though it was what
he had wanted, somehow this unilateral action lacked the fire of
their prior experiences. One word to Vex, and she would turn on
exactly the right amount of passion – but that was not what he
wanted, either. 'Minionettes would not have been proof against
Chthon's myxo . . . '

'But Aton wouldn't have been sent to Chthon, and this battle
never would have started.'

'And you never would have been born – or me,' he said completing his act.

Vex cried out in anguish as he climaxed. For a moment he
thought he had killed her, as Aton had killed Malice. In an agony
of remorse, he leaned over her – and now she smiled 'I *told* you I
could survive. I'm quarter-human, you know.' Then she fainted.

She had survived – but he was hardly reassured. She was so
beautiful, and under that lush female exterior remained so much
of the impish child that distinguished her from all the other
minionettes in his estimation. That child had captivated him completely. Yet she was not truly his, any more than if she were chained
to the wall like a slave for his convenience. Had she loved him as he
loved her, she surely would have died. But – she had wanted it this
way, for whatever reason, and the Hvee was bright.

He put that line of thought aside and tackled his other problem. He had to reorganize the forces of Life, to turn the battle about. That was what he was being paid for. Vex was right: this might be Ragnarok – but the actual alignment of Good and Evil was uncertain and the outcome could not be predetermined. He needed to review the troops, study new options, develop new strategy.

Chthon could see every portion of the caverns simultaneously. Wherever there were animals . . . and Chthon could send its animals anywhere. Unless—

Unless a portion of the caverns were completely cleared of animals. That would deprive Chthon of its perceptions, and allow the minionettes to make surprise attacks – from that opaque region.

But how could every living creature to be eliminated, even the tiny flying insectoids? And how could he deceive Chthon about his intentions, even though he could keep the cavern entity out of his mind? Better to let Chthon think he was still acting in predictable ways, until he could diverge with complete surprise.

He left Vex, only attuning himself to her aura so as to be assured no harm came to her. This was a power he retained after his experience with Chthon: he could not control the animals of the caverns, but his natural fragment of minion emotional telepathy had been enhanced. Just as he had shown Chthon the key to effective action against the minionettes, Chthon had shown him the key to a more controlled mental power. He ran to the cave where Aton worked, heating and working the precious metals into rings over a powerful gas jet.

'I have to get around the caverns faster,' Arlo said. 'And I need a good weapon. Could I borrow Sleipnir?'

Aton considered. He had a patch of glassy rock over his eye, shielding it from the rebound of the instence flame, and wore heavy gloves on his hands. He hardly looked like an artisan – but he was. His ring were very finely crafted. 'Son, we're part of this batlle too. Our truce with Chthon can't last much longer. Get Coquina out of the caverns, and I'll ride Sleipnir myself in the service of Life's army. You can't control him as I can.'

'How can Mother leave the caverns?' Arlo asked. 'The chill

would kill her!' But it was true: the hostage state of his mother had to be abated, for Chthon could kill her as readily as the chill could.

'Not if they set up heated facilities on the surface and monitored her telepathically. It might not work, but we can't depend on Chthon anymore.'

'That's right' But Arlo was uneasy. Why hadn't Chthon already acted against Aton and Coquina?

Considering his mother, he realized why: if anything happened to Coquina, Aton would be immediately free of any emotional restraint. He would be open to the lure of the minionette: his daughter Vex. That would be too much to resist, and Arlo would lose her despite her concession to him. Then he would have no choice but to return to Chthon. But – the elimination of Coquina for such a reason would alienate Arlo from Chthon irrevocably. He would never cooperate with the killer of his mother – *or* with the one who set in motion the chain of events that cost him his fiancée.

'No,' Arlo said. 'Mother stays here. Chthon will not harm her. But if we moved her from the caverns, and then she died, Chthon would gain.' Because then her death would not have been of Chthon's doing, and Arlo would know it.

Aton looked at him, eyes narrowed, and Arlo was reminded forcefully that his father was half-minion. How much telepathy did he have? 'What about Vex?' Aton asked.

That was more complicated. If Vex died, Arlo would lose his main reason for rejoining Life. But again, if she died as a result of Chthon's action, Arlo would be doubly determined to wipe out Chthon. While she lived, that prospect for interaction between her and Aton remained – which could disunify Life's force and send Arlo back to the cavern god. Chthon was gambling with events, perhaps knowing that there was more than an even chance for success this way even though the physical battle might be lost. The war was being waged on many levels. 'She is also safe,' Arlo said.

'But you and I are not?' Aton inquired.

Another complex question. If Aton took up arms against

Chthon, and died, could Arlo blame the cavern entity? Yet that would eliminate any prospect of an Aton/Vex liaison. So probably Aton was safe too. As for Arlo himself – Chthon would not kill him so long as there was any chance of converting him. But if there were no chance and Arlo's activities threatened Chthon's own existence, then there would be no choice: Chthon would act against Arlo. And if Arlo died, Aton, Coquina, and Vex would become expendable. 'We are less safe than the women,' Arlo said, 'but Chthon will not move directly against us, at first.'

'So you need transportation of your own,' Aton said, returning to the original subject.

'Two goats and a cart,' Arlo agreed, half in jest.

'The problem with animals is that they are subject to Chthon's control,' Aton said. 'We can make a wagon – but the animals would haul it only where Chthon directed. Actually, no wheeled vehicle would serve very well here—'

'No, of course not!' Arlo agreed ruefully. There went another prop in the mythology. Too bad, because the notion had its appeal, and he did want to follow the forms of the Norse example as much as possible, to reassure Chthon about his supposedly patterned thinking.

'Maybe a sledge,' Aton said. 'Something that slides over the irregularities.'

'Good idea!' Aton still had an excellent mind, and of course he was basically smarter than Arlo, as Odin was smarter that Thor. Still – 'It would take a strong animal to haul that.'

'Or a pair of them. But control—'

'How do you control Sleipnir?'

'I'm not sure. I think the caterpillar phase destroyed so much of his mind that there isn't enough left for Chthon to take over. But then, I'm not sure Chthon has ever tried.'

'Maybe if we freed a couple of caterpillar segments from a new caterpillar—'

'Worth a try,' Aton said. He put aside his ring and doffed his protective lens.

Arlo was surprised and gratified at his father's acquiescence. He realized belatedly that one of the horrors of the Vex situation was that it was forcing an antagonism, between Arlo and Aton – an antagonism neither wanted. How much better to work together!

Aton had tried to do right by his son, providing a human girl from outside. He had not known that a minionette would be substituted – or who that minionette would be. How could he? He had not known he *had* a daughter! In this devious transaction, the morality of the leadership of Life was thrown into question. Perhaps Life was the side of Evil, destined to be victorious. Did he want that? Yet whichever side he chose became the side of Evil if it won. The mythological parallel could not be accepted; yet it pervaded the struggle.

In this venture, simple as it seemed, of fashioning suitable transportation, father and son were not only doing battle against Chthon. They were opposing the baleful influence of Minion – whose blood, deriving from the common source of Malice, joined them both to Vex. A difficult human equation – yet perhaps it could be solved.

Aton fetched his huge double-bitted ax and handed it to Arlo. 'Rite of passage,' he said.

Arlo accepted it. He did not know the literal meaning of the phrase but understood that if he were to exercise leadership, this was the tool with which to prove it. His father was giving him every chance to be the man he had to be. He had half-feared jealousy or competition from Aton, but saw now that his father cared primarily for the welfare of Life and the success of his son. That was wonderful support!

They moved out. And – Vex appeared. 'Where?' she asked.

'Caterpillar hunting,' Arlo said shortly. This was one thing he didn't want her involved in, and not merely because of the danger.

'I'm in this fight, too,' she said. 'I can help.'

Arlo couldn't argue with that. . .actually, he could have summoned a minionette squad, knowing they would obey him now, but feared it would alert Chthon. He presumed that the sheer multiplicity of information coming in from all over the caverns would keep Chthon occupied, so that the cavern god would not pay attention to what Arlo was doing so long as it seemed innocuous or in keeping with the Norse framework. Ragnarok was no simple operation! And since Chthon could not enter his mind unless he permitted it, there was no give-away there. Aton and Vex were similarly secure; Chthon would have to observe them from the eyes of the animals in the region. This would look like a meat-hunting expedition.

Vex swung up on Sleipnir, riding the middle hump of the three rear sections, between Arlo and Aton. Aton guided her, of course, so that the animal would not object; perfectly legitimate attention. Did their eyes meet momentarily? Arlo wasn't sure. She was as lovely from the rear as from the front with a slender waist, generously expanding hips, and perfectly proportioned thighs. He had so recently had the use of that body, but already he wanted it again. Whoever had selected the original model for the minionette had certainly known his business! Of course, all the minionettes were alike, except for Vex's short hair and faintly human characteristics; that hair would eventually attain its full length and glory. But that didn't take away the perfection of his own minionette.

If she were really his own . . .

Why couldn't he take one of the other minionettes? Someone like Torment, the one he had met when he first learned of the invasion. Torment would be willing, he was sure, and she was every bit as pretty. Of course, she was old enough to be his grandmother – but that made no difference, really. She was *not* his grandmother.

It didn't work, even in his imagination. Only Vex was directly related to him. He had tried to suppress the minion element in himself, but could not; the fact that she was his sister did make a difference. It attracted him to her much more strongly, as though his emotion were sharpened by the cutting edge of his human guilt. He had been over this before in his mind and found no release.

Then what about the relation between Aton and Vex that fitted the minion pattern even more closely? And why was he dwelling on this now? Vex was his for the duration; she had agreed, and it was not the minion way to deceive.

Yet even as his eyes were on her back, her eyes were on Aton's back. What was she really seeing?

Sleipnir entered the treadway of the largest neighboring caterpillar. There seemed to be no limit to the expansive properties of these creatures; this one was hundreds of segments long, but always hungry for more. Perhaps it was because its vast bulk required a continual input of organic material. At any rate, the chances were good that it would have several large and recent segments not yet withered into formlessness.

Now they had two approaches: either trace it down or summon it to them. Both had their problems. The caterpillar could be many miles away, resting in some narrow tube so that they would be unable to approach it from the side. But if they summoned it. the creature would be on the offensive, fully alert and dangerous. Their chances of hacking off segments without *becoming* segments would diminish.

'I'll summon it,' Vex said. 'You two wait in ambush at a crossing.'

The obvious solution! But Arlo was not pleased. This was his project, and he should be the one to make decisions. He didn't mind deferring to his father, but Vex bothered him. If she started organizing things, she could soon choose which man she wanted to work with. . . .

No, he had no cause for ire. She had chosen to exclude herself. And this dangerous venture might solve their problem another way: if any one of them were killed, there would be no trio.

Arlo reacted to that thought with horror. He loved his father. he loved Vex, he loved his own life. He didn't want any of them to die! And if a personal decision were finally made, the rather delicate existing truce with Chthon would be broken, and the real trouble would start.

Vex trotted down the caterpillar path toward the potwhale

pool. Arlo and Aton moved in the opposite direction, seeking the best intersection. They were silent now, so as not to alert the prey.

'This ax,' Arlo asked once they got settled. He spoke in a low voice, hoping the sound would be carried downwind, 'Where did it come from?'

Aton was silent for a moment before answering. 'The leader of the prisoners had it,' he said at last. 'His name was Bossman. I killed him when he fell to the myxo, so the ax was mine.'

Arlo rubbed his fingers along his growing red beard. He wanted to know more, but knew the futility of pushing his father. Arlo was now larger and stronger than Aton, but knew that he lacked the intellect of the older mind. Arlo would gladly have exchanged some of his muscle for some of that knowledge!

Vex began her commotion, far down the passage. She jumped into the pool with a piercing cry and made a splash. The sound carried beautifully along the tunnel: obviously the caterpillar's trap was acoustically designed.

Arlo put his ear to the stone. Sure enough, the faint beat of marching feet had started. The caterpillar could not afford to be slow, lest the prey blunder out of the trap or fall instead to the potwhale. Arlo mused briefly on that: what did caterpillar and potwhale think of each other? Were they friends, or did each long to be rid of the other? Did they hold dialogue: 'Here, won't you share this morsel?' 'No thanks: age before beauty.' Arlo suppressed a smile. Caterpillar and potwhale were two of the oldest, ugliest monsters in the caverns.

The segmented monster moved with surprising rapidity. The marching beat accelerated to a run, all feet on a side striking the stone simultaneously. The creature could move very quietly when it chose – but now that the prey was apparently trying to escape, speed was of the essence. One thing about the caterpillar: its segments might lose their heads and fore-limbs, but their legs were always strong!

Now that the thing was plunging down the monster-trail,

Arlo had serious misgivings. He and Aton were safe; the caterpillar would not leave its path, and could not catch them if it did. But Vex – she was in the pool-circle. Suppose they failed to separate the segments, and she were caught?

There was only one answer: they had to sever the rear segments so that the caterpillar had no stabbing tail. In due course it would regenerate the spear-tail, but meanwhile would be no threat.

For an instant, one vast eye fixed on Arlo; then it passed on. Arlo stood as the juggernaut rushed by, transfixed by mental horror analogous to the physical horror of the thing's tail. Those facets, each reflecting his own image slightly distorted, as though his essence were being imprinted on the caterpillar's brain, so many views of a prospective segment . . .

Meanwhile, the segments shot past like the cars of an LOE freight train, making the green glow of the walls beyond blink on and off at a dizzying rate.

'Strike!' Aton cried.

But Arlo could not move. He had been mesmerized by the terror of that single yet multiple glance of the caterpillar's eye. He tried to stir himself, to bring down the ax, but his muscles would not respond.

'Now!' Aton cried again, nudging him.

Arlo tried again – and failed again. The ax did not swing, it fell – and the last hurtling segment of the caterpillar caught the blade and wrenched it out of his hands.

Arlo was left disarmed as the beat of feet faded. There was a great lump in his throat, and his eyes were tearing. Suddenly he felt much less like a man, and not at all like a god.

Obviously he was not the one to lead the forces of Life. Aton was the one. Intelligence, experience, and courage counted for so much more than youthful enthusiasm!

Then Aton showed his wisdom, as perhaps Odin had in some similar situation, one or two thousand years before. He did not rant or condemn or even ignore. 'I froze too, the first time,' he said calmly. 'Now pick up the ax and get moving; we'll have to tackle it at the pool before it gets Vex.' And he started down the path at a run.

Arlo's stasis snapped. He swooped up the ax and charged after his father. Sleipnir, who had been grazing on glow, followed.

The pool was close, within a mile in the old human measure. But the cavern predator had moved with such velocity that they had no chance to catch up before it got there. They would have done better to remount Sleipnir. Another mistake – and there was no room in this confined passage to board the steed now, as they would have had to leap over its head.

But the caterpillar had to slow at the pool entrance, for there it worked in competitive coordination with the potwhale. The larger segments barely squeezed through the aperture. There was another aspect of the trap: the caterpillar's body blocked the opening so neatly that there was no chance for the prey to squeeze by it and escape. Arlo wondered briefly how the creature widened the passages when it needed to; he had never seen a caterpillar cutting rock, but surely it had some method. Maybe the head was able to chip away at it.

Arlo and Aton drew up short. They dared not approach the massive spike of the tail! They would have to wait for it to clear the aperture.

Slowly, it did so. Arlo held his ax before him and edged through – only to discover a new obstacle.

The caterpillar's track circled the pool. Its head was designed to frighten the prey (and now Arlo appreciated how well it did so!), driving it around the circle toward the tail. Then the tail shot out to impale the prey, incorporating it as another walking segment of the creature. So the tail had crossed the aperture on its way back around the pool. The segments near the tail were now passing the entrance, still sealing it off.

'Damn!' Arlo swore explosively, finding satisfaction in the LOE expletive. 'I can't get through!'

Aton looked at him. 'Do you want to?'

'Vex is in there!'

'Strike, then.'

Arlo gaped. He had missed the obvious. He could hardly help Vex from inside the pool; the caterpillar and potwhale dominated that arena completely. It was necessary to attack *from the side* – and here they were in the ideal position!

'It is no shame to be confused, the first time,' Aton said. 'Remember: there is always another way – perhaps a better one. Always look for it.'

Valuable lessons! Arlo realized that there was more to assuming leadership than giving directions or deciding broad policy. He had to use his mind – and be ready to accept the advice of those whose minds were better than his.

He braced himself, waited until the slender waist between two segments of the caterpillar passed the opening, and struck. His blow was not as hard as he wanted because he did not have clearance for a full swing.

To his amazement, the ax cut cleanly through the cord, spearating the segments. Success! Apparently the caterpillar, so tough in other respects, was not constructed to withstand cutting from the side at the joins.

But the inertia of the creature was such that it continued to move. In a moment, the way was blocked by a new segment.

'All right', Arlo said. And he severed that one too.

After three more cuts, the caterpillar reversed its direction, and the aperture was finally clear.

The two men entered the pool room. This was a high-domed chamber similar to the one Arlo had watched the minionettes engage, but larger. It was completely round and filled with water almost to the rim of the caterpillar ledge. There was just room for a man to walk, and none to pass. At the moment the head and front of the creature were advancing one way; the separated tail, supported by ten segments, was going the other. Between them, the three individual segments stood, lacking direction.

Vex stood directly across the pool. She could not go far either way because the head was traveling slowly toward her, while the tail was closing the gap from the other side. There was, it seemed, enough of the body included with the tail segment to coordinate the whole, even though contact with the head had been lost. The feet marched rhythmically: ten up, ten down.

'Swim across?' Arlo called.

Vex shock her head. She pointed.

Already the monstrous black mass of the potwhale was surfacing. This was no trifle such as he had poked in potholes as wide as the span of his hand; this was a full-grown jelly thing over a hundred feet in diameter. In the center was the circular mouth, big enough to take in a man, and the ropy, long tongue.

The potwhale belched. A cloud of yellow vapor spread out, suffusing the dome with its appalling stench. Water rushed into the hole, draining the last of the slick skin surface.

The tongue cast about, blindly seeking prey. Arlo knew that it would find Vex quickly enough if she tried to cross the face of this creature. But the tail segment of the caterpillar had almost closed the gap. In a moment she would have to choose between dooms – as did every animal who foolishly entered here.

'I'm going across,' Arlo said. 'I'll cut off the tongue.'

Aton held up his hand warningly. 'Is that the only choice?'

Arlo forced himself to pause and think, diffcult as that was in the pressing circumstance. And a better way opened up. 'We can distract it with caterpillar segments!' he cried. 'Any that we don't need ourselves. That will stop both menaces.'

Aton nodded. 'Push a couple in, then move on to the tail. Cut off the very last segment, and the tail will fall. Less risk.'

Arlo started around the circle. The nearest segment was too far gone; it lacked any sign of a head, so that it would not be able to respond to directives, He wedged himself in between it and the wall, lifted his knee, and shoved. It toppled into the shallow water covering the fringe of the whale.

The tongue slapped toward it. The whale felt the weight, and was orienting on the morsel; it didn't care that it was part of the caterpillar-accomplice. Arlo's attempted passage across that surface would have been perilous indeed!

He went to the next separate segment and pitched it off. And the third; none were any good for his purpose. Then he came to the unified tail assembly.

Now he had a problem. He couldn't get by it, and it was too massive to lever into the pool entire. Also, there were several very nice segments in it – rock chippers with heads and fore-legs that should be serviceable. He wanted to save these.

Meanwhile, the whole unit continued to move, cornering Vex. In a moment the stab-tail would be in range of her.

Arlo jumped down. With three morsels between him and the tongue, he should be safe – for a while.

His feet shot out from under. The potwhale's skin was spongy and slippery, offering no firm footing despite its bulk, and it undulated under his weight. But there was not enough water to swim in. Arlo thrashed about, making no forward progress.

'Another way!' Arlo echoed. He lifted the ax with difficulty, about to chop it into the slick black flesh beneath, carving a foothold. But again he paused: surely the pain would attract the potwhale's immediate attention, and the erupting blood would make the foothold less secure than ever! What else offered?

He reached up and grabbed the foot of the nearest caterpillar segment. Now he had purchase. He clamped the ax between his knees and hauled himself from the leg to the next, hand over hand. He had found another way!

When he got to the terrible tail, projecting half the length of a man, he paused yet again. He had no leverage to chop at it! But at any moment it would shoot out, for Vex was now within its range. The last thing he wanted was to see her impaled.

He saw the tail shortening. That meant it was about to spring. Arlo grabbed the end foot with his left hand and swung the ax with his right. The blow was weak, the armor of the tail hard; the blade bounced off, almost cutting his own left arm. He could not stop it that way.

The rod shot out, its diameter decreasing as its length increased. Arlo hung on, bracing both feet against the wall and pulling. He succeeded: the tail was angled out over the water, missing its mark.

Only there was now no target. Vex had jumped off the ledge, 'Let *go!*' she cried.

Arlo looked at his hands and realized what was happening. The tail was geared to spear through the prey, then to incorporate the new entity into the scheme of the caterpillar by injecting some kind of pacifying chemical. Its surface was now slick with go and Arlo's hands were numb. 'I *can't!*' he cried.

Vex grabbed him and got her body under his arms. She shoved off hard from the wall, carrying him with her. She was amazingly strong – but of course that was a property of the minionette, to be able to take sadistic punishment. His hands tore free, and he saw how the surface of the tail had opened little pores in its elongated state. No doubt that fluid was much more effective when set into a massive wound, such as the puncture of a complete entity. His skin and callus protected him somewhat, but not enough. The effect was spreading.

Arlo fell and could not move. The caterpillar poison had entered his system, paralyzing him. He could see, hear and feel – but that was all.

'Oh, *no!*' Vex cried.

She set him down face-up on the blubbery back of the potwhale and splashed his hands in the water. But there was little water here, and it was already too late for washing to have much effect. She gave it up and handed herself along the caterpillar segment in the fashion Arlo had. 'Aton!' she screamed.

And Arlo realized how convenient it would be for her simply to leave him and take up with his father. She didn't have to *do* anything; she had tried to save him and had failed. What more could be asked? If he died, he could not return to aid Chthon's campaign, so her mission would be complete in that sense. Soon she would generate her own son from the loins of her father to carry on the tradition . . .

The tongue had brought in the third segment morsel. Now it was casting for Arlo. Still he could not move. Vex had reached the other end of tht tail assembly and Aton was helping her back up to the ledge. He knew this as much with his mind as with his eye; perhaps he was picking up images from the eyes of the other people. Vex had taken up the ax Arlo had dropped; fortunately it had not slipped down between the potwhale and the rock and on to the bottom of the pool. The two of them walked away.

Walked away . . .

Arlo fought, but the caterpillar venom held him immobile. Millons of years of evolution had gone into the perfection of this serum, and it was adequate to its task – even for the alien life-form Arlo was. Only on order from the caterpillar brain could he move – and then only his feet, synchronized with the caterpillar metronome. And there were no signals because there was no connection.

How had Bedside fought off this drug, to become a man – albeit a mad one – again?

The tongue slapped across one of his legs, curled about it, tugged. Arlo slid across the blubber toward the potwhale's mouth.

Another way . . . ?

The ten-segment it—had been marching and functioning, though it had no caterpillar brain ! Bedside's brain had also been able to control a small unit. So portions of a caterpillar *could* function. If the lead-segment handled it correctly . . .

I am a caterpillar, Arlo though. *I am marching home* . . .

And his legs began to move. He was a single-segment caterpillar.

I am running home!

Faster, as his legs caught the beat his mind provided. They were not responsive directly to his brain any more than his penis was, but like it they were influenced by vision his mind conjured. The brain was smart, the legs stupid; they could be fooled.

The potwhale's tongue clasped his leg tightly, hauling him up the rise surrounding the mouth regardless of his running motions. He smelled the rank intestinal gas that steamed up from that orifice, heard the grindings deep inside.

My feet are impeded; they must fight to maintain the cadence ...

His feet kicked wildly. His free foot smacked into the tongue, battering it against the captive foot. Again, harder.

And the tongue, hurt, slackened. The foot slid out of the loop. Arlo rolled down the incline, away from the mouth, feet still working. He turned over, his face rubbing across the black surface, and turned again, helplessly. And saw the forepart of the caterpillar.

Aton and Vex were astride it, one near the head, the other near the severed end. 'One ... two ... three ... heave!' Aton called, and they both shoved hard against the wall, just as the outer row of legs was coming down. Off-balanced, the caterpillar teetered.

'Heave!' And slowly the entire length of it toppled off the ledge, into the pool. The massed legs churned up a froth.

The splash was loud. The entire potwhale tilted with the added weight. Huge as the creature was, Arlo realized that it had to be shallow,. Flat like a leaf instead of round like a stone. Not nearly as massive as it appeared. A surprised honk emerged from the mouth. Then the orifice closed and the tongue sucked in.

Water poured over the rim. The monster was submerging!

Arlo, unable to swim because of the venom, knew he had exchanged one form of death for another. Instead of being eaten, he would drown. Even Chthon could not save him now – and Chthon did not have reason to.

Then strong hands gripped his arms. Aton and Vex swam for the rim, hauling him between them.

They had saved him.

The venom of the caterpillar was powerful. Arlo fought his way to consciousness, oppressed by suffocating heat – but still he was unable to move voluntarily. Not even his feet, now. Or his eyes.

But he could feel, and he could hear. Someone was stroking his brow. It was the gentle, cool touch of his mother, Coquina: cool because of her malady the chill. He was in her hot cave, and she was taking care of him, as she had when he had been a child. He was relieved; he felt safe here, and it was good to have her attention, and to have her know that she was needed. She had given up everything for the sake of his father Aton—and now she was losing Aton himself.

Footsteps approached, halting at the entrance, where Arlo knew a curtain of woven cave-vines contained the heat necessary for Coquina's survival. 'Come in , Vex,' Coquina said.

Arlo's mind reacted, though his body could not. What was the minionette doing *here*? In the nature of things, the two women should be enemies!

There was the rustle of vines being parted, a slight stir of warm air, and Vex stepped in.

'Put on some clothing,' Coquina said, a bit sharply.

After another rustling pause while Vex donned one of Coquina's dresses—tight fit, Arlo was sure! – she spoke. 'I brought fruit from Arlo's garden. Is he better yet?'

'Not yet. But thank you very much for the fruit.' Coquina was being very polite, very formal. 'I know the trip to the garden is dangerous for you, alone.'

'Aton went with me.' Arlo felt his mother's hand on his forehead freeze, almost literally: it seemed to become deathly cold. Small wonder!

Then Coquina stood. 'There is no need to tell me this.'

'Please – I must tell you. I – here.' Evidently Vex was holding out something. Arlo struggled to regain that ambience of perception he had had, to see things through their eyes. What was the object?

There was a brief silence. Then: 'He – gave you the hvee?'

Arlo knew exactly what his mother was a feeling: he felt hte same. If Aton had given Vex the hvee, all was over for Coquina— and for Arlo.

'He— sent it,' Vex said quiently. 'As— a gift for you. Please take it.'

What? The hvee would not be transferred like this!

Coquina accepted it. 'It does not wilt. How is this possbile?'

'Aton loves you,' Vex said. 'We did nothing in the gardens. He picked this flower; it oriented on him. See, it does not match my blue one from Arlo. You love him –'

'But how could you carry it?'

'How can anyone carry the hvee? I love him, too'.

Wrong, Arlo thought. The hvee loved its master, and loved the one who loved its master, but could not be transferred between common lovers. It was strictly *series*, not *parallel*. For when more than one woman loved a given man, there was rivalry, and that destroyed love and the hvee. So something was wrong here. The hvee should be wilting – and wasn't.

Coquina moved away from Arlo and went to Vex. *Oh, no!* Arlo thought. *They can't fight . . . not my mother and my sister, my two closest loves!*

'Aton has shown me something I did not know,' Coquina said gently. 'Come, child – sit by me. I shall not hold you long.' And her voice was oddly soft.

'I am confused,' Vex said. 'There is strange and terrible emotion here, and I don't know whether it emanates from you or Arlo, or from both.'

'My son is conscious? Coquina asked.

Of course Vex would know. She *was telepathic.* Arlo could have few secrets from her!

Vex must have nodded affirmatively, for Coquina continued: 'It is best that he know this too.'

'You know what I am!' Vex cried with sudden vehemence. 'You know how it must end! How can you speak to me?'

Now Arlo felt her emotion, in large part a blissful experience, in small part a black abyss. It was his own telepathy at work, coming at last, becoming stronger because of the urgency stemming from the incapacity of his normal senses. Three-quarter human,

that picked up Vex's negative emotion as positive; one quarter minion, that received it as it was. He really was a mixture of types. Yet
this duality was giving him a breadth of comprehension he could
not have had otherwise, as though it required two views to fathom
any given feeling. Chthon could see physical objects from many
views, but had no inkling of this mental holography.

'I knew your mother,' Coquina said. 'She was a fine woman—
Aton's first love. I was never jealous of her.'

'I did not know my father still lived!' Vex said in agony. 'He
was listed as dead because he went to Chthon prison. I met Aton
and did not recognize him because of that belief. When Arlo toled
me his grandmother was Malice-'

'Peace, child! I know you did not know. When you fled from
me at our first meeting, I knew you had to be a minionette – and
I recognized in your aspect your likely lineage. I remembered how
clever Uncle Benjamin Five was, and I comprehend some of that
man's motives. There was that of Aton in you—'

'I never intended to betray Arlo! See – I still wear his hvee, and
it lives. I have sworn —'

'I know, Vex. I understand. Let me explain about the hvee.'

Why was Coquina suddenly so calm? Arlo could pick up her
emotion now, separating it from Vex's; it was mainly positive, only
partly negative – which meant that it was all positive in origins,
owing to his own partial reversal of reception. She was not pretending; she was confident and relieved.

'I know what normals go through to love a minionette, now,'
Vex said. 'I never wanted to hurt anyone, but I can't be false to my
nature. Had Aton been dead, as I thought—'

Now a ripple of horror, inspired by the mere suggestion of
Aton dead. Coquina's love was a miraculous thing; Arlo had never
before glimpsed its depth. 'When Aton was a child of seven,' Coquina said, 'the minionette Malice, his mother and yours, visited
him and gave him the hvee. Even then, he loved her. Many years
later, he gave that hvee to me, forgetting its origin. I did not know
it was hers – but the hvee never forgets, and because I loved him,

it survived. Even when Malice died, the hvee lived – because it could not interpret what had happened. The hvee is not intelligent. But when I returned it to Aton, it knew his love for Malice was over — because she was dead and he knew she was dead and that it was really hers – and so it died.'

Vex had to work this out. "You knew Malice was dead – but not that you wore her hvee – so it lived?'

'Yes. The hvee loved me, because I loved Aton, who loved its true mistress. There must always be a chain and it cannot see beyond one link at a times Intellictual knowledge of one person about the end of the chain does not affect the hvee; it has to get close enough to comprehend its own, purely emotional way. Any breaks in that chain can kill it, if the break is adjacent.'

'But the hvee I just brought—there is no chain—'

'There *is* a chain. This is what Aton has shown us. The hvee does not distinguish between types of love; convention has relegated it to romance, but it is quite possible for a father to give it to his son, or to his grandchild—so long as true love exists. Sometimes close friends of the same sex exchange the hvee; this does not imply anything untoward.'

Arlo had not known this either. Where there was love— any love – the hvee could live. It didn't have to be sexual.

'But I could only carry Aton's hvee –' Vex said falteringly. 'I *knew* it was not intended for me —' She paused, confused. 'I bear Arlo's hvee!'

'Yes. That much is true. You love Aton – and you also love Arlo. Both are close kin to you; as a minionette, you must love them, so that you can love either – as events require. It is possible to love two; the hvee proves it.'

'Yet now you hold the hvee—'

'I shall give it to my son,' Coquina said. She put it in Arlo's hair, and her love was an almost tangible thing to his new awareness. 'See – it does not wilt.'

'Because he loves you,' Vex said. 'And I know he loves me too.

But how can it have passed between you and me, unless —' She halted, amazed. 'Unless you love me!'

'You are very like your mother,' Coquina said. 'And very like Aton. Much of what I love in him is really his reflection of his mother – whom I also loved. I never had a daughter –'

'But I am a minionette!'

'Minionettes are also human beings.'

'Yet Arlo – Aton –'

'We are coming into Ragnarok. If Chthon loses, *I* die, for I depend on Chthon. If Chthon wins, we may *all* die, for the cavern entity will have no further need of us. I rather think my son will die, too, in this awful combat. If Aton survives, it will be fitting that he return to Minion. I know you will take care of him when that time comes, and I would not have it otherwise. He was born to love the minionette.'

There was a long silence, but Arlo felt the gradually shifting and strengthening emotions of the minionette. Then: 'If you love me, why don't I feel the pain?'

'You are partly normal, child. Not *all* your emotions are reversed.'

'I never had a mother . . . '

'This is the sad thing about being a minionette. You are forced to orient exclusively on the opposite sex, in a sexual way, so that you never know the joys of true family existence. In this manner the pattern is constantly reinforced.'

'I think I have a mother now.'

'Yes. . . .'

Arlo's store of energy was exhausted. He sank back into unconsciousness – but it was a better state than he had been in before.

'We have to do something about those hands.' Aton said. 'The skin's gone. They'll be weeks healing.'

Arlo looked up at him. They were in the home-cave. Down in the tunnel was Coquina's section, too hot for normal comfort. Here it was pleasant. Evidently he had been shuffled back once the initial crisis passed. 'Why did you save me?'

Aton exchanged glances with Vex. Arlo saw and felt the futile longing that passed between them. Neither intended to yield, but both felt the magnetic pull. Arlo hoped they would not realize how well he could read their emotions, now.

'We need you,' Vex said. 'We did not save you from Chthon only to yield you to the potwhale.'

That was a fair answer. All three of them knew the situation: no need to rehearse it. Arlo looked down at his hands. 'Gloves, maybe. They don't hurt – in fact, I can hardly feel my fingers. . .'

'You took a dose of caterpillar compulsion,' Aton said. 'It will be slow to wear off. But we have to protect the skin, and we don't have proper bandages.'

'So we did get gloves,' Vex finished. 'From the minionettes.' She spoke as though she were not one herself, and it was no artificial distinction. 'Here.'

Gloves? They were giant metalweave gauntlets! Each finger was articulated by a construction of sliding, overlapping scales, so that it could be moved and bent freely without being crushed. Inside was webbing and padding, fastening the whole in place gently yet firmly. Very firmly. From the outside the gloves were crushproof; they could sustain hammer-blows without denting. But from the inside they were amazingly comfortable, featherlight despite their gross mass.

'Engineers' handwear,' Aton explained. 'I used a similar set on space ships, where temperature and pressure could vary widely across deadly extremes, but precise adjustments had to be made. You can thread a needle or handle red-hot iron—' he broke off.

'I know what a needle is,' Arlo said, smiling. 'A sliver of metal used in the manufacture of apparel. Coquina has one.' He looked at his hands. The gloves seemed to fit like living flesh. His skin was numb, but somehow the gloves transmitted the sensation of pressure to his interior receptors, making it seem as though the metal itself could feel.

Experimentally, he tapped the stone floor. There was no pain. He struck it, still receiving sensation without discomfort. He stood up, feeling weak and dizzy, and smacked his fist hard into the wall. It crushed the glow-lichen and chipped a fragment of stone away, but the shock to his hand and arm was minimal.

'Thor's gloves. . .' he murmured.

'We saved the best caterpillar segments, and made a sledge,' Aton said. 'I think it will serve.'

The two of them must have liked working together! But what could Arlo say? They had done it for him, and done well.

'Meanwhile, what is Chthon doing?' Arlo inquired.

'Winning the war,' Vex said succinctly. 'If we don't get organized soon, it will be too late.'

'I'll see about it,' Arlo said.

'Be careful,' Aton cautioned. 'Chthon gives few warnings.'

'Your eye!' Arlo cried, suddenly realizing. 'A warning?'

'How *did* you lose it?' Vex inquired.   •

Aton seemed reluctant, but answered. 'I was questing for better metals, back when I first started making rings. I needed accessible gold in an almost pure state, that I could remove with no more than hammer and chisel, and that's hard to find. I explored down past tunnels lined with ice and snow and found a closed-off region, an artificial dead end, a blocked passage deep below the normal run. I knew somehow that a fundamental secret of Chthon was concealed behind that barrier, and I wanted to master it. I started to pound through the partition – and the chimera came. I tried to fight it, but the thing moved so quickly. . . it plucked out my eye and left. It could readily have killed me, but Chthon sent it away. That was my warning: stay clear of the forbidden secrets of Chthon. So I gained knowledge of my limits and never trespassed again. And in a few days a chipper opened a rich vein of gold near my home-cave, and I knew Chthon had given me this in lieu of the knowledge I had sought.'

'Odin went down to the base of the great World tree Yggdrasil,' Arlo said, remembering as from a dream. 'There he found the Spring of Mimir, whose water gave inspiration and knowledge of things to come. And for a drink from that spring, Odin gave up this eye.'

'Lovely,' Vex said. To her, of course, it was.

They showed him the goat-cart. The two chippers were huge and well preserved, their forelimbs intact so that they could run on all fours. The sledge was fashioned of flexible wooden poles from the surface, cushioned by woven fibers. The front part of it was supported by the chippers, so that it did not touch the ground; it tilted down at an angle that made obstruction almost impossible. A vine-bound stalactite seat had been fixed on the rear, with strong handholds. It resembled a throne.

Arlo mounted it and took the reins. 'The goats are not really broken in yet,' Aton warned. 'Once they start, they tend not to stop, so take it easy. You have to work with them yourself, so that they will orient on you.'

'Sure,' said Arlo. He was feeling better already. He gave the reins a good twitch.

The two chippers launched themselves down the tunnel. Aton and Vex dived out of the way, lest they be trampled. The cavern walls shot past at an alarming rate. 'Hold! Hold!' Arlo cried, but they only went faster. They had not yet learnt the meaning or discipline of such a command, and they were powerful.

The sledge bumped across irregularities in the floor. Then the chippers hurdled a narrow river channel – and so did the sledge. It felt like flying. At first the experience was terrifying, but soon Arlo realized that the chippers were surefooted; they would not crash into any walls or leap off any cliffs.

Fine. Let them exert their energies. Arlo found that he could steer them, when he needed to, by jerking to one side or the other on the reins, because there were bits hooked into the corners of their mouths behind their teeth, and pressure there was painful. He felt that pain himself, through their limited minds. He directed them toward the wind caverns where the minionettes were camped.

The journey that would have taken hours on foot was much

shorter by sledge. Furthermore, he arrived fresher than he had been at the start, for the limited activity restored his body. He concentrated on the chippers' minds, strengthening his telepathic connection, acquainting them with himself as though he were the lead segment of their caterpillar. In a sense he was. His minion, Chthon, and caterpillar experiences all contributed to his mental authority. The chippers, tiring at last, were willing to accede to his demands. Since the mental directives turned out to be easiest and most effective, he finally removed the bits, leaving the reins as no more than a suggestion. No one but he would be able to control these fine animals!

Torment met him at the camp. She and the other minionettes knew without being physically informed that she was to be his liaison. 'We heard you had some trouble.'

'Bit of fun with a caterpillar. I'm better now. I understand you have trouble yourself.'

'We have lost one-third of our troops,' she said. 'We can replace them, but we cannot expend them at this rate indefinitely. The population of Minion is limited, and minionettes are hard to replace.'

'Come on here with me,' he said. 'I want to survey the caverns.'

She joined him on the sledge, stepping daintily. There was that in her appearance and manner that still set her apart from Vex, showing her to be a mature full-blooded minionette instead of a nascent one. These were appealing refinements. 'Your animals are beautifully tired,' she remarked.

He leaned over his chair and kissed her, savoring her aspect so like that of Vex, yet so enticingly distinct. Torment gasped and fell back, barely retaining her perch on the sledge. 'Are you trying to kill me?' It was no rhetorical or humorous question; she had been cruelly stricken.

'I want the goats tired,' he said. 'I am breaking them in.'

'If I seemed condescending, I will not be so again,' Torment said.

She had gotten the message. He wanted the minionettes broken in, too. He could not punish them in anger, but he could kiss them into oblivion. 'Chthon's creatures are now organized, under common command,' he explained. 'We can overcome them only if we have superior organization. Can you link with each other telepathically?'

'To a certain extent. The death of one of our own pains us all; there is no reversal among ourselves. So we tend to suppress it.'

'I'd guess there *is* reversal between yourselves,' Arlo said. 'Double reversal – that cancels out. You broadcast reversed, and you receive reversed.'

She nodded. ' You seem to be getting more intelligent.'

'I have had a great deal of experience in the past few days, and I am learning about telepathy. I want you to enhance your own telepathy, not suppress it. The minionettes must be unified.' He glanced around the stark wind tunnels. 'Now first I want to establish a secure base of operations.'

'We have sentries posted at all –'

He gave her a long loving look, enhanced by a jolt of positive emotion. She quailed. 'What do you have in mind?'

'Every living thing in the caverns is an agent of Chthon, except the human beings,' he said. 'Not just the caterpillars and chippers – the salamanders and pseudoflies too. You'll just have to clear a section of every living thing; only then can we plan strategy in secret.'

She nodded, and the motion sent ripples of color through her hair. It occurred to him that here in the green glow of the caverns the minionette's hair should not appear fire-red – yet it did. The image probably was formed in his brain as much as in his eye: another minor marvel of telepathy. 'We could do that in the old prison region,' she said. 'There are very few access points there. We have retained a few of the original prisoners as menials; should they be removed also?'

He sent a mental blast of ire at her to indicate his pleasure, and she smiled. 'You do have a certain way about you,' she murmured.

In hours they had sealed off the upper caverns and hunted

down every creature – human and animal – there. 'Now we are secure,' Arlo said. 'Now bring down the Vanir.'

'Vanir?' Torment asked, perplexed.

'The galactic allies,' he explained. 'In Norse mythology, the Vanir were originally lesser deities who warred with the arrogant Aesir. But the fray was even, and at length the Aesir made peace and admitted the Vanir to Asgard on an equal basis. The goddess Freyja, first wife of Odin, was of the Vanir; she was Valkyrie. With new gods like Thor being born of these Aesir/ Vanir unions, the distinctin becaame indistinct.'

'Valkyrie. . . minionette,' Torment murmured, 'Fighting maidens, coveyors of the dead to Valhalla. Very nice.'

'But some elements of the Vanir were the civilized non-human galactic species: the Lfa, EeoO, and Xests.' Then he reviewed the properties of the three galactic allies. 'I learned this from Chthon. Is my information correct?'

'Yes. Chthon seems to know a good deal.'

'Are they subject to the myxo?'

'We have assumed so. It is difficult to—'

'To work with aliens,' he finished for her. 'They have their own ways and needs and leaders.' He paused. They had now drawn up to the main camp again, and the other minionettes gathered about, listening. 'Well, they now have some notion of the stakes. If we lose this battle of the caverns, the entire galaxy will follow. I have seen it in a vision of the future. It will take thousands of years for all life in the galaxy to be exterminated, but it will be inevitable, with no hope of redress.

'Tell the Vanir I am assuming the leadership of the forces of Life because only I know how to oppose Chthon successfully, and that they will take their directives from me. I want their contingents down here in the secure caverns within twelve hours. Until that time, there will be no forays beyond the perimeter.' He looked around, smiling. 'I will make love to any woman who violates this directive.'

He concentrated on their lush figures, picturing Vex, making his penis rise so that all would know he was not bluffing, though of course he *was*. It was an effective threat; the minionettes drew back with a common expression of pain at the prospect of his specific enjoyment. Any of them would happily have submitted to rape by him, but not love.

'Meanwhile, we shall prepare several secret exits to the main caverns,' Arlo continued. 'We can put out the fire in one of the torch tunnels – I presume you can get fire extinguishers and heat suits – and lower a party that way, through the back tunnels. We shall also require a series of long, narrow wells through the floor. We'll need drilling equipment. Get it here in three hours.'

They did not question him. The minionettes scattered. Arlo turned his chippers loose to graze, then lay down for a nap. He knew he would be foolish to overtax himself before the real battle began; he was not yet fully recovered.

He dreamed of Valhalla, the hall of Asgard where the gods feasted. Thor was there, celebrating with his father Odin, chief of the gods, and so was Frigga, and golden-haired Sif and all the lesser gods.

Then Loki appeared. 'Come make merry with us,' Odin invited him. But Loki demurred.

'Why should I carouse with one who cuckolds his stupid son? Do you think I don't know the secrets of all you hypocrites?'

Arlo woke, sweating. What were Aton and Vex doing at this moment? They were now outside his telepathic range.

A signal caught his eye. He looked – and found a Xest standing beside Torment. It was exactly as in his vision, standing on eight spindly legs, with a globular body somewhat larger than a man's hand. It was bright orange; perhaps his vision had told him that, but in the flesh it surprised him. Almost immediately he realized that this was a stress color: gravity here was much beyond Xest normal, and it had to make a constant effort to adapt. Etiquette required that he not dwell on this.

'Apologies for waking you,' the minionette said. 'I am speaking for the Xest, who is telepathic like us, only more so. I merely translate its signals.'

Arlo found he could read much of the creature's mind directly, but elected not to advertise that fact. He did not know the galactic sign language at all well, never having had opportunity to practice it with galactics, so the translation was helpful. And he realized that something important was up. 'Continue.'

'Antipathetic pressures are on your mind.'

'They sure are!' Arlo agreed. 'This is Ragnarok, the battle of all time.'

Torment spoke again as the Xest signaled. 'Bedside – Loki – Chthon – these entered your mind while your guard was down. To spread dissent –'

Arlo's eyes narrowed. 'You mean my dream was not my own?'

'That is correct. It was projected from the enemy.'

Arlo nodded. He *knew* his father and sister were not betraying him; both were persons of integrity, however difficult that might be at times, and he had seen into their minds. The antagonist he faced was Doc Bedside, now organizing Chthon's power. Obviously Bedside wanted him out of the Life camp and back in his home-cave in a hurry. Why?

'Representatives from the other Vanir have arrived,' Torment said.

'Bring them in.' The Chthon matter would have to wait.

One Lfa and one EeoO entered. The first looked like a pile of fractured rubble with sticks protruding randomly. The second resembled a translucent pool of water that somehow needed no basin. It was a delicate blue throughout.

The Lfa came right to the point. Torment translated its peremptory signals. 'We govern half the galaxy. Humans govern a tenth. We do not accept your proffered leadership.'

Arlo smiled in such a way that the minionette had to smile with him. 'Have you been able to abate the nonexplosion wave?'

The Lfa shifted its bricks uncomfortably. 'Not yet,' Torment said.

'Can you abate it within fourteen Earth-days from this moment?'

'These things take time.'

'Time is gone,' Arlo said. 'This is Ragnarok. If we do not conquer Chthon within our deadline, the original chill-wave will intersect this planet, enabling Chthon to initiate the fluorine-oxy-
gen compounder wave, to be known as the killchill, that will destroy all life in the galaxy beyond this planet—and perhaps here
too, for the mineral intellect will have no further need of local life.
It regards us as fetid slime, a pestilence on the sacred matter of the
galaxy. Not even a microbe will live after the killchill passes; Life
will be eternally extinct.

'You will not be able to counteract that wave because you will
no longer exist. I am the only one who can find his way into the
secret heart of Chthon's caverns to destroy the broadcast mechanism – and to do that it will be necessary to destroy Chthon itself,
for Chthon *is* the mechanism. Are you ready to gamble that you
can penetrate that key region, or learn to nullify the nonexplosion
field so that you can blast apart this planet – in time?'

Now the EeoO signaled. *How* it signaled Arlo could not tell,
but Torment translated: 'Your campaign is useless.'

Arlo faced it. His gaze passed through its serene interior. Amazing how this thing could function without visible organs, nerves,
or bones! 'Why?'

'Chthon is aware of it. Chthon-controlled life permeates this
cavern.'

'I have the assurance of the minionettes that this is not so,'
Arlo said. 'Our dialogue should be private.'

The EeoO quivered, and Torment's mouth dropped open. "The
glow!' she exclaimed.

Arlo clapped his hand to his forehead. That was a mistake,
because the gauntlet he wore gave his skull a mighty crack. "The
glow!' Of course the EeoO was right. The green glow covered every wall; its light was essential to their vision. And it was an organic substance. If they burned it off, they would be dependent
on artificial light. That would complicate the campaign phenomenally. In any combat, the Chthon forces would have only to elimi-

nate the lights to assume a decisive advantage. And they were already winning.

No, perhaps not. If the forces of Life depended on the glow, so did the living forces of Chthon. Perhaps in the dark the fight would be even. But that still wasn't good enough.

'And the cavern entity knows your mind,' Torment continued translating from the EeoO's jiggles. 'You have been closer to it than any sane sapient living entity. Your leadership means that it is dealing with a known intelligence. That is why it does not act against you, only seeking to guide you subtly. It prefers your influence to that of some unanalyzed form of life.'

'Such as the Lfa?' Arlo inquired dryly.

He needed no translation to pick up the two creatures' agreement. Yet he was sure it would mean disaster if he yielded his leadership to them. He had to convince them to accept him.

How? His father was clever; Aton could have debated these balky aliens and made them look ridiculous. Arlo lacked that educational background, that ready wit, that minion-prompted sarcasm. And his motive was suspect, for Chthon obviously *did* want him in power. Was he really his own man, or was he forwarding Chthon's cause?

No matter. Alien domination of this campaign meant certain loss. He had to do it. Maybe he wasn't Aton – but he had an idea how Aton would have gone about it. There were little tricks of approach. Perhaps they would not work for Arlo, but he had to give it his best try.

His mind reached out – and it was as though it linked with that of his father. Illusion it might be, but suddenly his confidence grew.

Try them on the time scale, son.

'How long did it take the Lfa to colonize half the galaxy?' Arlo asked.

'Approximately half a million years,' Torment answered.

'We Humans colonized our tenth in three hundred years,' Arlo said. 'That is approximately three thousand times your rate –

and we were limited only by the fact that nothing was left to colonize. Does that suggest anything to you?'

'An impetuous velocity,' came the reply.

It's trying to get cute. Nail it. Make it give your answer.

'What type of entity would you assign to supervise the conquest of a difficult planet – in fourteen days?'

'I must take time to consider,' the Lfa signaled.

One down. Don't let the other get away!

Arlo turned to the EeoO. 'Have I made my point?'

'You must answer the question of Chthon's knowledge of your mind,' the EeoO replied.

This is a sharper entity. Appeal to its intellect.

'It should be obvious that if Chthon knows my mind best, the converse is true. *I know Chthon best.*' Arlo leaned forward persuasively, though he had no certainty that the gesture meant anything to the galactics. 'This is like a chess game – Torment, translate that analogy into terms they understand; surely they have similar exercises – wherein all pieces and all moves are conducted in the sight of both players. There can be no secrets. The more powerful, original, more reliable player wins – usually.'

'Your expertise is questionable,' one of the creatures signaled; Arlo was not certain which, since Lfa, EeoO and Xest were all moving now. But it was a good score to a vulnerable area, for Arlo had already muffed the green glow matter.

What would Aton do? *Counterattack!*

'Would you substitute *your* expertise? Would any of you go into the depths of Chthon blindly to tackle a planetary sentience in its home territory? Your chances may seem less than even, with me – but they will be virtually nothing with *you*. At least I have some notion of the rules of the game.'

And the three entities were without signals.

Nail it down!

'All right,' Arlo said briskly, as though they had formally accepted his position. 'We can't operate in complete secrecy but unless

Chthon can read my mind, it doesn't know exactly what use I mean to make of your contingents. If my strategy is original and sound, Chthon will not be able to counter it. I may ask you to do some seemingly foolish things. Do not challenge me on them; they may *be* foolish – so as to conceal my real intent. Only by keeping Chthon ignorant of the details of my campaign can I hope to prevail. Now I want you to bring down the drills and firefighting equipment and proceed as I outlined to the minionettes before.'

The Lfa and EeoO made motions very like a human shrug, and departed. Watching them move was an experience: one seemed to tumble over itself like debris down a slope, while the other slid gracefully along its pastel-hued base.

'You're lucky they aren't telepathic,' Torment murmured. 'If they had read the doubt in your mind—'

'Remind me never to try to bluff a Xest,' Arlo said.

'And get kissed again? Remind yourself!'

He smiled, making her wince. 'In fact, I'd better level with our Xest representative right now.'

'No need.' she said. 'The Xest understands. The Xest feels you are the most qualified leader for the endeavor.'

'I'm getting to like the Xest,' he said. Then he thought of something else. 'The Xest – they use the Taphid, don't they?'

'Yes. They import it –'

'Have them bring a good supply down here. We may need the Taphid when we lose.'

'When we—?'

'How would you like an affectionate hug?'

She departed without further word. The Xest projected a benign sentiment, and followed her.

Soon the equipment arrived. 'What's this?' Arlo inquired, picking up a Xest artifact. 'It looks like a hammer.'

'It is a power mallet,' Torment translated.

'The Xests' limbs are not as strong as those of many other creatures, especially on high-gravity surfaces. So Xest force is amplified by means of specialized tools. With this mallet one Xest can pound apart solid rock without personal fatigue.'

'Could I use it?'

'It should be feasible. Merely hold it firmly and depress the stud in the handle. It vibrates at sonic frequency.'

Arlo tried it. He put it to the wall and touched the stud with the thumb of his gauntlet. The stone powdered out beneath the point of contact.

'Very nice,' Arlo said. 'Do you have a larger model?'

The Xest produced a version whose head was the size of Arlo's two fists. Arlo tried it, and watched the thing blast a head-sized hole in the wall with one strike. Evidently that did not count as an explosion, or Chthon's repressive field would have interfered. But it was powerful! 'Thor's Hammer,' he said.

'Now Chthon undoubtedly knows what we have been doing,' Arlo told Torment. 'So we'll proceed according to schedule. Meanwhile, I'll finish my nap.' He lay down on the rock.

Torment looked at him silently.

'Hold my hand,' he told her. 'Put me to sleep.' *Perchance* to *dream. . .*

She knelt and took his hand. Arlo gave his turmoil and apprehension free rein, knowing that it came through to her like sweet music. He was leading the forces of life into disaster – and *he had no counterplan.* What was he to do?

Torment smoothed his forehead with her cool hand. 'You darling boy,' she murmured.

After a while he slept.

'He hasn't returned,' Vex said. 'Life has lost, as was fated at Ragnarok. Coquina is confined to her cave. What remains for us, in these few hours remaining?'

'Love,' Aton said. 'As it was fated to be.' He took her into his arms.

Arlo wrenched himself awake. 'I'm going home!'

Torment restrained him. 'Don't make decisions now; you're crazed by a dream-projection.'

'Go sit on a stalagmite – a sharp one,' Arlo snapped. He sent a mental summons to his two goat segments.

'This is of course in poor taste to suggest,' Torment said carefully. 'But is she worth it? We need you here, as the battle begins. We have women very like your minionette to console you, and far more experienced.'

'I'm aware of that. You come with me. Bring one member of each Vanir species – no, make that four EeoO, one of each sex. Relinquish command of the Life campaign to the Lfa leader.'

'The Lfa!' Now she was alarmed. 'There will be no imagination! Completely predictable procedure, child's play for Chthon to counter!'

'If you aren't coming. I'll go alone!'

She ran after him. 'Arlo, you're lovely like this! I can hardly refrain from embracing you. But can't you see – Chthon put that dream into your mind! I was with you, I felt it – the same signal the Xest picked up before! When you sleep, your guard goes down –'

'If I had a way to hurt you, I'd do it!' Arlo told her wrathfully. 'But it's impossible right now.' That damned inversion – his rage, her bliss. 'So you just shut up and fetch the Vanir.'

'Stop and think!' she cried. 'Chthon *wants* you out of here and back at your home-cave. You're playing into its scheme.'

Arlo came up to his chippers, who had stopped grazing and were ambling toward the sledge. 'Unseal the main exit.'

'No.'

He backhanded her across the face in fury. Torment accepted the blow unhurt, unable to repress her smile of pure animal pleasure despite her need to convince him intellectually. 'We won't let you walk into Chthon's trap.'

Arlo hitched the sledge, cursing as he struggled with the unfamiliar and crude fastenings. He finally got it right and started off. When he got to the sealed exit he dismounted, took his great hammer in his gloves, and pounded a gaping hole through the mortar.

By the time he finished, Torment had returned with a Xest, a large Lfa, and four EeoO units: translucent blue, green, yellow, and pink. 'If you insist on this disaster, we're your bodyguard,' Torment said, and they all piled onto the sledge.

'Suit yourselves.' He snapped the reins, though his real command was mental: the bits were gone. The two chippers, recharged by their rest, took off. The sledge was heavy with the weight of the group, so that the fibers of it sagged, but the chippers were so powerful it seemed to make little difference. They careened through the passages at a dizzying rate.

As they moved, Arlo spoke into Torment's ear, 'I doubt Chthon can hear us talk right now, or read your signals, and we'll know if there's any myxo siege against any of our little group. I believe you all understand that it is not madness but doom I have brought you into.'

Torment didn't bother to translate. 'We know,' she agreed grimly.

'Small as we are, we are the real invasion spearhead. The main attack, back at the sealed cavern, is only a decoy, a diversion.'

'Yes.' But she looked surprised.

'By seeming to fall into Chthon's trap, we lull it into complacency. But we shall soon be ambushed. We shall have to elude that trap just before it snaps, seemingly by accident. Now let me talk to the EeoO.'

Torment signaled to the four translucent entities.

'Soon we shall pass a series of dry holes,' Arlo said. 'They are ancient gas vents, long since inactive. The vents are narrow, and they twist through the rock, so that no solid living thing of any size can pass through them. But a liquid might – and the holes drain into a common chamber in the heart of the planet. It is very near Chthon's wave-generating circuitry.'

Torment signaled, then gave their reply. 'We comprehend.'

The sledge came to the vents. 'I can't stop the chippers without giving it away,' Arlo said. 'The EeoO will have to jump.'

The E, e, o, and O entities jumped, bouncing up like balls to get free of the moving sledge. They landed, rebounded, and rolled across the rock behind. They would soon liquefy, dissolve into pools, and seep through the vents until they merged in the deeper caverns Chthon thought were secure. But Arlo had learned more than Chthon had told him, during their interaction; he knew many of the secret secrets.

Mindless in their melted state, the E's and O's should broadcast few telltales of sentience. With luck, the new little EeoO emerging from the generative pool would be able to disrupt Chthon's circuits before the mineral entity caught on.

'Now the Lfa,' Arlo said. 'Can you disassociate, then reform as two or more subentities in some unobserved cavern?'

'Yes,' Torment translated. 'It is not normal procedure, but in emergency –'

'We shall soon pass the major gas crevasse of the planet,' Arlo said. 'The gas from this section funnels through to the fires near the prison region. If you can ignite the crevasse itself, Chthon's thermal ecology will be disrupted. The animals will panic, perhaps throwing off Chthon's control, and the mineral intellect's own circuits will suffer.'

'I shall make the attempt,' the Lfa signaled.

'Here,' Arlo said. And the Lfa tumbled off, breaking up into scattered parts of junk as it struck the stone.

'Now the Xest. We are approaching the probable site of ambush. We shall try to avoid it narrowly, distracting Chthon so that the activity of the EeoO and Lfa is not noted. You brought the Taphid?'

'Yes,' the Xest signaled. It was now almost blindingly orange.

'Thaw it in a hurry. Even Chthon will require some time to establish control over hungry Turlingian Aphids, and meanwhile they will provide excellent distraction for *us*. We shall drop them in the path of our pursuers.'

'But then we cannot –'

'Have no concern. In this situation, your personal debt limit is off. You may – and may have to! – replicate as copiously as possible. I presume your fragments reform into sentient entities rapidly?'

'Virtually instantaneously. That is why we require the Taphid,

for it acts rapidly without separating any individuals. One is loath
to dispense with it. Are you sure -?'

'What is the debt limit for saving the existence of all life in the
galaxy?'

'That is not our mode of appraisal,' the Xest replied. And
Torment added on her own: 'Their whole philosophy is to restrict
the spread of life, so that their resources will not be squandered.'

'So that the restricted population can live comfortably,' Arlo
said. 'But there have to be *some* survivors. Wouldn't the debt you
incur by unrestricted fissioning be theirs to expunge? Wouldn't
they be ready to assume that debt, as the price of life itself?'

'You make it wonderfully clear,' the Xest responded.

Had he – or was the creature merely being polite to a savage?
Well, he had its acquiescence, and that sufficed. 'Our shock troops
have already been launched. It is the job of those of us who remain
to make as impressive a distraction as possible. Chthon must believe that *we* are the shock troops. It will watch us most closely,
uncertain whether I have been fooled by the dreams. That uncertainty is our asset.'

'A return to your home-cave would not distract Chthon,' Torment said. Arlo was not clear whether she spoke for the Xest or for
herself. 'Better that we make a direct attack that cannot be ignored.'

'Yes,' Arlo said. 'Since I had not planned on that, it is good.'
He realized that this probably meant he would not see Vex or his
parents again. But this was war, and he had a job to do. 'There are
regions of the caverns I have been barred from. So has my father.
He spoke of a blocked passage beyond ice caverns. . . . With these
gloves and this hammer I can break through. That should really
alarm Chthon – and we'll have one hell of a fight.'

'That is our purpose.'

'I sense the ambush, between us and my home-cave. It is the
wolf-thing.'

'From your mental image, it is not a thing we can readily
conquer,' Torment said for the Xest. 'Best to avoid it.'

'My inclination is to bash it on the skull with the Hammer,' Arlo said. 'Therefore, in the interests of unpredictability, I shall not. Like cowards, we shall flee it.'

Torment put her hand on his arm. 'Your sentiment becomes you.'

'No doubt!' he said, half-angry. He guided the sledge down the tunnels he knew, fearing and enjoying their forbidden nature. One was an almost vertical ice shaft, where the moving air was forced down into an opening funnel where it expanded and cooled rapidly. This was not the river of ice where he and Vex had played, but an entirely separate region. The walls and ceilings became coated with crystals, patterns of faceted ice, and the floor was a narrow glacier.

'We shall never thaw the Taphid here,' the Xest complained.

'Just wait,' Arlo said. Soon they debouched into a veritable snowstorm – then, suddenly, into a warm side tunnel and a dead end. The chippers had to stop.

'I christen this the Cave of Odin's Eye,' Arlo said with a flourish. 'Only recently did I learn its significance, though I have been here before.' He got out, hefting his hammer. 'You're both telepathic. If Chthon-creatures come – and it's likely they will – warn me.'

'There is a creature beyond that wall,' said Torment. 'I feel it: large, very large, loving. The Xest says it is the most powerful animal in the planet, and semitelepathic. Unsafe to approach.'

'Now I am even more curious,' Arlo said. He had picked up the same emanations. 'This must be one of Chthon's secret weapons.'

'It may destroy us.'

'Our first line of defense is the Taphid.'

'Still too cold,' Torment translated for the Xest. 'It takes time for the grubs to thaw. And once they do –'

'I know. I've seen them operate.'

Torment lifted an eyebrow. 'You have been to space?'

'In a vision. I have seen the future – when Chthon wins. I

mean to see that that future never comes to pass.' He clenched a fist, not in violence but in concentration, noting how the scales of the glove slid smoothly by each other no matter how tightly compressed. 'We'll wait on the Taphid, then. Torment, stand guard with the chippers. We don't know what we'll find, other than large and dangerous. But no doubt an excellent distraction.'

The Xest came to stand beside him. Arlo bashed the wall with the hammer – and it powdered out beautifully. In moments he had broken open a hole large enough for them to step through conveniently.

They entered a round tunnel, fifty feet in diameter. There was a rank odor, as of the dung-region of a dragon's lair. Arlo had an uncanny sensation of familiarity.

'Let's fish for it,' Arlo said. 'I'd like to *see* this thing.'

He formed a mental picture of a huge fat chipper stumbling about uncertainly: ideal prey for a large predator. Suddenly the picture intensified, so that the chipper became almost tangible. The Xest was adding to his picture!

Somewhere, a hugeness took note. The telepathic monster of this tunnel perceived the image, and there was a hunger. Arlo felt the massive motion begin.

It frightened him. The presence was too large, too menacing. Yet it was a weapon of Chthon, and he had to understand it, learn its weaknesses, so that the forces of Life could eliminate it. And he wanted to make a really formidable distraction, to hold Chthon's attention. So he waited, projecting the fat chipper image as augmented by the Xest, making it so bumbling and fat and real that his own mouth watered.

The rock began to vibrate. Abruptly Arlo realized: this was a huge maze-dragon, dwarfing the one he had encountered while carrying Vex. Its network of passages – how far did they extend?

He saw a pattern of threads extending through and around a globe, and realized that the Xest had put this picture in his mind. The Xest's telepathy was superior to that of the minionette; it could make direct informational perceptions and projections. And the picture told him – that the dragon's maze encircled the very planet.

What a monster! It had to be killed, for it alone could consume the entire army of minionettes. Being telepathic, it would be able to locate every sentient entity in the caverns – if it were loosed in them. And Chthon had provided Arlo no hint of this before; it was a weapon held in reserve.

Yet why should he be surprised? Chthon could make the unique hvee grow, crossbreed and mutate successfully here in the caverns; the simple increase in size of an already formidable breed of monster was well within the mineral intellect's power.

Of course the creature would not be able to squeeze through the majority of tunnels – but still, it was too terrible a threat to ignore.

Would his hammer kill it? Could he strike hard enough, in a vital spot? Surely the monster had a brain somewhere, and if that were crushed. . .

The chipper-prey wavered. The Xest was getting tired. Its telepathy was superior, but could not be maintained long. Arlo, on the other hand, could continue the effort indefinitely.

A new picture came to his mind: an elaborate belt, or girdle, radiating power.

Thor's belt of strength! The Xest was telling Arlo he had it. Yet he did not. What did this mean?

But as the Xest projected new, fleeting images, Arlo understood. It was the caterpillar venom! Not a poison, but a channelizer, to make newly incorporated segments durable enough so as not to be a liability to the whole. The stuff had affected his system, giving it that special reinforcement intended to make him an indefatigable marcher. But now it made him stronger in other ways, extending his mental endurance. He did, indeed, possess the belt of strength, the last of Thor's gifts.

Now the rock shook so violently that Arlo had difficulty keeping his feet. He braced himself on the scant ledge formed by the intersection of the feeder-tunnel with the main one, lifted the hammer, and waited. The dragon couldn't possibly brake in time; it would shoot right by the first pass.

There had to be many prey-animals here to feed such bulk. Yet the entrance was blocked. How did they get through? Probably they *didn't*; Chthon had arranged to close off this section only recently, within the past couple of decades, and had trapped a sufficient pyramid of lesser animals to serve. At least until Ragnarok.

Did the monster know that the moment the war between Death and Life was over, the monster itself would be expendable?

Fool! Arlo fired at it.

Now the dragon hove in sight, far down the endless passage. Its huge eyes glowed, spearing out their light to augment the lichen glow. Like a mighty LOE express, it steamed down upon them, traveling so fast that the air compressed ahead of it, making Arlo's ears crackle.

LOE express, he thought fleetingly. "' There isn't train I wouldn't take, No matter where it's going.'" That long-defunct female poet would't take *this* train!

Arlo held his position. His gaze seemed to meet the awful stare of the dragon. He drew upon his reserves, physical and mental, knowing that he would have only one chance. He braced so hard it was as though his feet were crushing down through the rock to embed themselves in the heart of the planet. If he could strike it cleanly –

The bait-image vanished. The onrushing monster faltered, no longer able to orient on its prey. The eye-beams switched back and forth, trying to pick up what the mind had lost. In a moment that questing light would bathe Arlo and the Xest, exposing them, dooming them without chance of resistance. Only by passing on course, intent on something else, could the dragon be vulnerable to Arlo's surprise blow. On guard, it would come teeth-first.

The Xest, frightened, had erased the chipper-picture.

Arlo tumbled back, getting out of sight as the blast of the dragon's frustrated passage pushed air out of the hole they had made. Furious at his companion's act of cowardice, Arlo swung his hammer at the Xest with all his force.

The blow scored. The Xest shattered explosively. Its eight legs flew out in all directions; its body puffed apart as if it were no more than an inflated bladder, punctured.

As the dragon disappeared down the tunnel, suction jerked Arlo after it. He reached out instinctively and clutched an outcropping of stone. The air howled through the gap in the wall behind him, carrying the fragments of the Xest like so many dried leaves.

Now there was remorse. *I'm sorry!* Arlo cried into the gale. But of course it was too late.

A piece of Xest banged into his back and dropped down. Arlo swept it up – and lo, it was already forming into a miniature Xest. He held it to his face – and its little telepathic image entered his mind.

It was a picture of thousands of Xests overrunning the caverns, looking for Chthon's secrets, unstoppable because they were so small, so alien to the cavern entity's experience. Some even clung to the dragon, hitching a ride right around the planet. But mixed with the image was a burgeoning concern. *Debt!*

'Don't worry,' Arlo said to it. 'Do your job. Harass Chthon. If there is any life-debt, the responsibility is mine. It shall be so recorded.' He paused, unsatisfied. He had guilt of his own to expiate somehow. 'If we win, I will give you a hvee. If it lives, I will know you have forgiven me for my crime against you – against all you thousand Xests. The debt is mine.'

With a projection of gratitude, the little Xest moved on.

Arlo made his way back to the chippers and cart as the wind abated. Torment waited, as directed. 'So you have relived mythology again,' she said.

'Oh?' Arlo glanced at her, surprised.

'Did you know that Thor and the giant Hymir went fishing?' she asked. Then, seeing that he did not, she continued: 'Thor put the head of an ox on his hook, and it was the great Midgard serpent itself that took the bait. But as Thor drew it up and met the monster's gaze, Hymir in terror cut the line, letting the serpent escape. Thor in rage smashed the giant with his hammer, but the damage had been done.'

The Midgard serpent – the creature so big its coils encircled the world under the ocean! Indeed he had relived the myth, though he had not read that particular story. And now the world-snake knew its enemy and would be alert.

In Ragnarok, Arlo knew, Thor had in the end fallen prey to that monster. Had he only been able to kill it in the first encounter. . .

'So stay away from it!' Torment cried. 'I think our diversionary ploy has been successful. Life is going to win!'

'Not by reenacting Norse myth,' Arlo said.

'We have copied that enough. Now we can diverge and wipe out Chthon.'

'I hope so,' Arlo said, thinking of Vex. Life might win – but would he survive to hold her again?

They moved out, the chippers eager to leave these depths.

Then Arlo felt a sharp pain in his foot. He reached down – and his glove brought up a salamander.

He had been bitten by the caverns' most poisonous creature.

'Arlo!' Torment cried. Then she saw the salamander. Her horror was like the breath of new love to his mind. 'Oh, *no!*'

'The wind must have sucked it in,' Arlo said bemused by the knowledge that he was finished.

She grabbed him, drawing her knife. 'I'll have to cut, draw out the venom–'

But it was too late. Arlo fell into her arms, unconscious.

Mythology was not to be reenacted, after all. Not in this detail.

CHAPTER VI

Life

Two men sat in the passenger lounge of the FTL ship. They watched the simulated stellar view.

'Shall we celebrate my birthday with wine?' the old man inquired, showing his bottle. 'Today I am one hundred and eight years old.'

'By all means, Benjamin—if your health permits.'

'Hell with my health, Morning Haze! What use is life without pleasure?'

'In that case, let's make it a party,' the minion said. 'Let's bring in my brother and the minionettes and *really* celebrate!'

'And our Xest pilot too,' Benjamin added. 'Actually, it has been just about thirty-four years since we won Ragnarok, and the Xests deserve full credit.'

Morning Haze departed while Benjamin poured out the fine old wine. In a moment the minion returned with the other: the Xest, Misery, Vex, and Arlo.

The Xest wore a fine blue-green glowing hvee, symbol of its decades-long friendship with Arlo.

The two minionettes were like twin sisters in the prime of youth, stunningly beautiful – yet one was sixty Earth-years old, the other perhaps a century more. The men, in contrast, showed their ages. Morning Haze was fifty-eight and Arlo fifty; both evinced the waning of the powers of their youth.

'How grand it is,' Benjamin said, passing out the drinks, 'to have my nephew's three children with me on this occasion! I am only sorry Aton himself could not be here.'

'That is unkind,' the Xest signaled.

'Oh, I am sorry,' Benjamin said. 'In my age I forget. You, Morning Haze, would be constrained to kill your father in the minion fashion, were he present, so that your wife/mother Misery would not go to him. And you, Arlo, would also have to kill him, so that your sister Vex would not go to him. And you two minionettes would have to kill each other to possess him. While all the time Aton loves only his legitimate wife Coquina, who will not leave the caverns though the technology now exists to abate her chill. So this separation represents the only solution; the elements of our wider family, like oxygen and fluorine, must not be allowed to combine.' Benjamin sighed. 'Forgive me if I seem insensitive; I have never had any great sympathy for the minion code, though I value each and every one of you as though you were my own. So let us be happy together, for the duration of this little family reunion, and —' He paused. 'Where is Afar?'

'I am here,' a young man said from the doorway. He was tall and powerful, with a piercing glance and a touch of cruelty about the set of his mouth.

'Ah, you so strongly resemble your grandfather!' Benjamin said. 'My nephew Aton—he had that look in his youth.'

'The look of madness,' Morning Haze said without rancor.

'Yes, isn't my son lovely,' Vex agreed.

Arlo's lips twitched. 'Lovely!' he said with heavy irony.

'I suspect my father has outlived his humor,' Afar said. 'Yet that can be remedied.'

Vex smiled at Afar. 'So sweet,' she said.

Arlo's muscles bunched, but he said nothing.

'This is what I don't like about Minion,' Benjamin said.

'Why *must* it be incestuous, with Oedipus and Electra pursuing each other so determinedly, son killing father down the generations? If only you married outside your line, as you are now free to do, owing to the lifting of the planetary proscription, none of this would be necessary!'

'It is the Minion way,' Misery said. 'We would not have it otherwise.'

'Even though you know it was all the result of a private concubine plot, a scheme to reap illicit fortunes by catering to wealthy and unscrupulous potentates?'

'The scheme failed. We endure.'

'Yet your husband killed your only son,' Benjamin reminded her.

'So that I could possess her longer,' Morning Haze said proudly. 'The impetuous lad grew overconfident and attacked before his time. I did not initiate the action, for that is not the way. I merely —'

'Merely led him on by feigning early loss of vigor?' Benjamin suggested.

'I was more intelligent than he,' Morning Haze agreed obliquely. 'I inherit that from my Human ancestry.'

Benjamin sighed. 'To disparage such a compliment would be to wrong my brother Aurelius, and the Families of Five carry more honor than that. Yet I could wish that the intellect of Five could have found a more gentle expression.'

'I shall give Misery another son in due course. Perhaps he will inherit more of that Five intellect, and time his action correctly.'

'You see,' Vex said brightly. 'Soon my son will kill my husband — or be killed by him. In either case, I will have a good man.'

'Chthon!' Arlo swore. 'I wish I'd married a normal woman!' He glanced at Afar, who made an elaborate shrug. Arlo, despite his age, remained an extremely powerful man, not one that even a young minion would lightly provoke to mayhem. 'Or at least a more amenable minionette, like Torment. She was normal, at the end.'

'Perhaps she died because you made her normal,' Misery suggested with a smile both pleasant and cruel. 'A minionette in that state would be like a hunting dog without fangs.'

'Too bad you did not retain your godly powers after Ragnarok,'

Vex said. 'You could have defanged me. Then I could have died of beautiful sorrow.'

'Damn your sarcasm!' Arlo cried, his rage making her smile brilliantly. 'I thought killing was done when we vanquished the mineral intellect.'

'Not so,' the Xest signaled. 'Throughout the galaxy the species of Life are warring. Human fights Lfa over some trumped-up charge of planet rustling; EeoO fights Xest over the price of the Taphid, which happens to originate on an EeoO planet. The resources of whole stellar systems are being wastefully depleted. Once the sentience of Chthon was destroyed, no one seemed to care about mineral values. Even among one's own kind, the Taphid is often neglected.'

'This is regrettable,' Benjamin said politely.

'It is a mess, all right,' Arlo said. He emptied his glass, looked around—and intercepted the look Vex and Afar were exchanging. His hand clenched into a fist. He no longer wore the gloves of power or carried the hammer; Thor had died at Ragnarok. Pity that Arlo had lived!

'One also regrets it,' the Xest signaled. 'How much better it would have been to have made some compromise with the cavern entity. When one and one's myriad debt-brothers fought in the caverns, we thought we were God vanquishing Evil. Now it seems we were at least partially mistaken.'

'So it seems,' Arlo agreed. 'There was much that was worthwhile in Chthon. The mineral intellect was my fried, before Ragnarok; I can't claim it was evil.' He turned from the Xest, feeling the remorse of genocide. Chthon had never been alive – yet they had killed it, and that had been a galactic crime.

His eyes lifted – and saw Vex in the arms of Afar.

The wrath that had been building for twenty years was catalyzed. Arlo put his great scarred hands about a small auxiliary computer unit, lifted it, and with mad strength ripped it from its moorings. He hurled it at the couple.

The minionette, warned by her telepathy, drew back.

The man was not so quick. The heavy unit smashed into his body.

'Brother!' Morning Haze cried. 'What have you done?'

Arlo looked – and saw that the two had not been embracing, just conversing. And that the man had not been his son Afar, but his granduncle Benjamin. How could he have mistaken them? The two men were entirely dissimilar!

Morning Haze kneeled beside the old man. 'He is dead. Any shock could have killed him, in his condition – and this was no minor strike. What did you suppose you were doing, Brother, throwing that thing at our patriarch?

'Brother, I thought It was my son,' Arlo said, chagrined.

'*With Misery?*' Morning Haze inquired, drawing his knife.

On top of everything else, Arlo had mistaken the minionette! His obsession with the ugly heritage of Minion had made him see what he feared, and precipitated a quarrel he abhorred. 'Brother, in my confusion I have wronged you. I proffer apology. My quarrel is not with you or your minionette, but with my own —'

Now Afar crossed the room. 'So my father *has* outlived his time!' Afar said. 'By his own admission, it was *I* he sought to kill. Therefore he has violated the Minion code, and I may kill him without equality of weapons.' His hand moved, and he brought out a blaster.

'This must be abated! The Xest signaled desperately, its multiple legs moving in a confusing pattern as it ran between them. 'A misunderstanding —'

Afar fired. His blast was directed at Arlo, but the Xest was now in the line of fire. The flame bathed it, destroying it utterly, without trace of debt. What was not vaporized had been cooked. The fringe of the blast washed over Arlo, singeing his hair and momentarily blinding him, but his limited telepathy told him where Afar stood.

'Now the battle has been joined,' Arlo said grimly. He kicked the dripping, gooey hulk of the Xest at his son at the same time as Morning Haze, mistaking his intent, charged toward him.

The two minionettes watched the bloody struggle with twin smiles of pure rapture.

CHAPTER VII

Phthor

Arlo woke sweating with revulsion and horror. *The vision of Life's ascendancy was as bleak as that of Chthon's.* Each victory meant awful death for those closest to him, in that microcosm reflecting the carnage of the macrocosm.

Had this vision been sent by Chthon? Arlo doubted it; the elements of it rang too true. His future life with Vex would be like that, and in the end he would indeed have to kill his only son or be killed by him, in the minion way. This was what loving her entailed, and they both knew it. He could not escape that destiny by deserting Aton and Coquina and leaving the caverns forever; his fate was inherent in his love for the minionette.

'Thank God you made it,' Torment said. 'I may have destroyed your foot, but I got most of the venom out. You're tough, and I think the caterpillar poison countered the salamander poison somewhat – but that was close.'

'You're beautiful,' Arlo said, kissing her.

'So are your dreams,' she said. 'I'd like to know their literal content . . . '

That she had turned normal and died. That had passed through his mind as he kissed her, which was why the kiss had not hurt her. 'The essence is this : we cannot afford Ragnarok. Our victory is as bad as Chthon's. *No matter who wins, Evil prevails.* Compromise is essential.'

'It's a bit late for that,' she said. 'The forces have joined in combat all over the planet.'

'The war must be stopped. It *shall* be stopped.'

Torment smiled, appreciating his angry determination. 'How?'

'My mother Coquina is confined in her hot cave, on pain of death. She really has no way to compete with the minionette.'

'No normal woman *does*,' Torment agreed with a hint of pride. 'But what relevance —?'

"For a moment I thought they would fight. If one killed the other, the problem . . . would not really be solved. Coquina did not fight, though she knows how. Instead she – compromised. And gained more than she might have lost.'

'Compromise comes hard to a minionette.'

'Chthon thought to use me – as did you,' Arlo said. 'I have assets derived from Life and Death. Now I have need to invoke them, for our galaxy depends on it.'

'Perhaps you had better rest. You are weak from the salamander toxin and the blood I had to squeeze from you to get it out.'

Arlo looked down at his foot. Now it hurt, and the toes felt numb. She had bound some cloth about it, taken from some hidden part of her uniform.

Infact, she had handled the matter very rapidly and competently. Vex would not have been so apt. There was a difference between individual minionettes, and Torment was worthwhile.

They rounded a turn – and before them was the chimera. Both of them recognized it instantly, though neither had ever seen it before. Birdlike and malignant, it faced them, hovering in place.

The chippers stopped, afraid. 'Oh-oh,' Torment said. 'Can't outmaneuver *that*. But maybe I can block it off until you get your gloves on it —'

'No use,' Arlo said. 'Look behind.'

'I don't need to. I can feel it. Another chimera.'

'And more in the adjoining passages. We are trapped.'

She glanced at the box containing the Xest's Taphid supply. 'I wonder —'

'Still not thawed,' Arlo said. 'And if it were, we'd be the first eaten. So no net gain.'

Torment turned to him. "I think I would have loved you any-way. Any minionette would.' Then she drew her knife. 'If we stand back to back, we may kill one or two before they finish us. I'll take out the first with my blowgun; I have a spare one for you, in case you misplaced the one I gave you before. Try to protect your eyes; they'll go for that first.'

'You, yes; me, no,' he said, remembering something Aton once had mentioned about the delicacies the chimera preferred. It was not reassuring.

Arlo knew it was no use. The chimera fed on more than eye-balls and gonads, and it could strike at the speed of sound. Knives, blowguns or even blasters would be of little avail against this covey.

Yet he had a mission. He concentrated, reaching out – and a soundless implosion occurred somewhere within his head and body. Diverse but unimaginably powerful elements were thrust together like the mechanisms of a nuclear device, and as they merged there was a qualitative change.

'What happened?' Torment cried, alarmed and dazed by the emotional turbulence surrounding the metamorphosis.

'Enough pressure can convert black carbon into diamond,' Arlo said.

The chimeras launched themselves. From each available direc-tion they shot like projectiles at the target. Arlo felt them in his mind just before he saw them move. Death . . .

Death!

The chimeras dropped to the cavern floor.

'They're dead – all of them,' Torment said in wonder. 'I can feel it. An instant of incredible bliss . . . something wiped them out!'

Arlo relaxed. 'Twice I have fallen prey to animal toxins – but survived. It was not because I was lucky, but because I have special resources. I am part human, part minion, part Chthon. Life has shown me its secrets – and so has Death. From each I draw power – and together they are – Phthor.'

'I will take you back to your cave,' Torment said, as though he were babbling. 'Your emotion is so twisted I cannot interpret it. You need time to rest, to recover – and we'd better get out of here before whatever finished those birds orients on *us.*'

Arlo concentrated. Again in his mind and being he fused the diverse elements of his makeup, his genetics, his knowledge, and his emotion. The essences of the oxygen of life and the fluorine of death, precisely merged, figuratively. Consciously he repeated what had been involuntary a moment before.

The pieces fitted together, forced by the need he saw – the need to stop Ragnarok, to unify the essences of Life and Death, to prevent the twin horrors of victory by either faction. He stood at the crux of the great Y, so much more than the spread of the World Tree Yggdrasil. Here the futures diverged, and now he understood the message of the mythological Ragnarok. No matter which side won, Evil triumphed – because the battle itself was suspect.

They must not be permitted to diverge. One horn of it could not exist apart from the other, by definition. The horns had to be unified, integrated, fashioned into the I-course of a single, successful future.

Awareness came, like that of Chthon. He perceived the caverns through the senses of the creatures wihin them – but not limited to the animals. He was receiving from the minionettes, the Xests, the Lfa, and the EeoO : all the life of both sides.

First the near ones : the moving passages as seen through the four eyes of the two great chipper-goats, the odors of rock and glow they fed on, the feel of stone and ice under their feet, un-pleasantly cold. The air currents as perceived by the antennae of tiny, flying frost-gnats disturbed by the sledge. The taste of stone and water as perceived by the glow-lichen. And the uncertainty and concern of the minionette Torment: she had to safeguard this man, for he was the unifying focus of Life's effort. Did that respon-sibility extend to his difficult personal situation? Should she at-tempt to remove his love from his sister, thereby alleviating his inherent quarrel with his father? Or was she rationalizing, yielding to the overwhelming temptation this complex and forceful young male presented?

'A son you bore me you would immediately reestablish the minion triangle,' Arlo told her. "If I really want to be free, I must marry a normal girl – as my father did.'

Torment stared at him, embarrassed. 'You can read my mind – literally!'

'With semitelepathy so common in the galaxy, is it surprising that true telepathy should at last emerge?' Arlo inquired. 'Let me show you something else.'

He concentrated on her. Torment screamed, clutching her head : a short, sharp cry of dismay from the root of her being. 'You have – gutted me!' she gasped, clinging to the chair of the sledge.

'No!' Arlo drew her to him, close, and kissed her again. This time he savored her exquisite body, her unparalleled beauty, her respectable personality. For the moment, he loved her without bitterness.

She melted, every bit a woman. Her hair took on a sheen of almost living flame. Then she drew back, startled.

'What was that?' she demanded.

Arlo merely looked at her.

'It was – unchanged love,' she said, shaking her head incredulously. 'There was no reversal!'

'You are now normal,' Arlo agreed. 'That telepathic emotion reversal could have been corrected generations ago, had the developers of Planet Minion researched more thoroughly. It is time the minionette merged into the human mainstream.'

Now she was horrified. 'Our whole way of life —'

'Will change. But there is more,' Arlo said. He concentrated again. Torment lifted one hand to her mouth and bit her finger. 'I can control your body,' Arlo said through her mouth. 'I could will you dead – as I did those chimeras.'

He let her go, and she collapsed weakly against the chair. 'That is Chthon-power, after the myxo —'

'I can do it without the myxo,' Arlo said. 'My way is more efficient because it is natural, whole.'

'What *are* you?" she demanded, suspecting some ruse by the cavern entity. If Arlo had been taken over –

'I am not the enemy,' Arlo said, smiling reassuringly. 'There *is* no enemy – except this foolish strife. I am Phthor – the integration of the power of Life and Death.' He paused, beginning to reach his awareness out through the planet, finding his range magnified well beyond what it had been during the fishing for the dragon : beyond his own prior power *and* that of the Xest. 'Perhaps, when this is over, I will marry you, and your children will be normal and telepathic. Now – I must stop Ragnarok.'

'This power is new to you' she warned. 'If you try too much, too soon —'

'There is no choice. This is Ragnarok.' Win or lose, he would forfeit his special powers when this was over; the second vision had informed him of that. But on the personal level, he had already done what was fated: normalized Torment. Could he change fate enough to prevent her death? If not, his agony with Vex would come to pass . . .

Indecision was not a minionette failing. 'Then we'd better hole up somewhere safe,' Torment said briskly. 'I'll stand guard while you – reach out. If Chthon doesn't know about this yet, Chthon will find out very soon. Then your life will be in more danger than ever before.'

'You are assuming that I am opposed to Chthon.'

Torment's knife whipped around – and stopped as his mind clamped down on hers.

'I'm on the side of sanity,' Arlo said, letting her go. 'I don't mean to destroy Chthon. Chthon is not evil – it is merely a different way. We have to work out a compromise for mutual survival. Each side has things the other side needs. Life has mobility, technology, reproductive capacity – the ability to change the physical aspect of the galaxy, and to adapt itself to what cannot be changed. Chthon has – proportion.'

She shook her head dubiously.

'Unchecked, Life wil destroy itself and the galaxy,' Arlo continued. 'Like thawed Taphids, consuming its very future for the sake of its immediate appetite. The Taphids perish after they feed, for there is nothing left. Some control needs to be exercised. Chthon is that control. Together, in harmony, the two will make of this realm a paradise – for both.'

'I don't understand it,' Torment said. 'But I defer to your judgement.' She put away her knife, and took the reins. 'You go about your business; I'll find a cubbyhole.' Then, as an after-thought, revealing her private concern : 'My children will be *normal*?' She was not wholly pleased.

Arlo yielded the management of the material concern to her. *Obey her*, he projected to the dull minds of the chippers, and implanted brief directives about the motions of the reins so that they would know how.

He had already sent his awareness out through the caverns. Now he intensified it. He felt the stone itself, and its trillions of fissures and bypaths and metallic threads, and the little chthonic currents traversing these, and the larger network – that sum total was Chthon itself.

As his perception spread, he assimilated the circuitry that constituted the cavern entity, and knew where Chthon's secrets were. The EeoO were pooled near the antiexplosion wave generator, ready to reemerge as separate juvenile entities and attack by secreting corrosive acids around the key circuits. But a huge sucker-creature was making its way towards that region, Chthon's counter to the threat. It would imbibe and digest the entire pool before the EeoO could complete its reproductive cycle – if it got there in time.

The Lfa had reassembled and was making its way to the great gas crevasse. Soon it would set about igniting that chasm. Chthon was not yet aware of it, so had taken no counter step. The multiple Xests were scurrying in and around the huge nether tunnel, distracting Chthon with their activity. Arlo reminded himself: he must remember to give his friend-fragment the hvee!

Farther out, the minionettes had emerged from their enclave and, under Lfa command, were systematically clearing the caverns of Chthon-possessed life. They were spraying glow-destroying acid on the walls, making the region opaque to Chthon's perception. They had unbreakable electric lamps for their own use.

Aton, Vex, and Coquina had united in the fashion of a normal human family and were barricading their warm cave. Outside it the giant wolflike creature prowled, seeking some way to enter. It was the same one who had almost killed Vex before and lain in ambush for Arlo's party hardly an hour ago. He remembered : Fenris the Wolf was Odin's mortal enemy. That wolf would kill Odin at Ragnarok.

Chthon was still following the script.

On the surface of the planet, known as pretty Idyllia, another confrontation was occurring. Old Doc Bedside had emerged from the depths to seek out older Benjamin Five, and Benjamin had come forth to meet him in single combat. The two, according to Arlo's first vision of the future, were mortal enemies. In mythological terms they were Loki and the white god Heimdall, possessor of the great Horn of Ragnarok. Both would die.

All through the planet, the battle was being joined. There would be intolerable mayhem, if he did not stop it now.

But could he stop an entire planet?

Arlo extended himself, drawing on his newly integrated abilities. He had, he realized, tapped into the same reservoir of power that the § drive used, the binding force of the universe. The problem was to translate it into usable energy, to control it and channel it and focus it as required. § was there, virtually infinite, but his being was a very small aperture for its expression.

He closed about Benjamin and Bedside, freezing them in place; he halted the huge wolf at the home-cave; he stopped the Lfa near the gas crevasse. He started on the minionette army, but it was too much to compass all at once, and the girls weren't doing much real harm, so he let them go.

Now he reached out for Chthon. Through the rock he quested, searching for his friend. *Chthon! Chthon!*

I am here, friend. Just like that, complete communication!

We are in Ragnarok, from which none will survive. The battle must cease.

Life must be exterminated, Chthon replied. *It contaminates the galaxy. Only when this region is clean can we associate with our companion-intellects in the universe.*

It meant the other mineral sentiences inhabiting other galaxies. *Life is sentience, too.* Arlo argued. *One sentience may not destroy another. Sentience in any form is sacred.*

No. Only mineral sentience.

And why should he have thought that Chthon would be amenable to Life's logic? *If we do battle, you may be destroyed. We must compromise.*

There can be no compromise with Life. And Chthon's utter loathing of the Life-slime came through like a blast of heat.

This is not reasonable! Arlo protested.

It is not reasonable, Chthon agreed. *It is absolute.*

'Arlo!' Torment cried. 'The Midgard Serpent comes!'

Arlo refocused his attention. She was right; the super-monster was chewing its way through the rock, breaking open a new passage – straight for Arlo's cubby. There was no question about its objective; he saw in its mind that it knew him as the enemy fisherman who had teased it with the vision of food and attacked it with the myriad of annoying Xestlets.

In fact, it had been informed of him long ago. Once it had been an innocuous, if gigantic creature, running about its maze, feeding on the animals it trapped. Then Doc Bedside had touched its mind, instilling in it an abiding hatred for all things human, especially those with minion blood. It was not intelligent, but it had strong telepathy; it could tell the difference between human and minion. In this manner, Bedside's mad brain had fashioned its malevolence. The doctor had done the same thing with the cavern wolf. The children of Loki, truly!

Arlo oriented on it, but the monstrous serpent resisted. Its mind was somehow insulated, perhaps by the sheer mass of itself, and required more than token suppression. Arlo concentrated, bringing it to a halt – and lost control of the rest of the battle. His tiny human brain simply could not handle sufficient energy for everything at once.

Benjamin Five held a scythe, Doc Bedside a scalpel. Benjamin's weapon was much larger, but clumsy in this context. He normally used it for clearing the weeds from a potential hvee bed, setting up for crop rotation. Bedside was extremely swift and accurate with his little implement, and he could throw it if he chose. But he was aware that if his throw missed or failed to score vitally, he would then have little defense against the scythe.

The two men were mortal enemies. Bedside had taken Benjamin's nephew Aton into the netherworld, and killed Aton's son Aesir. Benjamin had 'sounded the Horn' summoning the minionette army for the invasion of the underworld. Now they would settle the score as it had to be settled: individually. The hate of each for the other required this ultimate satisfaction.

Cautiously they circled each other, each looking for an opening. The beautiful flowers of vacationland Idyllia surrounded them: Benjamin unconsciously trod them into the dirt. This was no sports match; this was sheer hate.

The wolf pawed at the rocks barricading Coquina's cave. The things's metal-hard claws caught the edge of the stone and sent it scooting down the passage. Now a gap was open. The wolf jammed its gross snout through, but its head was too big to fit.

Aton stood on one side, raising the double-bitted ax. Vex stood on the other, holding one of the stalactite spears. He would go for the nose, she the eyes, while Coquina remained as bait in the back of the cave. Just before they struck. Aton and Vex glanced at each other, to coordinate their attack. But it became another lingering look of longing, in the presence of Coquina, for which both were ashamed.

It would be well, Arlo thought dispassionately, if Vex died. Painful as that would be, it would resolve the problem her life presented. Better to mourn for her than to die for her.

The Lfa reached the gas crevasse, well toward the bottom. It lifted an appendage, concentrated, and developed an electric potential between spread antennae. A fat spark jumped. The massed gas caught, sending a flash across the chasm, illuminating the void blindingly, showing the sheer cliffs above and below. But the gas was too cold, too rare; in a moment it extinguished.

The Lfa raised its appendage again. If the first ignition did not take, the second would. Or the third. Each flash would warm the pit until the fire could be sustained the – inferno!

The EeoO pool was shifting and flexing, almost ready to shape into its new entities. But the sucker-creature had reached that pool. It lowered its proboscis and began to draw.

Arlo wrenched his power back to the diverse locales of battle. He froze men, monsters, and Vanir in place lest Ragnarok pass the point of no return. And the dragon, loosed, advanced. With teeth and claws and sheer forward momentum, it pulverized the thin partitions of stone that separated the warren of passages. The entire region shook with its progress, and stalactites broke off and fell in a wide radius. Its breath was burning hot, blasting the dust and gravel out in a turbulent cloud before it. The Midgard Serpent!

Arlo was in a quandary. The dragon was too massive and powerful to control with just part of his mind – but if he focused his full attention on it, Ragnarok would resume elsewhere. He had to stop both the battle and the monster, or fail totally.

He could kill several of the smaller individuals – Bedside, the Lfa, the pool-sucker – but that would only serve to aggravate the poisonous animosities that had generated this schism. Peace through murder was no peace at all! He had to suppress, not hurt, all combatants, until a lasting compromise could be achieved.

For a moment he let the dragon be and stopped the battle. *Chthon!* He cried mentally. *Abate your attack! We must talk, compromise! For the sake of the friendship we have had –*

But Chthon would not answer – and that was answer enough. The cavern entity would not bargain or even listen. Its determination was implacable, and his friendship with it illusory. And the awful rumble of the serpent drew closer.

In sudden fury Arlo released the rest of the caverns and directed a devastating shock at his personal nemesis, the dragon. It halted, momentarily stunned – and Benjamin swung at Doc Bedside, the Lfa struck another spark, and the sucker-monster drew in a snootful of the EeoO pool. Aton and Vex struck together at the face of the wolf. Arlo was conscious of it all, for his awareness required only a fraction of his power.

Bedside stepped back, letting the scythe blade pass harmlessly. Then he lunged forward, scalpel extended. The gas crevasse lit up again, more brightly than before, with sheets of incandescence rising almost to the high ceiling. The EeoO gave a poolwide quiver of anguish as its substance entered the digestive tract of the sucker. And Fenris the Wolf sent forth such a mighty howl of aggravation that the three people in the cave fell to the floor, hands over their ears.

Quickly Arlo clamped his control on again. That stopped the critical encounters, though the tiny Xests still ranged and the minionettes had flushed a surly caterpilllar.

Now the Midgard Serpent resumed. Arlo could not use his mind against it again, lest Ragnarok proceed. He would have to fight it physically.

'What are you doing?' Torment cried, seeing him heft the Hammer in his Gloves.

'I must slay the monster,' Arlo said.

'You must be protected! she said. *I* will fight Midgard!'

He kissed her once more, while his mind saw all the minionettes at once, like multiple images of her. Yet she was distinct, for she shared this adventure with him, and she alone was normal. She was worthy of his love. 'This is for me alone. Take the chippers and sledge, make your way to the surface. Tell the forces of Life that Ragnarok must stop, even though I may die.'

She hesitated. 'But you haven't given me my children!'

She wanted *him*, not the children. And he wanted her. But there was no time. 'Any man will volunteer,' he said. 'You are lovely – throughout.' Then he touched her with his mind, and she had to go. She jumped onto the sledge, took the reins, and started the chippers on their way.

The wall burst apart. Stones flew into the cave, striking the chippers, killing them. Torment was knocked from the sledge. Choking vapor filled the cave : the foul breath of Midgard.

The monster's eye spotted Torment as she took a rolling fall. Its tongue snapped out, bloated and gummy. It plastered itself against the woman, adhering to her struggling body. Like a buzzing fly she was drawn into the twenty-foot mouth. The teeth closed, crunched. Arlo felt the momentary agony of her death.

His future with Torment was gone. Fate had not permitted this small change.

Arlo clasped his Hammer in both hands and brought it down on the nose of the monster, now in range because a serpent's face is smallest when its jaws are closed. The head of the Hammer sank deep into the leathery skin, gouging a hole. The monster let out a deafening hiss of affront, but opened its jaws only enough to bite Torment's body into quarters for ready swallowing.

The nose was no good : too soft. He had to strike the skull! But how could he reach it, since only the snout was in the cave?

Now Torment had been swallowed. The jaws opened wide again, making the mouth fill the cave. A few drops of blood fell from the teeth. The monster snapped at Arlo, but lacked room to maneuver and missed him. Irritated, it crashed its head against the ceiling, knocking it out and tripling the size of the chamber as loose rock fell aside.

Now it could take a decent bite! The jaws opened so wide that the upper teeth became a vertical wall. That wall advanced on Arlo.

Arlo backed away as far as he could – and stumbled over something. It was the Xest's box. It overturned and the frozen mass of the Taphid slid half out. No longer completely frozen – the ravenous creatures were beginning to stir.

Arlo scooped up the box as the terrible jaws closed. He hurled the Taphid mass into the maw, down the throat of the serpent. As the mouth closed convulsively, triggered by that small mass, Arlo saw the interior heat of it melting the remaining ice into slush.

'Let *that* be your reward for killing Torment!' he shouted. But his eyes were moist, and not merely from the stinging vapor. *Torment!*

Now he sprinted for the cave opening. Pain shot through his sliced-up foot where Torment had extracted the venom of the salamander. Arlo stumbled.

The monster lurched forward in pursuit, ramming its head through the cave exit and bursting the remaining wall and ceiling asunder. Its mind oriented on its fleeing prey. It belched, a few wriggling Taphids emerging with the gas. Relentlessly it followed.

How long would it take for the Taphids to consume the material within the serpent's mighty gut and start on the serpent itself? Arlo could not guess, for the monster was so tremendously massive, and he could not stay around to watch.

He was not far from the world-encircling tunnel of the dragon. He ran for it, gritting his teeth against the pain of his leg. He passed through the opening that the monster itself had made, skidded in a man-sized dropping, and crashed into the bottom. Now he had a clear route – but he could never hope to outrun the creature in its own warren. Provided the serpent remained in good health . . .

But he knew the caverns because of his total awareness. And he knew the monster would be delayed, having either to turn laboriously about, or carve its way through the rock to return to its natural path. That gave Arlo a head start.

Is this the way Thor fights? Chthon's derisive question came.

Arlo didn't answer. The mineral entity's display of emotion only betrayed its uncertainty. Arlo still held Ragnarok in abeyance, and Chthon was evidently unable to resume the main fray until Arlo was dispatched. If he could make it to the gas crevasse in time. If that gas entered this tunnel, and then were ignited – it would not burn long, but that might be enough to finish the monster.

The distance was short on the planetary scale, but long for a man on foot, especially with one bad foot. Already the serpent was reorienting, closing in on its own tunnel. There was not going to be time.

An animal, frightened by the nearby activity, had blundered into the warren. Arlo had not seen this type before, but it had six legs and looked fleet. He touched it with his mind and leaped upon its back. Now he had a steed!

He had guessed correctly; this thing was fast. The wind whistled past Arlo's ears as they raced along. Soon they came to the place where the tunnel passed directly under the gas crevasse. Arlo dismounted, letting the steed run on as a possible distraction. *I am minion* he projected into its mind, to improve its chances as a decoy. Then he knocked at the rock with his Hammer, again and again.

Behind him came the dragon, horribly swift. Why hadn't the Taphids slowed it? Or had its intestinal juices digested the Taphids first? Arlo hadn't thought of that before, and it was not reassuring. He might have to face a full-strength monster after all.

As Arlo made a man-sized hole in the wall and climbed upward on the rubble he was making, the serpent shot past. The sudden compression and rarefaction of the air in its vicinity knocked him off his feet. The decoy had worked – but that would not fool the monster long.

He opened an aperture into one of the vapor–exits of the crevasse. Arlo pulled himself up along the smaller tunnel as the gas poured through his vent into the main passage. The suction of the dragon's passage helped it along.

Then pressure built up again. The dragon was returning, head-first; evidently it had a loop for turning about near here. Air and gas whistled back out through the crack – but enough filled the tunnel so that the monster choked on it. Good – it could not breathe the gas! Arlo himself was suffocating, but he drew upon his special physical strength and hung on. He found the tunnel's merger with the bottom of the gas crevasse.

Above him the canyon opened, dark to his eyes, permeable to his mind. It had not maintained a fire, fortunately. Below him the dragon ground at the rock, using its pile-driver claws to plunge into it and hook it out in gross chunks. Its mouth was not really a rock-cutter, but more for chewing prey. And it was losing initiative, for it had an uncomfortable bellyache.

Arlo's perception passed through the monster's body. The Taphid had consumed the serpent's stomach and now was working on the remaining innards. But the vitality of the snake was such that even gutted, it could function indefinitely. Given opportunity, it would grow a new digestive system. Meanwhile, it was hungry – and it had already fixed on its prey.

Arlo readied his Hammer, waiting to time his blow exactly right. The serpent might be able to get along without its huge stomach, but it would die without its little brain. And if that didn't work, fire should. He needed something to use to strike a spark.

The entire floor of the crevasse below Arlo collapsed, falling into the yawning maw of the monster. Now the gas howled through, finding a vast new outlet. Arlo scrambled desperately, but the combination of vanishing footing and rushing gas carried him down into the maw.

But the serpent, its perception dulled by its intestinal problems, did not realize it actually had his prey in its mouth. It spat out the rubble, or rather blew it out with a galelike burp of gas – and Arlo emerged with the stones. He crashed into the side of the cave-in, feeling bones bruise. He inhaled involuntarily – and found that the gas was now mixed with air and dust. It would sustain him – long enough.

Something bit him. He pinched at his thigh with his left Glove and brought up a Taphid. About to crush it, he changed his mind and flicked it back into the maw. Every little bit helped!

He hauled himself up, gripping the Hammer with one glove, and caught hold of a finger-thick whisker sprouting from the monster's lip with the other. He scrambled over the dragon's face until he stood atop its skull – and now he struck, guided by his ambient perception of the creature's anatomy. Right at this precise point, *here* –

The blow sundered the heavy mantle of bone, transmitting

the cruel shock to the tiny brain beneath. This organ was extraordinarily sensitive. The Midgard Serpent thrashed wildly and died.

Success! Arlo leaped off its hurtling skull and ran toward the chasm outlet. But as the monster collapsed, it exhaled a cloud of its remaining internal vapor, digestive gas that burned Arlo's skin, suffocating him anew, and blinded him. The Taphids had been lucky to survive that corrosive atmosphere! Poison from vents near the teeth mixed with this, making the cloud completely deadly. Arlo staggered a few more steps, then collapsed.

As Thor had perished in the cloud of venom released by the dying Midgard Serpent, he thought, feeling his mental control slipping as his body died. An almost perfect parallel that could hardly have been scripted by Chthon –

But that was what Chthon wanted him to believe! As long as he did, he was doomed, as the cause of Life was doomed, and any sane compromise was doomed. He had to seek his own destiny, not a reenactment . . .

Then he felt the multiple bites of the Taphids. They were swarming over him, having been belched out with the last great spasm of the serpent. He lacked the vision and the strength to pick them off, and in any event they were already burrowing voraciously. What appetite! They must reproduce in the very act of eating, to consume so ravenously!

Destiny? It was too late! As Arlo's control slipped, Bedside's blade cut into Benjamin's body. Benjamin grabbed Bedside's two ears, flung him about, and shoved him against the pointing blade of the fallen scythe. Blood spurted from both men as they continued their death embrace.

Fenris the Wolf twisted his head about, orienting on his enemy by sound. His jaws snapped sideways – and caught Aton at last. One gulp, and the man had been swallowed as the two women screamed.

The sucker imbibed the remainder of the EeoO pool, leaving only a film of jelly.

The Lfa generated another spark – and this time the crevasse caught and held. Flame ballooned up to the high cross-passages, sucking in cool air, and plunged down toward the bottom vortex where the gas leaked into the dragon's tunnel.

Arlo felt the heat incinerating his body, killing the Taphids in the process – and had a final realization. He had allowed himself to be deceived by a decoy! He should have struck, not at the dragon, but at Chthon's killchill circuitry! Then the deadline would have been postponed, allowing him to force a compromise between Life and Death, saving them both.

With what was left of his mind, now heating in its fragile housing of bone, Arlo flung a blast of § energy directly at that delicate submechanism that was Chthon's ultimate weapon. He could not destroy it physically, but he could alter the impedances, change the flows of current, make it into something else, neutralize it –

Chthon fought him. But Chthon, too, had been weakened. The chasm blaze was melting adjacent circuits, shorting some, interrupting others, interfering with the orderly process and feedback that was sentience. The two fading minds, animate and mineral, struggled over the killchill unit, buffeting its mechanism back and forth, while the increasing inferno sent heat through rock and passages, changing the composition of delicate diodes and resistance-sections.

Desperately, Arlo tried to demolish the structure before his own mind collapsed. As desperately, Chthon sought to trigger it off, though the guiding chill-wave had not yet arrived. As a result, it changed. It drew into itself in a kind of short circuit all the reserve powers of Chthon, coalescing about very special, potent substances, merging oxygen and fluorine in an entirely new and thorough manner, not restricted to organic material but all-inclusive, tapping violently into § without the limiting fuse of Arlo's brain, resulting in – Phthor.

Symbol	Element	Atomic Number	Atomic Weight
O	Oxygen	8	16, 17, 18
F	Fluorine	9	19

Sector Cyclopedia, §426

Epilogue

Phthor
Destruction
Ragnarok
First future : victory for Chthon
Cleansing the galaxy of contamination.
Second future : victory for life
Inevitably destroying its own sentience, unrestrained : the
Taphid.
Third future : compromise
Failed.
Fourth future : Phthor
Otherwise known as the birth of a quasar
Most powerful explosion of a galaxy
Akin to the violence of the Creation itself.
Life and Death : all gone
Ragnarok
Destruction
Phthor.

We in the external universe observe
We note the result of victory
Or of mutual loss.
This new bright quasar shines
An example
A warning
Showing the way to the greater good

Compromise.

> We record the case history
> And present it here for eternity :
> An example
> An education.
> We accede to what must be.
> We : the mineral intellects of the universe.
> We end our war with Life.
> We renounce – Phthor.

AUTHOR' NOTE

I wrote this sequel to *Chthon* because the first novel had gone out of print and I wanted to put it back into print. So much for divine authorial inspiration. The publishing establishment was much the same in the 1970's as it has ever been: resistive to the preferences of writers. They assumed that *Chthon* would not sell many copies, because it had already been published in mass market paperback. One publisher even put it as a matter of honor: it had a bargain with its readers never to publish anything that wasn't new. So when my literary agent offered *Chthon* and *Phthor* as a set, DAW accepted the latter but turned down the former. We declined. However, when a better established writer—I believe it was Gordon Dickson—made a similar offer to that publisher, it was accepted, and his "old" material was republished. So it was evident that rules that applied to me did not necessarily apply elsewhere. This was before I became a bestseller with light fantasy; *then* the rules changed for me too.

But we persevered, and in due course BERKLEY did accept the package, taking the old book in order to get the new one, and the two novels were published a month apart at the end of 1975. In the next dozen years, both went through several editions, doing well, and lo, *Chthon* outsold *Phthor*. So much for editorial judgment.

Given that the novel's genesis was commercial, how was it to write? Actually, not bad. Some books I write for love, and some for money, and the odd thing is that they can turn out equivalently. What really counts is what happens within the book, once the writer gets into it. There can be surprises, and a competent writer can indeed make silk from sow's ears. I discovered that there were a number of unfinished aspects worth pursuing. What happened to Aton and Coquina after they moved to Chthon? What about Chthon's war of destruction with the septic slime we call life? How about a better look at those fascinating planetary caverns? Then I got into thematic material: what could follow an Oedipus story? What mythology could there be tat wasn't Greek? Thus came Electra and Norse, and I liked them. Electra naturally complements Oedipus, a woman's interest in her father being similar to a man's interest in his mother and, as it turned out, a necessary stage in the life of a minionette. Norse mythology has Ragnarok, the destruction of the sides of good and evil, an especially useful concept in this case. And structure: what could match the double hexagon shape of *Chthon*? I settled on a Y, the fork representing the key separation of alternate futures. So I enjoyed working it all out.

In fact it turned out to be quite sophisticated in some details. The Y is hardly in a class with the hexagon, and there's not a lot of parallelism, but the devious interaction of the characters was a challenge. So was the problem of alternate futures, neither of which was worthwhile. How could I write my way out of that one? I finally figured out a positive conclusion, despite the destruction of all participants. So while I feel it is not the novel *Chthon* is, I remain quite satisfied with it. In fact, proofreading it a quarter century later, I found that I had forgotten whole major segments, so it was like reading some other writer's novel, being surprised by the twists of its story. I have always tried to write the kind of fiction that I would like to read, but it's hard to be objective about it. In this case I was able to verify that I really do like the way I write, when it has become unfamiliar. I also found that it does indeed fill out the first novel, so that the two together make a complete story.

At any rate, now the set of novels is available again, and readers can judge whether the critics are right about my writing ability degenerating ever since.